DESERT DEVIL

SAND AND SHADOWS BOOK 2

COLLEEN HELME

MANETTO BOOKS

Desert Devil/ Colleen Helme. -- 1st ed.

ISBN: 9798429825694

Dedication

In loving memory of
Tucker Cole Jordan
Forever Loved and Forever Missed

ACKNOWLEDGEMENTS

I'm so excited to bring you book two of Ella and Creed's story. When I started this series I had an idea of where it was going, but the scope of the story has changed in ways that have taken me by surprise. That's what I love about writing. It's always a process, and one that requires many hours of thought, heart, sweat and tears. Through it all my hope is that you will find something within these pages that are worthwhile. If it brings you a moment of escape, quiet reflection, or enjoyment, I will consider it a success.

Once again, I'm so grateful for my daughter Melissa, who is such a wonderful source of inspiration and support. Your involvement has been instrumental in helping me shape this story in the way it needed to be told.

Thanks to my wonderful husband, Tom, for believing in me, and supporting me. He's even learned to cook! How awesome is that? To my wonderful family, Tom, Jason, Erin, Mike, Orion, Melissa, Don, and Clayton for your continued encouragement and support. I love you all!

A big thanks to Kristin Monson for editing this book and making it better. You are the best!

I'm so grateful for my amazing audio producer, Stevi Incremona, for bringing Ella's story to life on audio. Thanks for teaming up with me! You rock!

BOOKS BY COLLEEN HELME

SAND & SHADOW SERIES

Angel Falls

Desert Devil

Twisted Fate (coming soon)

SHELBY NICHOLS ADVENTURE SERIES

Carrots

Fast Money

Lie or Die

Secrets that Kill

Trapped by Revenge

Deep in Death

Crossing Danger

Devious Minds

Hidden Deception

Laced in Lies

Deadly Escape

Marked for Murder

Ghostly Serenade

Dying Wishes

High Stakes Crime

Devil in a Black Suit ~ A Ramos Story

A Midsummer Night's Murder ~ A
Shelby Nichols Novella

NEWSLETTER SIGNUP

For news, updates, and special offers, please sign up for my newsletter at www.colleenhelme.com. To thank you for subscribing you will receive a FREE ebook: *Behind Blue Eyes: A Shelby Nichols Novella*

CONTENTS

CHAPTER ONE

I stepped down the hallway and paused in front of room two-one-two-seven. At three in the morning, most of the patients were asleep, and it was relatively quiet. Taking a breath, I pushed the door open and stepped inside.

The boy lay quiet and still, hooked up to several machines. The halo around his head held his neck in place and kept him from moving. His curly, blond hair was pushed back from his forehead, and, even with his eyes shut, his dark, long lashes went on for days. For a fifteen-year-old, he looked small and helpless, surrounded by all the machines that monitored his vital signs.

This was the first time I'd been able to visit him, but I'd been drawn to this room since my first shift at the hospital. I'd had to wait until now, when things had settled down, before I could visit him without drawing unwanted attention. I still didn't have a lot of time, so I stepped to his side and took his hand.

To my surprise, his eyes fluttered open and his gaze met mine. I smiled to put him at ease. "Hey Tucker, I'm Ella. I didn't mean to wake you."

"S' okay." He blinked a few times, trying to wake up.

"I just wanted to see how you were doing. Is it okay if I sit with you for a minute?"

"Sure."

"You can go back to sleep if you want."

"It's all I ever do anymore."

I smiled. "That's because sleeping will help you get better."

Tucker's breath hitched, and his eyes brightened. "You think I'll get better?" The desperation in his tone sent sorrow into my heart. Through no fault of his own, this poor boy had broken his neck in a freak accident.

The doctors had little hope that he'd ever walk again. Tucker's parents had been devastated, but this young man had put on a brave face, telling everyone he'd be okay... and he'd walk out of this hospital and prove them wrong.

Now, alone with me, his eyes filled with tears, and worry tightened his brow. He'd tried to be brave for his parents, but now he couldn't hold back the emotion.

As he blinked his tears away, I tightened my grip on his hand. "I don't see why not. You just have to give it some time, and let your body heal. Can you do that?"

He tried to nod his head, but couldn't with the halo around it, so he pursed his lips instead. "I think so."

"Good. Now try not to worry. Close your eyes and go back to sleep. Everything's going to be okay."

His eyes closed, and a tear rolled down his cheek. "What does that even mean?"

"It means that it's okay to be scared, but don't lose hope; you're stronger than you think. Now rest and go to sleep." He glanced at me with half-closed eyes. I smiled and sent him a reassuring nod. He let out a breath, and his eyes dropped shut. He relaxed and, a few seconds later, his breath came deep and even.

Now that he was asleep, I closed my eyes and concentrated on my connection to him. Still holding his hand, I placed my fingers against his wrist and felt the beat of his heart. Sending my awareness through our connection, I traveled up his arm to his neck and centered on the source of his injury.

There, I felt the swollen tissue and the herniated disc that had damaged his spinal column. Through surgery, the disc had been successfully treated, but the injury to his spinal cord was irreparable.

Using my gift, I sent my healing power into his neck, starting with the swelling and proceeding to the injured nerves of his spinal column. Stimulating the nerves and bringing them back together was a slow process, but soon the tissue began to regenerate. I sharpened my focus, pouring all my energy into the tissue until it had strengthened and fully reconnected.

Several minutes later, I knew the moment the injury had completely healed. The swelling was gone, and the vertebrae reset, allowing his neck and the rest of his body to resume its normal position and functionality. My breath whooshed out of me, and I pulled my focus away.

Opening my eyes, I panted, feeling like I had just run a marathon. Thankfully, Tucker's eyes were still closed. As I studied him, I noticed that his face held a slight flush of healthy color that hadn't been there before. With his spine restored, he'd be able to walk again and live a normal life.

Totally exhausted, the exhilaration of using my gift to help him gave me the strength I needed to get up and walk out of there. With one last glance at his peaceful face, I opened the door and stepped into the hallway.

Holding the outside door handle, I made sure the door closed without the usual loud click. I turned to leave and nearly crashed into a cart being pushed by an orderly.

"Oh! I'm so sorry," the woman said, covering her mouth with her hand. Her long, dark hair was pulled back into a low knot at the base of her neck, and her dark eyes flashed with embarrassment. "I didn't see you there."

"It's okay. I was just... I was trying to be quiet."

"Of course." She nodded, glancing at the door. "That's the poor boy with the broken neck. How is he? I feel so badly for him."

She stepped down the hall in the same direction I needed to go, so I moved beside her. Still a little weak, I couldn't quite keep up with her pace. She noticed and slowed her step, sending me a look of concern. Before she could ask if I was okay, I picked up the conversation where she'd left off.

"I know. It's heartbreaking, isn't it? But maybe with some therapy, he'll get some of the use of his arms and hands back at least."

"That would be something. I pray for him every day. Such a tragedy."

"Yeah, for sure." I'd never seen her before, but she acted like she knew me. Maybe she'd been in one of my patient's rooms and I'd missed it. Orderlies like her were nearly invisible in a hospital this size, but I usually wasn't so preoccupied that I couldn't be friendly. "I don't think we've met. I'm Ella St. John."

"Oh... it's nice to meet you. I'm Reyna Torres." Her surprise that I'd introduce myself seemed genuine. "I've only worked the night shift for a few days, but I'm always happy to make new friends, although... I have to say that I've heard of you."

"You have?"

Her eyes widened. "Oh... nothing bad of course. It's all been good. I mean... you're new here, so people have talked about you a few times. But in a good way. You're a really good nurse... at least that's what everyone says." Her gaze met mine, and she gave me a rueful smile. "So... I'm happy to run into you."

I chuckled. "Yes... well... it's nice to meet you, too, Reyna. I guess I'll see you around."

She nodded and continued down the hall, while I stopped at the bank of elevators. I pushed the button for the main floor and stepped inside, grateful to be alone so I could lean against the side and catch my breath.

It concerned me that she'd seen me leave Tucker's room, but there was nothing I could do about it now. If she'd been praying for him, that meant she'd be sure to follow his progress. By tomorrow, she'd know that something drastic had happened. I just hoped she wouldn't put it together with my visit.

The rest of my shift passed uneventfully, and a couple of hours later I arrived home just before eight in the morning, bleary-eyed and tired. Creed welcomed me, holding a spatula in his hand and stirring a frying pan filled with eggs.

"Hey beautiful." He hugged me tight before pulling away to tend to our breakfast. "How was work?"

"Good, but I'm exhausted." I dropped my purse on the counter and sat down, grateful to sit and get something nourishing to eat. "I'm glad I have the next few days off. I'd forgotten how draining three twelve-hour shifts could be."

Creed dished the eggs onto a couple of plates, added buttered toast, and set one in front of me. He carried the other to the counter beside me and sat down.

I dug in and groaned. "This is so good. Thanks."

"Sure." After a couple of bites, he told me his plans for the day. "I've got that commercial I'm working on today, so I'll be gone until six, but at least you'll be here when I get home for a change."

My lips twisted. He didn't like that I'd taken the night shift, even though he knew that it worked out better for me. I'd explained that I could use my healing gift easier in the middle of the night, without the attention it might bring, but that didn't mean he liked it. "Yeah. I can't wait to sleep beside you tonight. I've missed that."

We'd been married for a total of two weeks. It was hard to believe how fast our lives had changed. Now we were learning how to make it all work. It had been easy for me to get a job at the hospital, and this was my first week back at work.

Creed had started back to work as well. His agent had several offers for Creed to look over, and he'd started with a commercial and had a few other projects lined up after that. We finished up our food, and Creed took our plates to the sink.

I still hadn't moved, and Creed studied me, picking up on my weariness. "You look a little pale. What did you do?"

I sent him a smile, pleased that he'd noticed. "You know what? It's sure nice to have someone around who cares about me. I'm not real used to that."

Creed came around the counter and wrapped his arms around me. His warm embrace was like a charge of electricity, filling me with strength. He kissed the top of my head and pulled away. "So what happened?"

"I helped a fifteen-year-old boy with a broken neck. He was paralyzed, and I managed to heal him while he slept."

"Whoa. That's huge."

I nodded. "Yeah. It took a lot out of me, but I'll be fine after a couple hours of sleep and this food. Thanks for that."

He took my hand and tugged me off the stool. "Come on, let's get you to bed."

"I thought you had to leave."

"I've got a few minutes."

I let him help me undress. Before I could throw anything on, he bent down to kiss me, pushing me back against the bed. "Damn. If I don't leave now... they'll probably kick me off the job."

I smiled and pushed against his chest. "Go. I promise that I'll still be here when you get back."

With a sigh, he pulled away. "I think I'd rather stay."

I chuckled. "Yeah... but now you'll be thinking about me while you're gone, so it's all good."

He huffed. "What do you mean? You're all I ever think about."

Unable to resist, I pulled him down for a kiss. He was the most beautiful man I'd ever met, and he was mine. He still took my breath away, and I realized it wasn't just his looks or the sex. It was the way he looked at me with such tenderness in his eyes, like I truly was the center of his universe. In those moments, I knew I'd do anything for him, and it scared me that I could love someone so much.

He groaned and pulled away, panting for breath. "I guess I don't need that job after all."

"No... it's okay. You should go." I sat up, reached for his big t-shirt, and pulled it over my head. "There. Now you can go. Besides, I need to take a nap."

His lips quirked up in a tiny smile, and he let out a dramatic sigh. "All right... but at least we're even."

"What do you mean?"

"After that kiss, I think you're the one who will be thinking about me all day." He turned toward the door and grabbed his keys from the counter, along with his motorcycle helmet. "Oh... my mom wants you to call her. There's a couple of last-minute things she wants to go over."

"Okay. I'll give her a call. I love you."

"I love you too." He sent me a sexy grin and slipped out the door. Part of me wished he didn't have to go to work so soon, but I was glad I got to see him before he left. That didn't always happen. At least we had the rest of the weekend to make up for all the time we'd been apart, and I looked forward to it.

I got comfortable under the covers, but sleep eluded me, mostly because of the events from the last few weeks. There were times when I wondered if I'd dreamed it all. Not only was I married to the most handsome man on the planet, but the mystery surrounding my birth and my parentage had been answered.

Father John, the priest who'd raised me as his daughter, wasn't my real father like I'd always believed. But that wasn't the only thing that had changed. After meeting Aiden Creed through a crazy accident, my healing powers had blossomed.

Instead of just soothing pain and speeding the healing process with my touch, I'd actually been able to completely heal injuries. First, it was Creed's broken leg, and then a young man's head injury.

Totally baffled by this change, I was ready to go back home to New York to get some answers from my father, but, instead, Creed and I were forced to go to Las Vegas to settle a debt.

The man doing the forcing, Sonny Dixon, needed Creed to win a poker tournament. When that didn't happen, Sonny wanted us dead, but he was coerced into letting us go by a mob boss who happened to be my friend's uncle.

Still, it didn't stop there. In a fit of rage, Sonny sent Creed's former friend, Dom, after us. Dom tried to kill Creed, but I got in the way and took the bullet instead. I should have died... in fact... I think I did, but a power beyond my own brought me back.

Later, Creed and I made it to New York and finally asked Father John what was going on. He didn't know a lot, only that I'd been saved as a child by a heavenly messenger, but not why I could heal injuries.

That's when he appeared... the messenger. He wasn't an angel, but I think a saint is pretty close. St. John the Beloved told me I was given the gift of healing to help him. He wasn't real clear on how I was supposed to do that, mostly instructing me to follow my heart.

Then he left, telling me that Creed and I were meant to be together. By then, we had fallen in love, and we were married that same day, under my father's watchful eye. Now, here we were, back in Los Angeles, trying to figure out our lives. I still had so many questions, but I was learning to rely on my intuition, even though I hated the uncertainty.

I closed my eyes and sighed. Healing Tucker this morning had totally worn me out, but since I'd been drawn to him, I hoped that meant he was someone I was supposed to heal. I wanted to help everyone, but I didn't have the strength for that.

Healing came with a downside, zapping me of most of my energy. At least food and sleep helped revive me, and I wouldn't change it for anything. Still, after three days of using my gift, I didn't know how long I could keep this up. In the back of my mind, I worried that using so much of my own energy would prematurely age me. My father, John, didn't seem to think so, but how did he know?

Giving in to exhaustion, I turned on my side, and promptly fell asleep.

My ringing phone roused me, and I checked the time, finding it close to two in the afternoon. Pushing to my feet, I padded over to counter where I'd left my phone and answered. "Hello?"

"Hey Ella. I was just... oh crap! Did I wake you up?"

I recognized Lauren's voice and frowned. Creed had told me to call his mother, but I'd forgotten all about it. "Uh... yeah, but it's okay. What do you need?"

"I'm so sorry, I should have waited."

"That's okay. What is it?"

She began explaining the last-minute changes to the party she was throwing for Creed and me. We'd agreed to her plans to host a wedding party, since she wasn't there when we got married. I'd also had to agree to wear a wedding dress and exchange vows with Creed a second time in order to make it up to her.

Who knew she'd be so stubborn about that? Of course, I'd never known my own mother, and the only real mother figure I'd had was one of the nuns at my school, so what did I know? At least it was a couple of weeks away, so I didn't have to panic yet.

"And don't forget that Avery is getting discharged from the care center tomorrow," Lauren continued, pulling my thoughts back to the conversation. "We're having a celebration dinner here. You're still planning on it, right?"

"Yes. Of course."

"Good. We can talk about the rest of our plans then. I'm sure Avery wants to be included, but I'll go ahead with the changes we discussed."

"Okay. Sounds good. See you tomorrow."

We disconnected, and I shuffled back to bed, flopping down on my back. Avery, Creed's little sister, had been one of the first people I'd completely healed. She'd been hit by a car and had suffered major brain trauma.

Only it wasn't an accident. She'd been caught up in the same circumstances in Las Vegas that we had. In fact, she was the reason Creed had gotten involved with Sonny Dixon in the first place.

Avery had hooked up with Creed's childhood friend, Dom Orlandi, in Las Vegas, and he worked for Sonny. During her time with him, she'd unwittingly become a witness to Sonny's murderous ways. Because of that, Sonny had arranged the accident that was supposed to kill her.

Now she was poised to testify against Sonny. The old worry tightened my chest. After Dom had shot me, he'd gone after Avery. He'd drawn Creed to her care center with threats against Avery, but finding out that I was still alive had changed everything, especially when I'd used my touch to suck the life out of him. I'd immediately sent it back, but it still shocked me that I could do that. St. John hadn't liked hearing about it either, and he had cautioned me never to use my gift like that again.

After that, Dom had become an ally of sorts, promising to tell us if Avery was in trouble from Sonny. But the worst of it was that he knew my secret... that I could heal, as well as kill with my touch. It was unfortunate, since I didn't trust him for a minute. I kept expecting the other shoe to fall, but, so far, so good.

With my mind going a mile a minute, I knew I'd never get back to sleep now, so I put on my exercise clothes and went for a long walk along the beach. Creed's apartment... our apartment... was only a block away and the best part of living here.

I wore sandals to the beach and then slipped them off to walk barefooted through the sand and waves. The salty breeze and lapping waves always revived me. After an hour, I headed back to the apartment feeling totally refreshed.

I couldn't wait to see Creed again. Sure, we'd only known each other for a month, but I couldn't imagine my life without him. How had I ever managed before? I got a shower in before he came home. After that, all my worries and concerns were forgotten.

The next day, Lauren brought Avery home. We headed over for dinner with a big surprise for her. With all that happened in Las Vegas, she didn't have a car anymore, and we'd found one for her.

It hadn't been easy, but we'd managed to sell her car to my friend, Seth, who owned a car shop in Sandy Creek, the small town where I'd lived when I met Creed. He'd also sold my Jeep for me, which gave us enough money to buy a used car for Avery, and a motorcycle for Creed.

I pulled up in Avery's sporty, blue, Mini Cooper, with Creed following behind, and parked in his mom's driveway. Snatching a big bow from the passenger seat, I set it on top of the car and joined Creed at the front door.

After a quick knock, Avery pulled the door open, smiling and happy. She practically jumped into Creed's arms before tugging out of his embrace to throw her arms around me.

I'd never seen her in regular clothes before, and she looked so happy and healthy that it was hard to believe she'd been in a coma and unable to walk or talk after her accident. "You look amazing!"

"Thanks," she said. "I'd forgotten how much I liked wearing jeans and a tee. Come on in. Dinner's just about ready."

"We will, but first, we have a surprise for you." Creed motioned toward the car with a huge grin. "Like it?"

Avery's eyes grew round, and she gasped. "What?"

"It's yours." Creed handed Avery the keys and she squealed with excitement.

"Really? It's for me? Oh my gosh!" She rushed to the car and opened the door. "It's even a convertible! And it's blue! I've always wanted one of these!"

Creed couldn't keep the grin off his face, and I had to admit how fun it was to see Avery so excited. Creed's mom, Lauren, came out onto the porch, and we spent several minutes looking over the car.

"You guys are the best. Thank you so much." Avery hugged us again, tears leaking from her eyes. "I can hardly believe it."

She couldn't wait to take it for a spin, and Lauren was happy to go with her. Creed and I waited on the porch while Avery drove it around the block. After all the excitement, Lauren hustled us inside to eat before the food got cold.

During dinner, I asked Avery if she had any favorite stories to tell me about Creed, and she didn't hesitate to regale me with all the times he got into trouble. Not about to be outdone, Creed got even with her by mentioning a few of her own embarrassing moments. Even Lauren told a story or two, pride gleaming in her eyes. According to Creed, his mother hadn't always been so attentive, so I was grateful to know that he'd been somewhat biased in his thinking.

I knew that he'd felt responsible for his sister, but I hadn't realized it had also included his mother. Growing up without a father had hurt him, and he'd blamed his mother, but nearly losing Avery had changed everything. Now they were a family.

After cleaning up, Avery pulled me aside, concern tightening her eyes. "Can we talk for a minute? Just you and me?"

I glanced at Creed, who was chatting with Lauren about his job prospects and the commercial he'd just finished. She'd been in the movie business, but had never hit it big, and I knew she had high hopes for Creed. "Sure."

Avery drew me down the hall into her room, leaving the door slightly ajar. "I just have to ask you something." She fidgeted with the edge of her shirt, and her lips thinned.

Taking a breath, she met my gaze. "I know you healed me. I don't know why or how you did it, and I don't mean to be ungrateful, but I'm kind of worried."

My brows rose. "About what?"

"When you healed me, did you do something more?"

Confused, I shook my head. "What do you mean?"

She shrugged, but it was half-hearted. "Like... I don't know... make me smarter?" At my widened eyes, she continued. "I can't explain it, but... I remember things that I had a hard time with before. It's almost like I have a photographic memory. Once I read something, I don't forget it."

She shook her head. "That never happened before. In fact... I was just barely average in school." Her troubled gaze searched mine. "Do you think it will go away?"

I frowned. "Honestly... no. I think you're stuck with it."

Her breath caught. "Are you sure? I mean... that would be amazing... but, I don't want to get my hopes up." She shook her head. "It's my worst fear that it will just someday go away, and I'll be back to my normal self. I don't want that to happen. I like being smart. In fact, Mom brought a laptop to the rehab center, and I started taking an online course for computer programming.

"I've already plowed through the first course, and I'm halfway through the second. I can see it all in my mind so clearly, and I'm learning to read and write code. It's like a whole new language that I already understand. Can you believe it?"

"Wow... that's amazing."

Her head bobbed with enthusiasm. "I think I want to learn everything I can about computers, and I want to go to M.I.T. or Stanford, if I can get in. I'm re-taking the S.A.T. next week. I think it could really happen... but not if all of this suddenly goes away."

I could understand her uncertainty, but I didn't see how it would ever change. I thought back to the day I'd sent my healing energy into her brain. Had I overdone it? Was it my fault she was smarter? I didn't think so. I'd just helped her out the best I could.

I took her hands and squeezed them. "I can't tell you anything for sure. I just know that whatever your brain can do now is the way it's supposed to be. I don't think you need to worry about it going away."

"Really?"

"Yes. Live your life. Make plans, and follow your heart."

She nodded, resolve tightening her lips. "I will, Ella. I promise. I won't waste it."

I smiled. "I never thought you would. Now let's get back before your mom thinks she's missing out and comes looking for us."

We joined Creed and Lauren, who abruptly changed the subject of their conversation, like she didn't want me to know what they'd been talking about. She then expertly shifted her focus to me and my need for a wedding dress. Naturally, Avery joined in, more than willing to help Lauren plan the party.

Avery insisted on helping me find the perfect dress. She turned on her computer and quickly found the website to the shop she and Lauren wanted to visit. After what seemed like hours, I managed to pick out a few dresses to try on. That satisfied Lauren, and she scheduled an appointment on my next day off.

Once we got home, Creed pulled me into his arms. "Thanks for doing this whole wedding thing. You're making my mom and Avery happy, even if it's a pain for you."

"It's not a pain." I frowned and pulled back, gazing into his beautiful, blue eyes. "Is that what Lauren thinks?

"Not exactly. She's just surprised that you're so willing to let her plan everything. Most brides aren't like that, so she doesn't know what to make of it."

I sighed, hoping I wasn't too much of a disappointment to my new mother-in-law. "It's just not something I ever thought would happen. To be honest, I've never really thought about a wedding party, or even getting married... but I am looking forward to celebrating our marriage. I guess the details aren't as important to me, so I don't mind letting Lauren plan it all. In fact, I have a pretty good idea she'll do a better job than I could. Have I disappointed you?"

He raised a brow, then his lips twisted into a sexy smile. The intensity of his gaze made my heart race. When he answered, his voice came low and unhurried. "I kind of liked the way we got married, so I'm not disappointed. But this is important, too. For one thing, we hardly have any pictures of us. I want something more to mark the occasion, so this will make up for that."

He let out a derisive huff. "In fact, every time I tell someone I'm married, they think I'm joking. It's like you appeared out of nowhere and we married on a whim. This will make it more official."

"I never thought of it that way, but I see what you mean." I splayed my fingers across his chest and leaned up to kiss his neck, inhaling his intoxicating scent. "I guess I'm the mystery woman who swept you off your feet. They probably think I've cast a spell on you."

I leaned in to kiss that sensitive spot below his ear, and he sucked in a breath. "They wouldn't be wrong about that."

"Right... until they meet my father and see that he's a priest. Then they'll think you *had* to marry me. Maybe I'd better tell him not to come."

"Angel..." He cupped my cheek and gently rubbed his thumb across my bottom lip. "I don't really care what people think. I just want to show off my beautiful bride." He leaned down to press his lips against mine, sending heat spiking through my chest and down to my toes. He deepened the kiss, and I forgot all about the wedding party.

As he reached down to pull my shirt over my head, I placed my hands over his to stop him. His eyes narrowed with confusion, and I sent him a seductive grin. "You know... since we don't have many nights together, why don't we play some poker?"

His eyes darkened with desire, and a slow smile spread across his handsome face. "You're on, but you know you're going to lose, right?"

My lips curved up in a seductive smile. "That depends on your definition of losing."

CHAPTER TWO

W e had the next day to ourselves, and I enjoyed every minute of it. Time spent with Creed, combined with food and rest, helped my energy return, and I hated knowing this was the last night we'd have together for a while.

The next morning, Creed headed into the studio, and I met Lauren and Avery at the bridal shop. Luckily, the dresses I'd picked out were available in my size, and I was even a little excited to try them on.

The first one looked amazing, but the second one was better. Still, it was the third dress that had it all. Made of corded, white lace, it was form fitting around the bodice and flared out below my hips. The style accentuated my nearly non-existent curves, making my waist look even smaller. The lacy boat neckline gave my shoulders more width, and the plunging V-back made it sexy, but not enough to embarrass my father.

Lauren clapped her hands and gasped. "Oh, Ella. That's the one. You have to get it."

"It totally is," Avery added. "You look so beautiful. Aiden will be speechless."

My heart did a little pitter-patter, and I had to agree that this was the right dress for me. I'd never understood the thrill of finding the perfect wedding dress until now, and I was totally enchanted.

"I think you're right. This is the one." I hadn't dared look at the price tag. I knew it would be huge, but, after looking at Avery's and Lauren's excited faces, I couldn't let them down.

As I studied my reflection in the mirror, I knew I wanted this dress even more than they did. I wanted to be fancy and beautiful, even if it was only for a few hours. I shoved the practicality of buying something so expensive out of my mind. This was one thing I could do for myself, and I wasn't going to regret it.

The attendant came in, exclaiming how beautiful I looked. She checked the fit and determined that it needed a few alterations. Normally they would take a couple of weeks, but, since I didn't have that much time, I had to pay two hundred dollars extra.

After ringing up the cost of the dress, and everything else that went with it, I held my head high and tried not to blink... or faint. Still, Avery flinched a little, and even Lauren's eyes widened a bit. Avery hurried to tell me it was totally worth it. Biting my bottom lip, I nodded stoically and got out my credit card.

As we left the shop, my cell phone rang with a number from the hospital. "Sorry, but I've got to take this." I stepped away from them and answered. "Hello?"

"Hi, is this Ella St. John?"

"Yes."

"This is Carol Brown from the hospital administrator's office. Our hospital administrator, Dr. Kelley, would like to see you. Can you come in and meet with him?"

"Uh... sure. What's this about?"

"I'm sorry, but I don't know. I just know that he'd like to see you right away. It's a matter of some urgency."

Dread tightened my stomach. "Okay. I'll be there as soon as I can."

"Thank you Ella. I'll let him know."

"Who was that?" Avery asked.

I slipped my phone into my purse. "The hospital. They need me to come in right away. I guess that means I'll have to take a rain check on lunch."

Both Lauren and Avery voiced their disappointment, and we said our goodbyes. With my stomach twisting, I drove straight to the hospital. As I walked in, I wondered if I should have gone home to change into my scrubs first. The secretary hadn't said anything about working, and my shift didn't start until seven, so I hoped it wouldn't be a problem.

Still, my mouth went dry and my stomach fluttered. What was so urgent? Was I in some kind of trouble? Had someone from the hospital in New York told them I'd been sent to a clinic in the middle of nowhere because I'd refused to help a patient? But John would have taken care of that, unless he'd forgotten.

The administration office was on the ground floor, just off the main entrance. Turning down the hall, I stepped to the office door and pulled it open. Sitting behind her desk, Carol caught sight of me and sent a nod. "Hi Ella. Thanks for being so prompt. Take a seat, and I'll let Dr. Kelley know you're here."

I sat down while she put the call through and tried not to bounce my knees or chew on my lips, but the feeling that I was in trouble wouldn't leave. She hung up and nodded my way. "He's ready for you. I'll show you to his office."

Taking a deep breath, I followed her to a corner office. After a quick knock, she opened the door and ushered me inside. Sitting behind his desk, Dr. Kelley stood to greet me. He had a full head of gray hair, and wore a blue dress shirt with a striped blue tie, and a white doctor's jacket. Not a hair on his head was out of place, and his white goatee accented his round cheeks. He had a soft manner, but he was known for getting what he wanted and accepting nothing less.

"Thanks for coming in, Ella. Please have a seat." He motioned to one of the chairs in front of his desk. His large office had windows along one wall to let in the light. A bookcase lined the other wall, and another held his framed credentials.

After I sat down, he began. "I'm sure you're wondering why you're here, so I won't hold you in suspense. There was an incident the night of your last shift, and I needed to ask if you knew anything about it."

Alarm ran down my spine. "An incident? What do you mean?"

He sat forward in his chair with his elbows resting on the desk. "Did you happen to visit a fifteen-year-old boy named Tucker Jordan that night?"

Taken by surprise, I hesitated, and Dr. Kelley's eyes narrowed. "He said a nurse who introduced herself as Ella spoke with him. Was that you?"

"Uh... yes. I stopped by his room to check on him."

"But he wasn't on your floor. Why did you go to his room?"

"I was on my break, and I just wanted to keep him company. Some kids have a hard time at night when they're alone... and after what he'd been through... I just wanted to see how he was doing."

Dr. Kelly sat back in his chair and sighed. "I see." He couldn't hold my gaze any longer and glanced down at his hands. "This may sound odd, but the boy... he's insisting that he talk to you."

I kept my tone light. "Okay. I'd be happy to stop by his room."

Dr. Kelley met my gaze. "There's more to it. He's... well... I don't know how to put this, but he's made a complete recovery. To say we're baffled is an understatement." He pressed his lips together. "The surgery was successful, but the damage to his spinal column didn't give us much hope that he'd ever walk again. Now he's walking and ready to be discharged from the hospital."

He shook his head. "It isn't every day you see a miracle like that. Anyway... he's ready to leave, but he wouldn't go home until he spoke to you."

"Oh." I swallowed, worry tightening my chest. "Did he say why he wanted to see me?"

Dr. Kelley's lips thinned. "He thinks you had something to do with his recovery." He caught my gaze. "I'm sure he's just searching for an explanation. I think we all are... but since there isn't one, go easy on him, okay? He's waiting in the conference room with his parents."

I swallowed. "Okay."

Dr. Kelley came around his desk and motioned to the door. "I'll be coming with you." I nodded and followed him down a short hallway. He stopped to open the conference room door, motioning me to go in first. I stepped inside to find Tucker and his parents sitting on the far side of a large, oblong table.

Tucker spotted me, and a big grin lit up his face. "You came!"

I grinned back, unable to resist his happiness. "Hi Tucker. You're looking good."

He hurried to my side and threw his arms around me. I hugged him back, surprised and grateful that he was whole and healthy once more. My throat closed up, and I couldn't speak. Tucker pulled away and motioned toward his parents. They'd followed him to my side of the room, and Tucker introduced us.

"Mom, Dad, this is Ella. She's... she's the one I told you about."

His father's eyes held both wonder and a dose of skepticism. "Nice to meet you," he said, shaking my hand.

I turned to his mother, and she threw her arms around me. "My son told us you helped him. I just wanted to thank you. I can't begin to understand what you did or what happened, but..." She swallowed, and her eyes filled with tears. "They said he'd never walk again." She turned to Tucker. "But look at him." She cried softly, and her husband took her in his arms.

Tucker couldn't take his eyes off me. "Are you an angel?"

My breath whooshed out. "Oh... well... no, of course not." I glanced at Dr. Kelley, watching his brows dip and a frown form across his face.

Tucker followed my gaze and sucked in a breath. "Sorry... I guess that was a stupid thing to say."

"No... not at all." I smiled to reassure him. "If a nurse or a doctor is doing a good job, they can seem like angels, so it makes total sense that you'd ask."

He nodded, but I knew my answer didn't satisfy him. I glanced at his parents and Dr. Kelley. "Could I have a moment to talk to Tucker alone?"

Dr. Kelley's mouth dropped open, and Tucker's parents froze. A few seconds later, Tucker's mom broke the spell and pulled on her husband's arm. "Of course. We'll wait in the hall."

His dad met my gaze before he allowed his wife to pull him out the door. Dr. Kelley hesitated, but followed them out as well. As soon as the door shut behind them, I turned to Tucker. "What do you think happened, Tucker? It's okay, you can be honest with me."

He hesitated before blurting it out. "I think you did something. I don't know how... but you healed me. I know it sounds crazy... but I woke up while you were sitting beside me. Your eyes were closed, and I felt something change in my neck... like a wave of heat, and my muscles got all tight. After that, my whole back was kind of sore, and I fell asleep. But when I woke up later... everything was working. I could feel the bed beneath my legs... and I could move again."

He met my gaze with a challenge in his eyes, almost daring me to deny the truth. I couldn't do it. "You're right, Tucker. I have what you'd call healing hands. When I came to visit you, I hoped that using my gift might help you. It looks like it did."

He nodded. "It did more than that. I'm walking, and my neck doesn't even hurt anymore. But I don't understand... how did it happen? Is it going to last? Do I need to do something to keep it?"

"No... not at all. It's given freely with no strings attached. I just ask that you keep this to yourself, okay?"

"But my mom... she thinks it's a miracle. I told my parents it happened after your visit, so they know you had something to do with it."

I sucked in a breath and closed my eyes. "Right. Of course. I'm sure you were all trying to make sense of it. The doctors probably are too, but I really don't want this to get out." Why did Tucker have to wake up while I'd been healing him? Now I was connected to his miraculous recovery.

Tucker studied me for a moment. "It's okay Ella. I'll tell them you were praying for me, and God healed me. That's the truth, isn't it?"

I held his gaze and nodded. "Yes, it absolutely is."

"Okay. Good." He stuffed his hands in his pockets. "I won't say anything more about your part, if that's what you need."

My shoulders relaxed. "Thanks Tucker. That would definitely help, and I appreciate it."

"Sure... and... just so you know..." His lips twisted into a small smile. "You haven't fooled me."

"What do you mean?"

He lowered his voice. "I know you're an angel, but I won't tell anybody that either."

I let out a breath and grinned, not about to correct him when he was so sincere. "Thanks... and... I'm really happy to see you back on your feet."

He nodded, and his eyes filled with tears. "Thank you Ella. I wish there was some way to show you how grateful I am."

"Just live a good life, Tucker... that's more than enough."

"I will... I promise."

The door opened, and Tucker's dad poked his head in. "Is everything all right?"

"Yes," I answered. "We're done." I glanced back at Tucker. "Hey, you take care now... all right?"

He nodded. "Thanks Ella." He gave me a quick hug before hurrying out the door to his parents. I stayed where I was, unsure of my next move. Worry tightened my stomach. Dr. Kelley was sure to question me. What was I going to tell him?

The door opened again, and Dr. Kelley motioned me out. "We need to talk, but first, let's join the others waiting to say goodbye to Tucker." I followed him out of the office and into the hallway where several doctors and nurses waited at the exit to say their goodbyes.

Quite a few nurses wiped their eyes, and I heard more than one of them mention 'miracle' and 'miraculous recovery.' It surprised me that Tucker had been given a clean bill of health so quickly, but, watching him, it was plain to see that nothing was wrong.

To my surprise, Reyna, the orderly I'd met that night, stood among the group. While everyone focused on Tucker, giving him high fives and clapping, she studied me. Our gazes met, and she quickly glanced away, but not before I saw the speculation in her eyes.

Damn. I'd done too much, too fast. I should have healed him more slowly, maybe over a few days, so it would have been more believable, but I wasn't sure I could have managed that. Once the process had begun, it needed to be completed. Now there was no denying that something miraculous had happened, and I was right at the center of it.

The doors closed behind Tucker, and everyone stood still for a moment to watch him walk away. Most people shook their heads in wonder before heading back to their responsibilities. I caught snatches of their conversations. This was a day to remember… a miracle had happened right here in the hospital. Who would have thought?

Reyna made her way toward me, but Dr. Kelley motioned me back to his office before she could reach us. I left her behind and followed him. We both sat down in our respective seats, and he studied me with his hands clasped tightly together on top of his desk. "What did you make of that? I've never seen anything like it."

I rubbed my sweaty palms on my pants. "I don't know. What did his doctor say?"

Dr. Kelley snorted. "He could hardly believe his eyes. He ran all the tests twice, but with Tucker standing and walking, he couldn't come up with an explanation. There was nothing he could find that would explain his recovery." He raised his gaze to mine. "The boy thinks it was you. What did you tell him while you were alone?"

I shrugged. "I told him that I was there to keep him company and to pray for him." I took a breath. "I know it seems crazy, but maybe the injury wasn't as bad as everyone thought. I mean… I never saw the scans, but maybe they missed something?"

Dr. Kelley let out a breath and sat back in his chair. I knew he didn't believe that, but saying his recovery was a miracle was too much for him. "Yeah... maybe so."

His eyes got that far-away look, so I stood to leave. "Is it okay if I go now? My shift doesn't start until seven, and I'd like to get a few things done at home before work."

"Oh... sure. Thanks for coming in, I know it meant a lot to the boy."

"Of course. I'm glad I got to see him before he left." I raised my brows and shook my head, hoping to look convincing. "It's kind of hard to believe that he just walked out of here. I guess miracles really do happen."

"It sure looks that way."

As I left his office, I heard him mumble under his breath that it wasn't the only miracle happening around here. My neck prickled, and I hurried down the hall to the exit. Stepping outside, I began the walk to my car, only to find Reyna waiting for me.

"Ella. I had to talk to you." She glanced behind me before motioning me further into the parking lot. "I swear I didn't tell anyone I saw you come out of his room. So if you're in trouble, it's not because of me."

"I'm not in trouble."

She relaxed. "Good. I would never want that." We stopped in front of the parking complex, away from everyone. "I just wanted you to know that your secret is safe with me."

"My secret? What are you talking about?"

She shook her head. "You don't have to play dumb with me. I know you healed him. You... you're special. I felt it the first time I saw you. I believe God sent you. You're one of his helpers, and I'll do everything I can to keep your secret and help you remain anonymous.

I hesitated, unsure how to respond. Denying it seemed like a slap to her faith, but acknowledging it was not something I could do.

"It's okay." She squeezed my arm. "You don't have to say anything. I just wanted you to know that I'm on your side."

I swallowed. "Thanks Reyna. Are you working tonight?"

"Yes."

"Okay. Good. I'll see you then."

Reyna sent me a nod and turned away. I made it to my car and slipped inside, closing my eyes and leaning over the steering wheel. What had I done? Not only were people beginning to notice, but now Reyna knew my secret.

Would she keep her word?

I spent the rest of the day cleaning and doing laundry. I had to leave for work before Creed got home, so I couldn't tell him what had happened. After arriving at the hospital, I knew I might be under higher scrutiny than normal, so I was careful about how I used my gift.

Not only that, but Reyna seemed to be everywhere I looked, like she was watching my every move. She sent me a few reassuring smiles, but I wasn't sure I could trust her. At least things stayed pretty low-key, and I only used my gift to soothe and speed things along, rather than completely heal anyone's injuries.

Still, by the time I got home the next morning, I was exhausted, and I needed to talk to Creed. Luckily, he sat at the kitchen counter, eating a bowl of cereal. He took one look at me and frowned. "What's wrong?"

"You'll never believe what happened." I rushed into his arms and sighed with relief to feel his strength surround me. "It's not really bad... but I might be in trouble." I pulled away to sit on the stool beside him.

"The hospital administrator called me yesterday and asked me to come in early because Tucker, the boy I healed, wanted to see me before he left the hospital." I explained meeting with Tucker and his parents. "He asked me if I was an angel. After I got his parents and Dr. Kelley to leave the room, I told him I had healing hands."

Creed's eyes widened. "What? You told him that?"

"I had to. He'd already figured it out, and I didn't want to lie to him."

Creed shook his head. "Why not? You can't let this get out. If people find out what you can do, it would be a disaster."

"I know, I know. He's not going to tell anyone."

"You can't know that. Besides, you said he'd already told his parents... and now Dr. Kelley knows?"

"No. That's not what happened. Just give me a minute to explain."

Creed rubbed his face and let out a breath. "Okay. Tell me everything."

"To begin with, Tucker told everyone I was there in his room, but he didn't say that I'd healed him. After we spoke alone, he said it looked like I was praying, so I told him I was. We decided that he'd tell his parents and Dr. Kelley that God healed him... which is basically the truth."

Taking it in, Creed nodded. "Okay... I guess that's a good explanation, since you can't really argue with it, but, from now on, you've got to be more careful. You can't keep healing people all at once like that."

"I know. I'll try to take it slow. That's what I've done in the past, but Tucker was a different case. I couldn't stop the process once it had begun, and it was my last night on the job for a while. But next time, I'll try and heal them over a few days when it's possible, so no one suspects anything."

"Yeah... that's a good idea, but I'm not sure that it will get you completely off the hook. I mean... if someone gets wind of this, it could be bad." He checked the time. "Dang... I'm going to be late. I wish we had more time to talk about this."

"Yeah... I do too." I'd wanted to tell him about Reyna, but now it would have to wait.

He pulled me into his arms and held me tight. "Angel... the nights you work are hard. I miss you, and I hate not sleeping with you at night. With everything going on in our lives, it's like I never see you during the week. And now there's this extra worry that you'll be discovered, and I don't know how to help you."

"I agree, but I don't know what to do about it. I'm supposed to help people, but how can I do that without getting noticed? It's so frustrating."

"Maybe you should slow down a little. I think changing to the day shift would be an improvement. That way we could talk about these things when they happen, instead of days later. I might be able to help that way." Hope filled his eyes. "Will you think about it?"

I wanted to give him all the reasons I shouldn't take the day shift, but he was right. Things were starting to unravel. "Sure. I'll think about it."

"There was a time you wanted to go back to Sandy Creek. Maybe we should."

I shook my head. "But... your career is here, and... I don't know... it seems like I can help more people here than in that little town."

"I know. Let's talk about it later... but for now, please be careful, okay?"

"I will. I promise."

"Okay. I'll see you... tomorrow... I hope." He kissed me before heading out the door, leaving me aching without him. Damn. He was right. Something needed to change. Before we'd come back to L.A., I'd entertained the idea of heading to Sandy Creek where we'd first met. But, after seeing all the good I could do here, I'd put that aside.

Now I wasn't sure of anything. Still, I could see about switching my night shift to days. Tonight, I'd talk to my supervisor and see what I could do. Maybe I could make the switch in a couple of weeks after the wedding party. It would certainly give me something to look forward to.

Until then, I'd have to be more careful.

The next two nights nothing drastic happened, and I was able to keep my promise. I spoke to Reyna a couple of times, and she asked me about my family and where I grew up. Before I knew it, we had developed a friendship, and she opened up about herself, telling me that she was a single mom and working hard to give her ten-year-old son a better life.

"I'm hoping to earn enough money to go to school and get my nursing degree. I have enough saved up to start school next summer."

After that, I felt more comfortable around her. She loved helping people, and I couldn't help being impressed. Once, one of the doctors asked me to help him, and the nurse at his side didn't like being dismissed. Reyna had been in the room and quickly asked the nurse to help another patient, redirecting her attention.

Another time, Reyna asked me to check on a sick man who'd been sitting for over an hour in the waiting room. Waiting that long wasn't uncommon, but his condition had deteriorated quickly, and he needed immediate help, which I was able to give him.

It surprised me how observant she was, and I began to trust her.

I got home from work at seven forty-five that morning and found Creed still in bed. "Creed. What are you doing? Are you going to be late for work?"

He groaned and turned over to face me. "My call time isn't until ten."

"Oh."

"Come here."

I dropped everything and climbed into bed. It didn't take long before my clothes joined his on the floor. The safety I felt in his arms relieved the tension from the long night at work. His hands roamed over my body in a tender caress, and the love in his eyes sent my heart racing. "I've missed you so much."

"I've missed you, too. You're the most important person in my life."

Our lovemaking was sweet and savage at the same time. My need for him only seemed to grow stronger with each passing day, and I couldn't get enough of him no matter how much time passed.

Did all married couples feel this way? I couldn't imagine my life without him. He filled parts of my soul that I didn't know were empty. Love like this seemed precious and rare, and I knew I'd do anything in my power to keep it burning and alive.

An hour later, I lay in his arms, relaxed and sleepy. My eyes drifted closed, and he began to stroke my arm. "Angel... I'm sorry, but I've got to get up."

"No... don't go." I tightened my hold on him, and he lay with me for a few more minutes. Then he kissed my head and pulled my arms from around him. As he padded into the bathroom, I opened my eyes to admire his perfect backside.

He stepped into the shower, and I turned onto my back. Why had I ever thought it was a good idea to take the night shift? I needed him like I needed air, and I'd been suffocating. Had I even told him that I'd managed to change my shift?

At least there was time to talk now, and I rolled out of bed to throw on one of his t-shirts. I got out the pan to cook some eggs and toast and got started on breakfast. Soon Creed was dressed, and we sat down at the counter to eat.

"I have good news. I got my shift changed to days."

His eyes widened. "When?"

"After the wedding."

"Thank you, God."

I chuckled. "Yeah... and things are going pretty well at work. How about you?"

"My agent sent me to a few auditions. I'm not sure if anything will come of them, but you never know. I've got another set of commercials coming up, so that's good. I'm not scheduling anything else until after the wedding. You've got four days off then, right?"

"Yes."

"Great. I want to spend every minute together."

"Me too. There is one other thing I haven't told you yet."

Creed froze, picking up my reluctance. "Okay. What?"

I wasn't sure how to break it to him, so I just blurted it all out. "One of the orderlies figured it out... that I healed that boy." At his widened eyes, I quickly continued. "But it's okay. She's cool with it, and she's not going to tell anyone. She's even watched out for me a few times."

"Why would she do that?"

"She believes that what I do is a gift from God."

"So she hasn't asked you for anything?"

"No."

"Hmm." He finished off the last bite of his breakfast. "And you trust her?"

"So far, so good."

He took a deep breath and shook his head. "That makes me nervous. What do you know about her?"

I told him about her son and her dream to become a nurse, along with the other things I'd observed. "She's really nice, and she cares about people. I don't think she has any ulterior motives."

"I hope not. I guess time will tell."

It bothered me that he was so suspicious, but, after all we'd been through, I couldn't blame him. "It will be okay. You'll see."

CHAPTER THREE

On my next night shift, a multiple-car accident brought several people into the emergency room, and everyone had their hands full. With all the rushing to help stabilize the accident victims, it wasn't hard to use my gifts without being noticed.

One victim had been pinned inside her car for a couple of hours and was the last to arrive. I was helping another patient when they brought her in and didn't know about her until Reyna told me.

I had to finish stabilizing my patient and didn't get in to see her for another ten minutes. I hurried into the room in time to hear the doctor pronounce that she was dead, along with the time of death. My breath caught. As everyone left, I stepped to her side and placed my hand on her arm. She wasn't breathing, and I couldn't feel a pulse.

If I had been faster, I might have saved her. With my heart racing, I sent my healing power into her anyway. I'd never tried this on someone who was clinically dead before, so I didn't know what to expect. Still, it surprised me to feel nothing. My healing energy had nothing to connect to. Her light was gone, and so was she.

Reyna came to my side. "Can't you do something?"

"No. It's too late. She was already gone."

"But... you tried, didn't you?"

I stepped away. "Of course, I did."

Reyna placed the woman's arms across her chest and drew a sheet over her body. "It's so sad," she whispered. "She had three small children, and they'll never see their mother again."

I gasped. Was she blaming me?

Her gaze caught mine. "It's not your fault. I'm sorry if it sounded that way."

But was it? If I had gotten there just a few minutes earlier, could I have saved her? Reyna's expression didn't hold blame, but there was a tightness to her mouth, like she'd expected more from me.

My throat tight, I hurried out of the room. A doctor called to me, and I pushed the tears from my eyes to help him with another accident victim. The man had a few broken bones, and I could smell alcohol on his breath, but he would live.

We got him stabilized and sedated. As the doctor determined the course of action for the patient, he glanced my way. "Rough night."

"That's for sure."

He glanced down at the man and shook his head. "And he's the one who caused it all. It's so tragic. By morning, he'll probably wish he was dead, too. I hate this part of the job."

I swallowed. "Yeah... me too."

"He's the last one. Let's hope the rest of the night is more quiet."

I nodded, checking to make sure the IV was running correctly and the man was comfortable. I'd planned to help him with my healing touch, but I just couldn't do it now. Instead, I'd focus on the other accident victims and leave this guy to fend for himself. That wasn't very charitable of me, but I didn't care. He'd killed a young mother of three small kids. He didn't deserve my help.

By the end of my shift, I was totally drained. Instead of dwelling on the woman who'd died, I'd put my energy into helping the others. If anyone noticed, I didn't care, I just wanted to make sure I did what I could.

Creed was gone when I got home, so I crawled into bed without eating or showering. I woke up in the late afternoon and finally got cleaned up. Creed called to say he'd be late and asked how I was doing. I lied and told him everything was fine and asked him about his day.

Before I knew it, it was time to head back to the hospital for another shift. Knowing I had one more shift before my break was the only thing that got me through the night. Still, I barely managed to hold it together. Reyna noticed my heavy mood and tried to cheer me up, and I appreciated her thoughtfulness.

My last shift for the week finally arrived. The day before, Lauren had dropped off a few invitations for me, in case I had friends from work to invite. I brought a couple to work, but, after only being there a few weeks, I didn't feel like I knew anyone well enough to invite, except maybe Reyna.

As my shift ended, I saw her in the hall and decided to give her an invitation. "Hey. I know it's late notice, but I'd like to invite you to my wedding party. Don't feel like you have to come—"

"Oh... how wonderful. Thank you! Of course I'll come."

"You can bring your son, if you want."

She held the envelope to her chest like it was a treasure. "Thank you Ella. I'm honored. Have you invited anyone else?"

I shrugged. "I'm not really that close to anyone else here."

"Oh... well, then I'm glad you invited me. I'll be sure to come."

"All right. Well... I'll see you next week." I hurried to my car, wondering if I'd made a mistake. She sounded almost like she was doing me a favor by coming. Maybe I should have invited some of the others, but honestly, I wasn't that close to any of them.

My time off work passed way too fast, and I almost dreaded going back to the hospital. If not for Creed and his steady presence, I might have quit. He helped me through the guilt of losing the accident victim, and I tried not to let that influence my happiness.

Back at work, I did my best to help those I could without drawing undue attention. During my break one night, I slipped into the critical care unit to help heal a burn victim. He was a firefighter, and I knew if anyone deserved some help, it was him.

I came out of the unit to find Cody, a nurse on my shift, standing at the nurse's station watching for me. I made eye contact with him, and he quickly turned away, like he'd been caught and was hiding something.

After that, he seemed to pop up in my vicinity when I least expected it, and it put me on edge. I realized he'd been lurking around me a lot more often than I'd thought. A lot like Reyna. I began to scrutinize the behavior of others around me and realized that he wasn't the only one.

A few doctors and nurses had begun to ask for me when a difficult case arrived. It seemed like they had put it together that they had a higher success rate of recovery for their patients when I was involved.

Did Reyna have something to do with that? Most orderlies stayed in the background and never spoke to the doctors, so if she was mentioning me, it was subtle enough not to raise suspicion. Still, it seemed like everyone watched me, and I didn't like all the attention.

The next night, I concentrated on my job and pushed my worries aside. My shift blurred by in a haze, and I barely managed to get enough sleep before I had to be back at the hospital.

Creed worried about me, and I realized we'd hardly spoken this whole week. I tried to make up for it with a text or a phone call, but it was never enough. Thankfully, I could look forward to working the day shift after the wedding. I only had one night shift left before then, and I could hardly wait for it to be over.

As I arrived at the ER that night, I noticed Cody speaking in hushed tones to a woman just outside the hospital entrance. As I passed them, Cody glanced my way and froze. The woman jerked her gaze to me, and I heard her ask, "Is that her?"

A chill ran down my spine, and I hurried inside. Luckily, she didn't follow me in, but I didn't like her attention. Why was she singling me out? Had Cody been feeding her stories about me? This could ruin everything. I decided then and there to confront Cody and get some answers.

After putting my things away, I joined the rest of the team, and we got our assignments for the night. The shift began uneventfully, so I decided to stock the cabinets with supplies. If Cody was up to his usual antics, this might be the perfect chance to confront him.

Sure enough, Cody stepped into the room, and I whirled around to face him. "Why are you always checking up on me?"

My outburst surprised him, and he stepped back. "I'm not. I'm just doing my job."

"No. You're watching me. Why? And who was that you were talking to outside?"

"I don't know what you mean." He tried to step around me, but I blocked his way.

"Come on Cody. Tell me what's going on."

His shoulders slumped, and he turned to face me, his mouth a grim line. Glancing behind him to make sure we were alone, he lowered his voice. "I shouldn't be telling you this, but Dr. Kelley asked me to keep an eye on you. Ever since you got here, a lot of unexplained incidents have happened, and people are talking."

I lowered my head. "What are they saying?"

"They're saying that you must have something to do with it. Dr. Kelley told me that, in the last three weeks you've been working here, not one your patients has died. But it's not just that. They've all made miraculous recoveries. Like that kid who broke his neck. You had direct contact with him, and he walked out of here."

Cody's intensity surprised me, and I took a step back from his aggressive tone. His shoulders dropped, and he hurried to explain. "Look, I don't think there's anything wrong with it, and I don't think it would have mattered so much, but people are talking. And now it's reached a reporter."

"What?"

"Yeah." He shifted on his feet. "That woman you saw me talking to was asking about you. She knows your name, and she asked me about the 'miracles' that have been happening around here. She wanted to know what I thought about them, and if I'd actually seen them happen.

"She said she was a reporter, and I don't think I'm the first person she's talked to. From all the details she knows about some of these cases, I think she's been talking to the patients. Apparently, they're more than happy to recount their miraculous recoveries with her."

His gaze bored into mine. "I didn't tell her anything, but she figured out who you were, and I'm afraid that she might hang around to talk to you." Concern narrowed his gaze. "So be careful."

I huffed out a breath. "Okay. Thanks for telling me."

"Look... I'm sorry if I've made you uncomfortable. Dr. Kelley just wanted someone to keep an eye on you. I think mostly for insurance purposes... or something like that."

"Insurance?" I shook my head. "Whatever. We'd better get back to work."

Knowing he was dismissed, he gave me a quick nod. I turned my back on him and finished filling up the cabinets. His revelation worried me, but it also made me angry. How was I supposed to help people if everyone was watching me? Did this mean I couldn't use my powers? But what if someone really needed me? I couldn't just let them die.

I was supposed to help people with my gift... at least that's what St. John had told me, so why was this so hard? Was I doing something wrong? I wanted to slam the cupboard doors shut. Instead, I clenched my fists and took a couple of deep, calming breaths. I knew getting upset wouldn't help anything, but, with so much going wrong, it was getting harder to keep my cool.

The next couple of hours passed with only minor injuries and illnesses that didn't need my special help. Three in the morning rolled around, and I took my break. If I could just get through this last shift, everything would be fine. I knew things had gotten out of hand, but, with some time off, and Creed's help, maybe I could figure out what to do about it. There had to be an answer to this. I just needed to find it.

As I finished up my snack, Reyna shoved the door open. "Ella. Come quick, they need you."

I jumped from my seat and followed her into an emergency room flooded with medical personnel. As I washed my hands and fastened my mask, she filled me in, telling me the young woman they were working on had overdosed. "The paramedics gave her Narcan, but she's barely hanging on."

I slipped to her side just as she flat-lined. The doctor gave the order to shock her heart. The first shock didn't work, but, after the second one, a faint heart beat showed on the monitor. Still, it didn't look good.

With my heart in my throat, I stepped close and placed my hand on her upper arm, praying she wouldn't die on me. Feeling her essence, I sent a blast of healing power into her bloodstream. I kept my power steady while I imagined the toxins burning out of her blood. Seconds later, her listless heart began to beat in a steady rhythm, and pink color flushed through her skin.

Her chest heaved, and she gasped in a breath. Blinking her eyes open, she regained consciousness. Filled with relief, I stepped away, hoping I hadn't been too obvious. She glanced around the room and began to talk. As the nearest nurse calmed her down, the doctor in charge caught my gaze.

He stared at me, his eyes unblinking and tense. Before I could look away, he nodded toward the door. Still catching my breath, I followed him into the hall. He turned to face me, rubbing his forehead like he didn't know what to say.

As he opened his mouth, two people came out of the ER and brushed past us. A few more entered passed by, leaving little room for privacy. "Could you come to my office please?" He waited for my nod before turning down the hall. With a deep pit of dread clawing a hole in my stomach, I followed him to a small office. He held the door open to let me pass, and I waited for him to talk, not about to give anything away before I knew what he wanted.

"I saw what you did," he began, shoving his hand through his hair. He paced back and forth in the tiny, square space. "That girl was barely alive, and you... you touched her arm.

Right after that, she came back. I know it sounds crazy, but there's no other explanation. Did you do something?"

Damn. I was obviously doing everything wrong. This was the recurring nightmare I always had, and it never ended well. I should have prepped for this sort of question. Back in New York, they'd grown used to the milder version of my healing hands, but here I could actually heal a sick patient completely. No one expected that.

I wasn't sure what to say. Should I lie and tell him it was the Narcan, and I had nothing to do with it? I hesitated long enough that he stopped pacing and folded his arms. He cocked his head and raised a brow. From his piercing stare, I knew I couldn't lie to him.

Taking a chance, I took a breath and spoke. "I don't know how to explain it, but... I have a healing touch. I know that sounds crazy, but I've always had it. With my touch, I can soothe the pain and distress people feel and help them heal. That's why I went into nursing in the first place. It just comes naturally."

He shook his head and narrowed his eyes. "This seems like a hell of a lot more than that."

I shrugged, trying to make light of it, and hoped he didn't realize how fast my heart was pounding. "I'm not sure about that. I do what I can, but I believe a higher power takes care of the rest. I may have a healing touch, but I'm not God."

He closed his eyes. "Of course not. I'm just... this is beyond anything I've ever seen, and I don't know how to explain it."

"Maybe you don't have to. There are some things that can't be explained."

A knock at the door saved us from further conversation. The doctor let out a long breath before pulling it open.

Reyna glanced between us. She sent me a hesitant smile before speaking. "Sorry to interrupt, but the girl's parents are here."

The doctor glanced my way. "Maybe you're right, but I'm not ready to let it go."

He hurried down the hall, leaving me to worry about what he'd do next. Reyna stood in the hallway and tightened her lips. "Don't worry about him. He wants a scientific explanation, and there isn't one. Maybe someday he'll see the truth like I have."

My shoulders sagged. "Maybe." But I doubted it. I sent her a quick smile, and got back to work. After eating a granola bar, I had more energy, but it seemed like everyone was watching me now, and the stress was starting to get to me.

For the next few hours, I managed to avoid the doctor. It helped that none of the cases were life threatening, so I just did my job without using my gift, which was good, since my strength was just about gone anyway.

Finally, my shift ended, and I slipped out without encountering the doctor, Reyna, or the reporter. Needing to talk to Creed, I hurried home, hoping to arrive before he left for work. As I pulled into the driveway, despair filled my heart to find his motorcycle already gone, but at least we could talk when he got home.

Right now, I needed sleep more than anything. Healing that girl had taken a lot out of me, and I was exhausted. At least I didn't have to go back to work for four days. That should give me enough time to figure things out.

Of course, the big wedding party was tomorrow night. Despite my misgivings, I wanted to enjoy this special occasion. For one night, wouldn't it be nice to forget about my healing powers and be normal? Too bad fitting in with Creed's friends and family brought a whole different set of uncertainties, and I wasn't sure which was worse.

With all that to worry about, I wasn't sure I'd able to fall asleep. But, after showering and slipping into bed, I was out like a light.

***

Sounds of voices woke me, and I stirred. Checking my watch, my eyes widened to find that it was after six p.m. and I'd slept for nine hours straight. Recognizing a voice I hadn't heard for a while, my heart sped up.

I jumped to my feet and pulled on some scrubs before hurrying around the closet divider to find Creed talking to my father. "Dad! You're here." I rarely called him Dad, and it took him by surprise. As I flew into his arms, unbidden tears filled my eyes.

"Ella."

He caught me up in a hug, and relief poured over me. I swallowed to get under control before pulling away. "I didn't know for sure if you were coming."

He grinned and took a step back to look me over. "I couldn't let my daughter get married for a second time without me." As he studied me, his brows furrowed. "Are you getting enough rest?"

"No. But I've got the next four days off, so that should help." I stepped into Creed's arms and hugged him tightly. Pulling away, I kept a tight hold around his waist. "I've been missing my husband. It's like we never see each other. But that's going to change, since I'm switching to days."

Creed's hold around me tightened, and he drew me down to sit beside him on the couch.

"That's great news," John said, sitting in the cushioned chair beside the couch. "Creed was just telling me about your schedules, so I'm glad you were able to switch. But why did you take the night shift anyway? It seems like someone with your credentials could get just about any shift you wanted."

"You know why... because at night I can help more people without being noticed."

Creed shook his head. "That's what she thought at first, but I'm not sure it's been working out so well. It turns out that people take notice when miracles start happening."

"What do you mean?" John asked, his brows dipping.

They both glanced my way, and I let out a sigh before telling John about the boy with the broken neck and all the attention that brought me. "He's one of several patients that I've helped, and, no matter how hard I try to keep things secret, it seems like someone always puts it together that I was there." I chewed on my bottom lip, knowing they weren't going to be happy with the latest development. "But that's not all. There was a reporter at the hospital last night asking about all the miracles."

Creed stiffened beside me, and John's mouth dropped open.

"She didn't talk to me, but she found out who I was."

I quickly explained that the hospital administrator had even asked another nurse to keep an eye on me, and their alarm grew. "A doctor last night actually wanted to talk to me about it. I knew if I lied, he'd see right through me, so I told him I had a healing touch, but it was in God's hands. I hope that was the right thing to do."

John sat up straight. "I hope so, too, because you can't tell anyone the truth. I think saying it's in God's hands is the best way to go. People might label you, or mock you for your beliefs, but at least it's a good way to explain it."

I let out a breath. "Yeah. I just wish I could stay under the radar. I'm supposed to heal people, but when I do it gets noticed, and I'm in trouble. If I can't do what I'm supposed to do, then why do I have this gift at all?"

"Don't say that." John's brows drew together. "It was given to you so you could help people. No one said it would be easy, but I'm sure there's a way to make it work." John rubbed the back of his neck. "What about Sandy Creek? I thought you planned to go back there. Did something change your mind?"

"Well... we were always coming here first, but now I'm not sure anymore." I shook my head. "I know I'm supposed to be intuitive about this, but I haven't had a moment to figure it out. I mean... besides working at the hospital... which I thought was the right thing... we've had this wedding to plan. But it's not just me. Creed has his work here too. Maybe once the wedding party is over, we'll have more time to talk about it."

John nodded and sent me a reassuring smile. "I'm sure you can figure it out. There is usually more than one way to go, so, while you're at it, you might think about changing your perspective."

"What do you mean?"

He shrugged. "Just take a look at all of your options. Maybe you can use your gift in other ways that don't include working in a hospital."

"Like what?" That thought had never crossed my mind.

"Lots of people need help, Ella. Not just those in the hospital."

"But..." I hesitated, knowing I shouldn't dismiss his idea outright. "Okay... maybe you're right. Maybe there is another way to help people, but I still need a paying job."

Creed stirred next to me, and I glanced his way. "What is it?"

"I have a lot of work coming in, and my agent's been making the rounds. There's a good chance I'll have one or two offers coming up. If any of them work out, we'll probably be okay on my salary if you need to quit."

"But I don't want to quit."

"I know... I'm not telling you to do that. We're just throwing out ideas here, right?"

My lips tightened. "Sure."

John leaned forward, resting his elbows on his knees. "There is something I've been meaning to tell you." He ducked his head and clasped his hands together. "I should have told you before you left New York, but the timing was never right. Maybe now it is." He caught my gaze and took a deep breath.

"Gabriella, when you were still a child, I received a notice from an anonymous donor. To this day, I'm not sure who it was, but now I think it had something to do with St. John. Anyway... the donor had opened an account in your name, with me as the custodian. The account held a big chunk of money meant for you. I dipped into it to help pay for your education, but that was just a drop in the bucket.

"The money's been growing all these years, and there's enough for you to live on... probably for the rest of your life... so you don't have to worry about money. I didn't tell you because... well... I know the value of hard work, and you haven't needed it. But now... it's almost like a way for you to use your gift to help people without worrying about making money."

Shock washed over me, and I got a little dizzy. "What? I have money?" I shook my head. "I don't understand. Who would... you think St. John did this?"

"I don't know for sure, and I know it's a surprise, but it makes sense now, where it didn't all those years ago."

"It doesn't make sense to me. Working at the hospital is all I've ever wanted. It grounds me... not doing that just seems wrong."

John gave my knee a squeeze. "I'm not saying you need to quit. It just gives you more options. Don't worry, Ella. There's time to figure it out."

I sighed and slumped against Creed. "Yeah... okay." I pinned John with a hard stare. "Is there anything else you haven't told me? Cause... we might as well get it all out now."

John's lips twisted. "No. I think that just about covers everything."

I shook my head and met Creed's gaze. "Well... it looks like you're getting more than you bargained for. You still want to 're-marry' me?"

Creed tried unsuccessfully to hold back a grin. "You're just full of surprises... but I think I can cope with the shock." His lips quirked up, and I gave him a quick kiss, unable to resist his sexy smile.

"Well... at least I know you didn't marry me for my money." I glanced between Creed and John. "But let's keep this between us for now, okay?"

"Of course." John's shoulders relaxed, and he exhaled like he'd just gotten rid of a big burden. "So what's next?"

Creed glanced at his watch. "We're meeting my mom and Avery for dinner in twenty minutes."

My mouth fell open. "We are?"

"Yes... didn't you see the text I sent you?"

"No. But that's okay. I'll just have to hurry."

I slipped into the bedroom and searched through my clothes for something appropriate to wear. I found a pair of jean shorts I liked and layered them with a tank top and a breezy blouse. After throwing on some beaded jewelry and a cute belt to dress it up, I headed into the bathroom. Combing through my thick, white-blond hair, I decided to leave it down to brush my shoulders for a change.

After adding some eye makeup, along with blush and a swipe of rose-colored lipstick, I didn't look quite so pale, but my blue-violet eyes seemed a little haunted. I shook my head. Could my life change any more drastically? Here I was, married and living in L.A. with this crazy gift, when just a couple of months ago, I was working in a small-town clinic and bored with my life.

I'd wanted to find a purpose, and now the vastness of it all was overwhelming. It almost made me want to go back to that simpler life when the only worry I faced was which scenic hike I wanted to try next. Of course, the last one had nearly killed me, so what did I know?

Could I actually do this? Become the person St. John had asked me to be? I wasn't sure. It seemed like the harder I tried to do what I was supposed to, the worse I made things. Maybe my father was right. Maybe I was doing it all wrong. But what did that mean?

"Ella," Creed called. "You almost ready?"

"Yeah. I'm coming." I squared my shoulders and took a deep breath before stepping into the living room.

CHAPTER FOUR

The drive to the restaurant on the beach wasn't far, and warmth filled me to remember the first time I'd been there. It was the night Creed and I had arrived in L.A. several weeks ago, and the moment I'd realized how much I loved him.

As we got out of the car, I caught John's raised brows and wary eyes. I had to agree that, with the peeling paint and overall shabby appearance, the restaurant wasn't much to look at.

I took John's arm and smiled. "Don't worry. It doesn't look like much on the outside, but the food is excellent, and we can sit on the deck overlooking the ocean to eat. You'll love it."

His left brow quirked up and I grinned before tugging him inside. We strolled through the restaurant to find Lauren and Avery sitting at a corner table on the deck. Lauren wore a lovely, magenta, silk blouse with a scarf that brought out her beautiful skin tones. With her lively blue eyes framed by long lashes, and long dark hair sweeping over her shoulders, her striking beauty took my breath away.

Avery's features were a close match to Lauren's, only her hair was cut short in a pixie style that made her look much younger than she was. At least her clothes were more similar to mine, although she looked so effortlessly put together that I couldn't compare. Between the two of them, they were more artfully elegant than I'd ever be.

Creed greeted his mother with a kiss on her cheek and gave Avery's shoulder a squeeze. With his dark hair the same shade as his mother's, along with his deep-set blue eyes and chiseled jaw, it was easy to see the resemblance. Just looking at the three of them together was a feast for the eyes, and it was difficult to look away.

I glanced at John, who gaped with undisguised admiration at the beauty before him. As Creed introduced them, John pulled out his most charming smile and greeted them both warmly before we took our seats at the table.

At first, Lauren and Avery seemed a little uncomfortable to eat dinner with a priest, and I realized how different he must look to them, wearing his white collar and black shirt and slacks. But John quickly put them at ease, mostly at my expense. He regaled them with stories of my childhood, embarrassing me as much as possible and unintentionally sending my self-esteem into a nosedive.

The conversation turned to the wedding, and John shook his head. "You're really going to make them exchange vows again?" He caught Lauren's gaze. "With a priest and everything?"

"Oh, heaven's no," Lauren said, waving her well-manicured hand. "Nothing like that. They're just going to say a few words about their undying devotion to each other and make us all cry." She winked at Creed. "It'll be like renewing their vows... nothing too serious."

My eyes widened, and I caught Creed's gaze. "You mean I have to give a speech?"

"Don't look so surprised. Just tell everyone how much you love me and how you knew, from the moment you laid eyes on me, that I was the only man for you."

"So you want me to lie?" At his answering chuckle, I continued. "And what are you going to say?"

"You'll just have to wait and find out."

I closed my eyes and shook my head. Public speaking was not one of my strengths, and speaking about my feelings was even worse.

"Don't worry, Ella," Avery said. "You'll do fine."

"So how many people are coming?" John asked.

"Just close friends," I answered. From the corner of my eye, I noticed Lauren stiffen and glanced her way. "Right?"

"Oh... yes, of course. Most are Aiden's friends and relatives, but I did invite a few of our close acquaintances and people in the business as well. They're all very excited to meet you, Ella."

A tiny wave of unease washed over me, but I smiled to cover it up. Still, why had I ever agreed to this? Parties with lots of strangers were not something I ever enjoyed, and I knew I was being put on display for all of Lauren's friends. This was not a world I'd ever been exposed to, and my discomfort rose. How could I fit in when I wasn't even on the same level?

Taking in Creed's handsome face and dark good looks, my unease grew even more. He was a semi-successful actor on the verge of something big, and I was just a nurse from New York. If it hadn't been for our chance encounter, we never would have met. What if this party made him realize that I didn't fit in with his world? Would he have second thoughts?

"Did you pick up your dress?" Avery asked.

I blinked. "My dress? Was I supposed to do that?" Alarm tightened my stomach.

Avery laughed. "No silly. I was just joking. I picked it up for you."

"Oh... good. Thanks."

"We're so lucky The Luxe Hotel was available for the party," Lauren said. "They have a wonderful venue with an intimate setting for exchanging vows. After that, we'll have plenty of room for dancing and greeting guests. It will be wonderful."

"With you in charge, I'm sure it will be." Creed smiled at his mother, and I hoped she didn't resent me for not helping her out more. Since it was all her idea, I'd been happy to let her take care of it. Now I hoped I'd done the right thing.

"Yes," I chimed in. "Thank you, Lauren. I'm sure it will be perfect."

She reached over and patted my hand. "I'm glad you let me do it. Just remember... if you don't like something, it's not my fault."

"I'm sure I'll love it."

"Ella's easy to please," John said. "She's never been much of a party girl, so having you take care of this is a real blessing."

Lauren smiled, her happiness undeniable, and shame that I'd ever thought poorly of her washed over me. She asked John about New York, and the conversation turned to other things. Soon, it was time to say our goodbyes and head home.

"Ella," Lauren said, taking my arm as we walked out. "I have a professional makeup artist and hairdresser coming to the hotel, so don't worry about any of that. Just make sure you're there at four. Avery will bring your dress and accessories, and we'll have everything else ready."

"Oh... okay." Had she done that to make sure I'd look better than normal because I needed all the help I could get?

"Don't worry," she said, mistaking my frown. "Avery and I will be taking advantage of their services, too."

I nodded and tried to smile. "Sure. I'll be there at four."

Lauren turned her attention to John. "You'll come early too, won't you? Aiden could use some company while he gets ready. He's wearing a black tux." She hesitated. "I didn't get one for you, but it's not too late if that's something you'd like to wear."

"Oh... no." John shook his head. "Thank you, but I brought my best priestly clothing. I assure you, I will look splendid."

"Oh, okay." Lauren's brows drew together, and it was easy to see she had no idea how John would be dressed, and it worried her. "We'll see you tomorrow then. It was great to meet you, Father... John. I'm so glad you were able to come."

"Me too," he agreed. We said our goodbyes and got into our car. As we pulled out of the parking lot, I turned to John. "So, are you staying with us? You'll have to sleep on the couch, but it's not too bad."

John chuckled. "Uh... no, but thanks. Creed booked me a room at The Luxe, so it will be easy to meet you when you come at four. I'll just plan on seeing you tomorrow."

"Oh, nice." I glanced at Creed, realizing he'd taken care of everything while I'd been wrapped up in work. "Thanks for doing that."

His lips twisted, but he refrained from giving me a hard time about it. "Of course."

At the hotel, Creed pulled into the parking lot to unload John's luggage. Before John headed inside, Creed turned to me. "You want to check out the place while we're here?"

"Sure... that's a great idea. I probably should have done that before now."

Creed shrugged. "It's okay, Ella. I know it's not your thing, and my mom's been happy to do it."

A pang of guilt swept over me. He made me sound like I didn't care. But I did. It was just all happening so fast.

After John checked in, we took a look at the outdoor Sunset Terrace room Lauren had booked. With its twinkling lights, beautiful olive and elm trees, lush hedges, and tranquil water fountains, it seemed almost magical.

"Wow. This is amazing." I glanced at Creed, and excitement bubbled up inside me.

He grinned back. "Are you actually excited about this?"

"I am now."

He let out a huff, but kept from rolling his eyes. "Finally."

"I'm sorry. I know I haven't been as involved as I should." I glanced around, taking it all in. "But this is perfect."

John followed us in and let out a low whistle. "This is nice. Lauren told me all about it, but seeing it is even better."

My heart lurched. She'd told my dad and not me? I knew it was my fault. I'd been way too busy, and I felt terrible. I stiffened with sudden realization. "Oh my gosh!" My hand flew to cover my mouth. "John... we have to pay for this."

John held up his hands. "Don't worry. I already took care of it."

Relief washed over me. "Oh, good. I'm glad you could use the money in the fund for this. I'm sure it wasn't cheap. I just feel bad that Lauren did all the work. I should have done more but—"

"It's okay." Meeting Creed's gaze, John continued. "We all understand. You've had a lot on your plate." He pulled me into a hug. "And I look forward to seeing my daughter in her beautiful wedding dress."

"Thanks, Dad."

He set me away from him. "Okay... well, it's late, and you've got a big day tomorrow." As we said our goodbyes, he lifted a hand. "Oh... one more thing. A night's stay here at the hotel for the two of you was included with the package, just in case you didn't know."

"Sweet!" I glanced at Creed, who didn't seem surprised. "Did you know that?"

"Yup." He pulled me against his side. "Come on, let's go home."

"Goodnight," I called to John. He waved, and we headed back to our car. It was late, but, since I'd slept most of the day, I was wide awake.

Back home at the apartment, I kicked off my sandals and sank onto the couch. Creed sat down beside me, and I snuggled into his arms.

"Thanks for taking care of everything," I told him. He grunted and I shook my head. "I hope I'm not too much of a pain."

He took my hand and twined our fingers together. "You've been busy. It's hard trying to figure all this out with your gift and everything. What you can do is a big responsibility, and I want to help you with that. After what you told me today, I'm a little worried about all the attention it's bringing you."

"Yeah... me too. It would have helped to talk about it with you before now. I'll try and do better in the future."

He shook his head. "It's okay. I think it had more to do with our schedules, but, now that you've taken care of that, it will be so much better."

"No kidding. Just think... we'll get to sleep with each other every night."

"I can't wait."

"Me either." Now that we had the whole night to ourselves, I wanted to share all my worries. "There is one other thing I haven't told you."

His brows rose. "What's that?"

"I think the reason I haven't been very enthusiastic about the wedding party is because most everyone there, besides John, will be strangers to me. They're all people you know or who are tied to your family. I'm going to be the odd one out, and I'm just a little nervous about it."

He nodded. "That makes perfect sense. But I'll be with you the whole time. You won't be alone. Avery will be there too. I'm sure she'll want to stick close."

"Yeah, she's great. I'm just worried that I won't fit in."

"Angel... you don't have to fit in... in fact, I'd rather you didn't. I know this isn't your thing, and I'm really glad about that. Sometimes these parties can feel forced... like everyone's playing a part and trying to outdo everyone else. But this is a celebration for us, so I'm hoping it will be a little different.

"You know my mom and I are part of that "Hollywood" world, and she wants to show us off, but her intentions are good. I really appreciate you going along with it, since I know it means a lot to her. But don't ever feel like you need to fit in with that crowd. You're like a breath of fresh air... and that's the way I want to keep it. It's one of the reasons I fell in love with you, and I would hate it if you ever changed."

"But what about you? That's your world, too."

He paused. "You're right... I am part of that, but you keep me grounded. I think we do that for each other. Even though our worlds are miles apart, let's never lose sight of what's important."

"And what's that?"

"Us. Whatever it takes, we stick together."

I grinned. "Okay. I'll try to remember that tomorrow night, especially if some ex-girlfriend shows up."

His lips twisted and he shook his head. "I went over the guest list with my mom, so unless she changed something, we should be good."

"Are you serious?"

He chuckled but didn't deny it. Before I could say another word, he tickled my ribs, and I struggled to get away.

"Oh no you don't." I smacked him and launched an attack of my own. Soon, we were both breathless, and I was sprawled on top of him. I lowered my lips to his, and he kissed me back, eagerly tugging at the hem of my shirt.

"I'm sure glad John's staying at the hotel," he said. "I nearly died when you offered him the couch."

I laughed. "Yeah... I caught that look on your face. It was pretty funny."

He growled and tightened his hold around me. Before I knew it, he'd twisted me onto my back and kissed me until I couldn't think straight. In fact... I really couldn't think at all.

After lounging around the next morning, we finally got out of bed and ate some breakfast. It was the first time we'd eaten breakfast together for a while, and I wasn't sure that would happen when I had to be to work at seven in the morning.

"Will you get up at six and eat breakfast with me before I go to work?"

He let out a huff. "And lose out on my beauty sleep? I don't think so." At my frown, he shrugged. "But I'll more than make up for it, since we'll be sleeping together for a change. I guess you could find a different job where you don't have to get up so early."

I sighed and shook my head. "That's not going to happen. I mean... not that I don't enjoy eating breakfast with you, but I don't want to quit working at the hospital. Do you think I might have to?"

Creed rubbed my arm. "Maybe things will be different working on the day shift? I know John said there were other ways to use your gift, but let's not worry about that right now. Today's a big day. Have you figured out what you're going to say for your vows?"

I huffed out a breath and rolled my eyes. "Well... since I just found out about it last night at dinner, I don't have a clue."

He snickered. "Do you want me to help? I can give you a few pointers. I could even write the speech if you'd like. You could start by saying that you were so entranced with me that you hit me with your car to keep me around."

"That's terrible. It's not even funny."

His smile widened. "Okay... that's fine. But I hope you don't mind if I put it in my speech."

"Don't you dare."

"I guess you'll just have to wait and see."

I shook my head. "If that's the case, then you're going first."

He cocked a brow. "Sure... on one condition."

"What's that?"

"Since we both need to shower, you have to wash my back."

I grinned, remembering the first time I'd helped Creed shower. His leg was broken and I'd enjoyed having the upper hand. Getting him in and out of the shower was a moment I'd always remember with fondness... especially the part where his towel fell off.

Warmth filled my heart. We may not have known each other long, but I knew he was mine, and I looked forward to telling everyone at the wedding how much I loved him.

We met John in the lobby of the hotel, and my eyes widened to find him wearing his cassock and looking official. It seemed like he'd gone a little overboard. "You look nice, but a suit would have been fine. I mean... we're already married, so it's not like you have to perform our ceremony."

"I know, but I rather like this outfit... it reminds me of Neo in the Matrix. Only with a collar."

A small laugh escaped me. "I never thought of it like that, but you have a point." It hit me that my father wanted to make a statement, but I wasn't sure what it was. "So why are you really wearing it?"

He stood tall, and his unwavering gaze met mine. "I guess I want to make a point that, even though this is a wedding party, there's a deeper meaning behind this occasion. You've already made vows to each other, and I don't want the spiritual part of your marriage to be forgotten."

I nodded, understanding him perfectly. I glanced at Creed and found him nodding as well. Sure we'd come back to our normal lives, but that wasn't all we were. I had this amazing gift, and Creed was part of that. St. John had told Creed he was my protector, and we both needed to make sure that was our priority.

Putting everything that had happened in the last month into perspective, it suddenly felt like we were on the precipice of something big, and I hoped we could handle whatever came next.

Lauren and Avery entered the hotel and greeted us in the lobby. Lauren had Creed's tux, and Avery came with my dress, along with hers and her mothers. We said goodbye to John and Creed, then one of the hotel staffers led us to a special bridal suite so we could get ready, while John took Creed to his room to change.

Lauren had me undress and slip on a white terrycloth robe to get started, and I realized this was going to be a major production. A makeup artist arrived and got to work on me, while a hairdresser worked on Lauren and Avery. I tried to remain upbeat and positive, letting Lauren and Avery do most of the talking.

I turned my head and did whatever I was told, and, after a while, I began to relax a little. I even got caught up in the excitement, especially after Lauren and Avery kept proclaiming about how amazing I looked.

I finally got to see what they were exclaiming about a few seconds later. The makeup artist finished and turned my chair to face the full-length mirrors along the length of the wall.

I stared at my reflection for several seconds before it registered that it was really me. Holy smokes! I looked like a super-model or someone famous. The dark eyeliner around my eyes made them seem even bigger than normal, and, with the hint of smoky eyeshadow, the deep violet-blue color seemed almost ethereal. My normally pale skin had a rosy glow, and my lips looked even fuller than usual and sported the perfect shade of pink to match my skin tones.

Finished, the makeup artist moved to work on Avery, and the hairdresser took her place. He ran his fingers through my hair to assess the best way to style it. After getting a feel for what he had to work with, he asked me if I wanted it up or down. Since I had no preference, I told him to figure it out.

I wasn't sure my hair was long enough to style it up, but that didn't stop him from going in that direction. He spent several minutes matching the color with a myriad of hair extensions he'd brought and finally settled on one.

Someone asked if I wanted to listen to some music, and I agreed, as long as it was soothing. Hearing a beautiful, classical piece helped me relax, and I closed my eyes.

Maybe now was a good time to figure out what I was going to say. Only... my thoughts were too scattered to make much sense of them, and, after rambling on and on in my mind, I finally gave up. I'd just say what was in my heart and hope that was good enough.

At last the hairdresser put the finishing touches on my hair and turned me toward the mirror. Worried that I'd hate it, I took a deep breath and opened my eyes. Relief washed over me to find a beautiful coiffure that looked more natural than I would have believed. It was the perfect combination of curls and fullness, with the added touch of shimmering rhinestones to make me look elegant and alluring, without being a big puffy mess.

For never wearing my hair or makeup like this, I worried that Creed wouldn't recognize me, but it was too late to change now. Avery and Lauren seemed to love it, so I tamped down my worry and hoped Creed would be happy.

With all three of us looking beautiful, it was time to get dressed. Our dresses hung on a clothes rack, and Lauren and Avery insisted on getting dressed first so they could help me with my dress once they were done.

As I watched them, I totally understood why we'd needed to start at four. I'd never spent so much time on my appearance in my life. Finally, it was my turn to get dressed. Lauren and Avery took great care helping me step into the lacy dress. They treated me like I was royalty, and I tried not to enjoy it too much.

After slipping my arms through the bodice, I straightened to suck in my stomach so Lauren could zip it up. The dress was designed with corded lace that beautifully detailed the fit-and-flare silhouette style. It fit even better than when I'd first tried it on, and the Sabrina neckline was perfectly paired with the alluring V-style back.

Lauren played with the bottom folds until she was satisfied and turned me toward the full-length mirror. My breath caught, and I swallowed my surprise. I looked amazing. Gratitude washed over me that maybe I would fit in after all.

"Oh Ella," Avery said, holding a hand to her heart. "You look stunning. I can't wait to see the look on Aiden's face. He's going to pass out."

Lauren chuckled. "He's not going to pass out, but I think he'll fall in love with her all over again. You are a beautiful bride, and I couldn't be more proud."

"Thanks Lauren, that means a lot."

"Of course." A small table by the door held a beautiful bouquet of flowers, and Lauren picked them up. "These are for you. I hope you love them."

The small bouquet held pink and white roses that cascaded down in a waterfall of color, and were accented with matching ribbon. "Wow. It's gorgeous. Thank you."

"Good. Before we go, I asked the photographer to come in and take some pictures. Let me see if she's out there."

I took the amazing bouquet, and Lauren opened the door. Outside, she found the woman, who quickly came inside and took several pictures of us and a few of me by myself.

Once she was done, Lauren turned to me. "I think it's time. Are you ready?"

I took a deep breath and let it out. "I think so."

"Avery, go get her father."

After Avery left, Lauren explained that my father would walk me to the terrace garden where Creed would be waiting. The guests were all seated, and, once I joined Creed, my father would welcome everyone and say a few words. Then Creed and I would exchange our vows, and we'd be married... again.

"Oh... I didn't know my father was doing that."

"Yes, we got it all ironed out this morning."

"Okay... nice. What happens after the vows?"

"After that, you'll get lots of pictures taken while the chairs are removed so you can meet the guests. Not everyone was invited to the official vow exchange, so more people will be showing up throughout the evening. But we'll have food, and dancing, and of course pictures... lots of pictures. Oh... and there's a videographer as well. I knew Aiden wouldn't want to miss out on a wedding video."

I nodded, shocked at how much had gone into this 'little' party, and that she had made so many decisions without me. I didn't realize how important a wedding video was, but at the moment, I had to admit I was grateful. Thank goodness John had been involved to pay for it all since we had the funds.

I followed her out the door and found my father waiting for me. With a quick smile, Lauren left us there to find her place in the terrace garden. Now that I knew his role in this venture, I could understand why my father wore the cassock and looked so official.

He smiled, and his eyes misted over. "Gabriella... you look beautiful. I am so proud of you." He held out his elbow, and I placed my hand around his arm.

"Thanks, Dad... and thanks for raising me as your own."

"It was one of the greatest joys of my life." He swallowed and managed a tremulous smile. "Shall we go?"

"Yes."

We began the short walk outside to the terrace yard. I barely registered the photographer, the videographer, the beautiful setting, and the white lights shimmering in the trees. Once my gaze landed on Creed, he was the only thing that mattered.

My step faltered a bit to see him standing there waiting for me. I'd never seen such a handsome man in all my life. The black tux fit his form to perfection, and the sparkle in his eyes, along with his sexy smile, took my breath away.

John took his time, proudly walking beside me until we reached Creed. Avery stepped forward to take my bouquet, and John placed my hands in Creed's before stepping around us to face the crowd. Creed leaned in close to whisper. "You look more beautiful than an angel."

I smiled, squeezing his hands tightly. "Thanks. So do you..." My eyes widened. "I mean... for a guy."

Creed's lips turned up, and his eyes sparkled with mirth.

John began. "We'd like to welcome all of you here to celebrate the marriage of Aiden Creed and Gabriella St. John."

Just hearing him announce our names together sent a thrill through me. Even though we'd been married by a saint, and then a justice of the peace, this ceremony seemed to finally make it all real.

John continued to speak about the sanctity of marriage and how our love brought us together. Before I knew it, he was telling us it was time to exchange our vows. He glanced at Creed. "Aiden, let's start with you."

Creed met my gaze, and my heart lurched in my chest to have this amazing man looking at me with so much love in his eyes. "Ella... we met on a lonely stretch of road during a rainstorm when my car broke down. You ran into me and broke my leg."

Chuckles of delight came from the audience, and I tried not to wince.

Creed's lips turned up in a rueful smile. "It was a painful way to meet, but, if you hadn't come along right at that moment, I would never have met you. So... even though our journey began a little rough, I'd do it all over again just to have you in my life.

"You gave me your trust, your patience, and your love. I am a better man because of you. You may have nursed me back to health, but you mended much more than a broken leg. You mended my heart, and you fill my days with happiness.

"I call you 'Angel,' because that's what you are to me. The first time I called you that was the day I began to fall in love with you, and I've been falling more in love with you every day. You are my beautiful Angel, and I promise to stand by your side, to love you, cherish you, and honor you all the days of my life. Come what may, Gabriella St. John, I love you, and I will love you with all of my heart until the day I die."

I blinked back my tears and tried to swallow the lump in my throat. My heart was so full, I wasn't sure I could speak. Creed squeezed my hands, lending me strength, and I took a deep breath and began my vows.

"Aiden... as painful as our first meeting was, I believe that we weren't brought together by chance. I believe that you and I were destined to share our lives together. In you, I've found my best friend, my lover, my protector, and my equal. You help me grow and make me a better person. Because of you, I can face the challenges of each day and know that I am not alone.

"I promise to love you, respect you, and cherish you all the days of my life. Whatever our future holds, I love you Aiden Creed, and I will love you with all of my heart until the end of time."

Creed blinked the tears from his eyes and mouthed, "I love you."

John cleared his throat to control his emotions and continued the ceremony. Nodding at Creed, he said, "You may now exchange the rings."

My eyes widened. We'd looked at rings a few weeks ago, but we hadn't bought them. Before I could panic, Creed reached into his pocket and pulled two ring boxes out. Handing me one, he opened the other and took out the beautiful diamond ring I'd admired but didn't think we could afford. He placed it on my finger with a wicked gleam in his eyes.

I marveled at it for a moment before opening the box he'd given me. I took out the simple, titanium band etched with Celtic symbols Creed had picked out, and managed to slip it onto his finger. In the next instant, Creed gathered me in his arms and kissed me.

I vaguely heard some cheering and clapping from the guests before we pulled apart and turned to face them. With smiles all around, Creed took my hand and raised it high in a sign of victory. We were quickly ushered into a spot beneath a beautiful, white-flowered pergola, while the chairs were moved to the back around several tables. Our photographer cornered us for several photos, and surprisingly, I enjoyed being the center of attention.

Several minutes later, Lauren and Avery joined us, hugging and kissing us both. "That was amazing," Avery said. "It was the most beautiful ceremony I've ever been to. You guys are so perfect for each other, and you look like royalty."

"Thanks Avery." I smiled, my heart so full I was afraid it would burst.

"It was wonderful," Lauren said, giving Creed a hug. "I'm so proud of both of you." She turned to hug me before pulling away. "I hope someday I can fill that spot a mother would have in your life... at least, I'd like to try."

"Thank you Lauren. I'd love that."

John shook Creed's hand while patting him on the back. He released Creed to hug me. "I'm glad you did this, although I liked how you got married the first time just as much."

I grinned. "They were both wonderful in their own ways."

More people came to wish us well, and I enjoyed meeting Creed's friends and relatives, along with some of his co-workers. The terrace began to fill up with people, most of them new arrivals who hadn't been at the ceremony.

A long time later, after we greeted nearly all of the newcomers, a few of Creed's friends pulled him away, and I stood there, uncertain about what to do. Avery came to my rescue, introducing me to some of her friends. We wandered to a table for a drink and nibbled on some amazing hors d' oeuvres.

We spoke for a few minutes longer, but soon Avery and her friends got distracted, and I was left out of the conversation. I glanced around the room, hoping to spot a familiar face. A woman came to my side and I gasped. "Reyna. You came."

I hardly recognized her. She wore a deep crimson dress, with her long, dark hair flowing down her back in beautiful waves. Her dark eyes and skin, combined with her ruby red lips, made her seem exotic and nothing like I was used to.

"Ella. You look amazing. Congratulations." She gave me a quick hug. "I'm honored you invited me." She glanced around the room. "I have to say I didn't expect to see so many celebrities... including your husband. You didn't tell me you were marrying a movie star... and such a handsome one at that."

I pulled away, a bit surprised by her scolding tone. "No, you're right, I didn't. But he's much more than that to me."

"Of course he is... I didn't mean to imply anything. It's just not what I expected... with you being..." She glanced around the room before meeting my gaze, "...so special and all. But I couldn't be happier for you."

"Thanks. I'm glad you could come. Did you bring your son? I'd love to meet him."

She shook her head. "Oh... no. You know boys and weddings... not something they're too interested in. But I would love to introduce you another time. Maybe after you come back from your honeymoon?"

"Sure... or any time, really."

"How long will you be gone?"

"Well... we're not going on a honeymoon right now. But we're planning to go somewhere special later." I hated admitting that we hadn't planned a honeymoon. Creed had mentioned it, but I'd been too absorbed in my work, and now I felt like an idiot. What kind of wife doesn't want to go on a honeymoon?

"Oh sure... that makes sense. I hear a lot of people do it that way. Then they can have something else to look forward to."

"Exactly." She gave me the perfect way out, so I had to take it.

Luckily, Avery came to my side, saving me from the awkward moment, and I introduced them. After we exchanged pleasantries, Avery told me that her aunt wanted to speak to me, so we made our excuses and left.

"You looked like you needed rescuing," Avery said, pulling me toward her aunt. "Is she really an orderly at the hospital?"

"Yes, but now I'm beginning to wonder. At work no one really notices her, but tonight she looked amazing."

"Yeah... she's a knock-out. Anyway, come with me, I wasn't kidding about Aunt Jody wanting to talk to you."

She pulled me toward a woman that was the spitting image of Lauren only with lighter hair and a little older. I'd already met her, but it was so brief that I didn't remember anything she'd said. With a warm, bright smile, she included me in the circle of family members who had gathered together, and my heart swelled to be part of a big family. I'd never had that, and it amazed me to realize how much it meant to me.

"Where's Aiden?" Avery asked, glancing over the crowd. "He should be here. I'll go track him down."

She left my side, and a beautiful woman took her place, stepping in front of me with bright eyes and a smile that seemed a little too big. "Hi," she said, her voice perky. "I'm a friend of Aiden's, and I've been dying to meet the woman who captured his heart."

The woman looked slightly familiar, but I couldn't place her. I gave her a polite smile, but her attitude of superiority left me cold.

"I'm Whitney Hughes," she continued, not put off in the least by my less-than-enthusiastic smile. "I'm in the cast of

My Crazy Life and I met Aiden when he had a bit part on the set."

"Oh... yeah. I've seen that show. I thought you looked familiar."

"Yup... that's me. Some of us were a bit shocked to hear he'd gotten married, but I guess something must have clicked between you two. Anyway...congratulations."

"Thank you."

"Did Aiden tell you the exciting news? I'm so thrilled for him."

I shook my head. "What news is that?"

Her eyes widened. "Oh dear... I thought for sure he'd told you... but maybe he wanted it to be a surprise." She glanced away, but I caught a glimmer of malice in her eyes. I may not know what game she was playing, but I could definitely spot trouble when I saw it.

I didn't respond, and she squirmed in the silence, her gaze skimming over the crowd. She glanced back at me, so I arched my brow and tilted my head. "Was there something else you wanted to say?"

She let out a nervous chuckle. "Oh... no. Not about that. I just thought... well, it was nice to meet you. I'd love for us to be friends. You know how it is in this business... a good friend is hard to find, and the more people you know, the better off you are."

"Yes. I imagine that's true."

She scurried off, and I finally caught sight of Creed heading my way. His concerned gaze met mine, and his lips quirked up with an apologetic smile. As I moved toward him, Lauren, and a man I didn't know, came between us.

"Aiden! Why didn't you tell me?" Lauren motioned to the man beside her. "Rod just told me you got the part. I didn't even know that you were auditioning."

Creed's brows drew together. "What?"

"He couldn't have told you," Rod said. "I just found out a few hours ago myself." He placed a hand on Creed's shoulder and squeezed. "But it's good news. They want you to co-star with Peyton Lind on *Crossfire*. You got the part!" He turned to Lauren. "She's the principle star of the show, but they want Creed to be her partner."

Turning back to Creed, he continued. "They were impressed by your audition and really liked the chemistry between the two of you. This is huge. It's almost like having your own show. I mean… she's the star, but this could be your big break."

I stepped to Creed's side and took his hand. I'd heard of Peyton Lind. She was an up-and-coming actress who'd played a star-crossed lover in a recently canceled TV series. Were they saying that Creed had been cast opposite her in a new TV show?

Creed glanced at me, his eyes clouded with worry. "Ella, I had no idea. This is a surprise. I honestly didn't expect to get the part." He let out a breath and squeezed my fingers before glancing at Rod. "Are you sure?"

Rod chuckled. "Yes… it's true. You did it. You got the part." Rod stepped in close, separating me from Creed, and gave him a hug, pounding his back. "Congratulations man… you've done it. All that hard work has finally paid off. I couldn't be more proud."

"Thank you." Creed's grin split his face. "This is unreal."

"Well… get used to it." Rod turned his attention to me.

"You must be Ella." He extended his hand. "As you've probably guessed, I'm Creed's agent, and I've been dying to meet you. Congratulations to you both. I have to admit I was a bit shocked when Creed said he'd gotten married, but now I can see why."

He wiggled his brows at Creed. "And now you have even more to celebrate. Getting this part is just the beginning of so many possibilities." He patted Creed's shoulder again. "Let's get together tomorrow to iron out the details of the contract." He glanced my way. "Ella, it was lovely to meet you."

Tomorrow? Was he serious? Before I could say a word, Lauren stepped in to take his place. She threw her arms around Creed, holding him tight before looking into his eyes. "Oh, Aiden, I'm so excited. What good news. I always knew you had a bright future in this business." She squeezed his arm and caught sight of someone behind us. "There's Emily. I have to tell her. She'll be thrilled."

Creed let out a breath and turned to me. "Ella, I—"

"Creed!" A woman squealed. "I just heard. Congratulations." She threw herself into Creed's arms. "This is so exciting." More of Creed's friends crowded around us, and Creed got swallowed up in the excitement. He did his best to stay beside me, but people kept pulling him away to congratulate him. In this crowd of actors, Creed's good fortune was a bigger cause for celebration than our wedding.

Soon, I found myself on the outside edge of the crowd. Was this what it felt like to be married to a celebrity? My stomach got a little queasy. This was my biggest fear, and it was happening right before my eyes.

A man stepped beside me, and I welcomed the company until I recognized his low tone. "Hello, Ella."

A shiver ran down my spine. How did Dom Orlandi get in here? Last time I saw him, he'd tried to kill me, and he would have succeeded if not for my gift. Tall and lean, he gazed down at me, a slight smile creasing his lips, and I tried not to shudder. "It looks like Creed has abandoned you."

"What are you doing here?"

His brows rose. "I came to offer my congratulations."

I huffed out a breath. "Right. What's the real reason?"

"Well... there is something you need to know." He glanced over his shoulder. "I think you'll want to sit down for this."

He motioned to a table near the back wall and started in that direction. Talking to him was the last thing I wanted to do, but I didn't have a choice. At the round table, he maneuvered two chairs close together and waited for me to sit.

I sat beside him and tried to act cool and unruffled, but having him so close sent phantom pain into my chest where he'd shot me. I focused my anger on the fact that he'd dare show up here, and the pain subsided, leaving me calm and clear-headed.

"I've done what I could," he began, picking up a napkin and shredding it with his fingers. "But word has reached Sonny that Avery has recovered enough to testify against him. With the trial coming up, he sent me here to make sure she doesn't."

At my widened eyes, he continued. "I'm not going to hurt her. I'll figure out a way to put him off, but I'm not the only person Sonny asked for help. The other person is far more dangerous than me, and I thought you should know."

"Who is it?"

"His name is Gage Rathmore, and he's more powerful than anyone else I know." Dom's gaze darted around the room before coming back to mine. "If you can talk Avery out of testifying, I think I can convince Sonny to leave her alone." I began to shake my head, and he leaned closer. "Please. I can't protect her from Rathmore. With his involvement, she's as good as dead."

"But then Sonny will go free. After everything he's done, how is that right?"

"It's better than Avery dying. Tell her she can't testify."

My lips twisted. "You tried to kill Creed, and you nearly killed me. How can I trust you?"

"I'm looking out for her, just like I told you I would. That's the reason I'm here. You need to talk some sense into her. She has a new lease on life. I'd hate to see anything happen to her after all she's been through. You have a week at most, but I can't protect her after that. Just... let me know as soon as you can."

"If you really care about her, then prove it. Testify against Sonny yourself. Then Avery won't have to."

His brows rose. "You can't be serious."

"I'm dead serious."

He blew out a breath, and his hand squeezed into a fist. "He'll kill me."

"Better you than her."

"Dom?" Several feet away, Avery stood frozen in shock.

Caught off-guard, Dom glanced at her and swore under his breath. He hunched over to stare into my eyes and lowered his voice. "Don't let her testify."

I placed my hand over his fist, my power ready to pull the life out of him. "If anything happens to Avery, I will hunt you down and send you straight to hell."

With a gasp, he jerked away from my touch and shoved back from the table. Unable to hide his fear, he turned on his heel and stepped into the crowd.

CHAPTER FIVE

A very hurried to my side, her gaze glued on Dom's retreating back. "What was he doing here?" Her face had gone pale, and she leaned against the table for support.

I pulled her down to sit in Dom's vacated chair. "Have you heard from the prosecuting attorney about Sonny's trial?"

Her gaze followed Dom until he disappeared from sight. Then she glanced my way and bit her bottom lip. "I didn't want to say anything and ruin your wedding day. So what did Dom want?"

"He said he'd convince Sonny to forget all about you if you refuse to testify at the trial."

She let out a derisive sniff. "Yeah... right. That's not going to happen."

"There might be another way." I patted Avery's cold hands. "If someone else turns against Sonny, they won't need you."

Her eyes widened. "You mean someone like Dom?" She shook her head. "That's never going to happen either."

"Maybe not... but I'm going to see what I can do. If not him, someone else could be persuaded."

Regret tightened her eyes, and she shook her head. "Maybe... but... this isn't the time to be worrying about that.

In fact... this is your party, and you and Aiden aren't even together. I've been looking all over for you. I just heard about Aiden's offer, and I can't believe that he just left you sitting here all by yourself."

"It's okay. People were congratulating him and he got pulled away. It's not his fault."

She frowned. "Yes it is. He shouldn't have left you alone. I'm going to find him and talk some sense into him. You're a lot more important than some stupid TV show."

She marched off and I sighed. This was not how I'd expected my wedding party to go, but I didn't want Avery to make a scene either.

I stood to follow her, and John spotted me. "There you are," he said, hurrying to my side. "I just heard about Creed's offer. Did you know?"

I shook my head. "No... I think it surprised him, too."

Concern tightened his face. "I think taking that acting job is a mistake."

"Uh... yeah... it worries me too, but what am I supposed to do? This offer looks like a dream come true for him."

"That may be, but I thought his dreams changed when he married you."

"I know, I did too, but we never talked about his career, and we had no idea that I had money." I patted John's arm. "Don't worry. I don't think he's signed a contract yet. We'll talk about it and figure it out."

John shook his head. "There is nothing to figure out. He shouldn't take the job."

I sighed. I wasn't sure Creed would feel the same way. This was his big chance. What would happen if he gave it up for me? I would never want that. Glancing over the crowd, I spotted Creed. As his head turned my way, I waved to catch his attention.

Relief flooded over his tight face, and he pushed through the crowd toward me. Avery got to him first and started chewing him out. He stiffened before shaking his head and turning away from her. By then, I'd made it to his side, just in time to hear Avery say Dom's name.

He whipped back around to her. "What did you say?"

"Dom was here, threatening Ella, and you left her all alone."

Shock tightened his jaw, and he turned to me. "Are you okay?"

"He wasn't threatening me. He just wanted to deliver a message."

Creed jerked his head up to look for Dom, and I took his arm. "He's gone."

"What did he say?"

At Creed's harsh tone, the people standing around us turned to gawk. I squeezed Creed's arm and sent him a smile. He realized people were watching and relaxed his stance. "Let's talk over there." He motioned to a corner of the room and glanced at Avery. "Stand guard for us, okay?"

She nodded and turned to face the crowd while we walked away. Reaching the corner, I leaned into him. "He said Avery might be in trouble if she insists on testifying against Sonny." Creed swore under his breath, and I rubbed his arm to soothe him. "It's okay... we'll figure this out."

His brows drew together. "What did you tell him?"

I licked my lips, knowing that using my powers to hurt people wasn't part of my job description. "I told him to leave Avery alone or he'd regret it. After he told me that Sonny has a powerful friend who may come after her, it made me mad. I may have mentioned that there was another way to take Sonny down without involving Avery, and that Dom could turn on Sonny himself. I don't think he liked that idea, but maybe he just needs a little convincing?"

Creed's eyes tightened. "By you? Did you hurt him?"

My eyes widened. "No. Of course not."

"St. John warned you not to use your gift that way. That's why you have me."

"I know... but you weren't here." Creed flinched, and I regretted my words. "I'm sorry... I shouldn't have said that. He just surprised me... and it scared me a little, so I'm kind of defensive."

Creed sighed and rubbed his forehead. "I knew this day would come. I just didn't know it would be today. Do you think Avery's safe? Should we be worried?"

"Dom said she'd be fine for at least a week, and we have to let him know by then if she's going to testify."

"I don't think we can talk her out of it."

"I don't know what to think anymore. It's a mess. Everything's happening all at once, and it's a lot to take in." I tried not to grimace, but I couldn't hide my disappointment that it had ruined our day. "And now you've been offered a part for this new TV show. I wish I had known it was a possibility. Maybe it wouldn't have been such a shock."

"I'm sorry Ella, but I didn't expect to get the part. I got blindsided by Rod, and then everyone here ganged up on me. I'm sorry we got separated, especially since Dom showed up."

"It's not your fault." I swallowed my disappointment and mustered a smile. "I mean... this part you landed sounds like a dream come true."

His lips turned down. "It's a big deal, but having it happen like this..." He shook his head. "I figured if I got the offer, we'd talk about it and decide what to do together. Now everyone expects me to take the part, and I don't know how you feel about it."

"I'm happy for you... I just didn't expect it... and deep down... I'm not sure what it would mean for us. Not because it wouldn't be great for your career... but because of me."

He nodded, but he couldn't keep the regret from showing in his eyes. "Don't worry. If it's not good for us... then I'll turn it down."

From his dejected tone, I knew it hurt him to say that, and my heart broke. "We'll figure it out, and I would never ask you to do that."

His lips twisted, and he shook his head. "We'll see. But right now, we need to get back to our celebration. It's already gone off the rails, so, before anything else happens, I have a special surprise for you, and you're not leaving my side again."

He took my hand and pulled me toward the small dancing space in front of the four-member band. With a signal from him, the group of musicians stopped the number they were playing and started a new one. To the strains of "Angel of Mine," Creed pulled me into his arms. My heart melting, I smiled up at him, amazed at this sweet gesture.

"I love you, Angel. We'll figure this out together. All of it."

I nodded. "I love you too." I gazed up at him, hoping he could see all the love I had for him plainly in my eyes. All I wanted at this moment was to enjoy dancing with my husband and forget about everything else.

His eyes softened, and he held me tight. We began to dance and I inhaled his wonderful scent. As his strong arms held me close, we stepped together in perfect harmony. Everyone in the crowd turned to watch, and I caught sight of Avery and Lauren, both of them smiling with delight. John stood beside them, more worried than happy. As he met my gaze, he mustered a smile and dipped his head.

I glanced up to meet Creed's deep blue eyes, and he leaned close to place a tender kiss on my lips. The crowd broke into applause, and under the twinkling lights, we swayed together. Gratitude warmed my heart knowing that, for this moment, no one could pull us apart.

After the song ended, other people joined us on the dance floor, and we traded partners. John danced with me, while Creed danced with his mother. Several of Creed's friends took John's place until Creed had danced with Avery and his aunt. After that, he refused to dance with anyone but me.

Half an hour later, Creed sent me a sexy grin and whispered in my ear. "Ready to go?" I smiled up at him and nodded.

He swirled me around the dance floor one last time before pulling me to his side and raising his hand. "Thanks everyone. Enjoy the rest of the evening. My lovely wife and I will be going now."

Amid all the cheers and good wishes, we left the hall and made our way to the hotel lobby and the elevator to our room. In the lobby, a group of people surrounded Whitney Hughes and a few of the other celebrities from our party. When we appeared, their attention turned toward us, and several people let out exclamations.

To my surprise, they started our way, and Creed pulled me toward the bank of elevators. Before we got there, the group caught up to us and began to pepper us with questions.

"Congratulations on your wedding. Is it true that you only met a month ago?"

"Where did you meet?"

"How long have you known each other?"

"Creed, are you excited about working with Peyton Lind?"

In the ensuing silence, Creed opened his mouth to reply, but was cut off.

"Are you the nurse who works at Saint John's Memorial Hospital? What do you think about all the miracles happening there? Did you have something to do with them?"

My gaze flew to the woman talking. She was the same reporter from the hospital. With growing horror, I instinctively backed away. Her unusual questions silenced the others, and they all stared at me.

"Thank you for your interest," Creed said, slipping his arm around me. "I'm sure you're all curious, and I promise to answer your questions at a more appropriate time. As you can see, my beautiful bride and I are eager to enjoy the rest of our celebration... alone."

Amid the chuckles, he focused his most charming smile on the woman who'd asked about me. "As for my wife being the cause of miracles, I would have to agree." He glanced at me tenderly. "She definitely saved me."

He leaned down to kiss me, giving the reporters just what they wanted, and I heard several sighs. Pulling away, he ushered me to the elevator and pushed the call button. The doors opened, and Creed pulled me inside, pushing the button for our floor. With a wave at the watching people, he leaned close to kiss me again. Amid their cheers, the elevator doors slid shut.

Ending the kiss, I held his gaze. "Wow. You are amazing. That could have been awful, but you handled it perfectly."

Creed grinned. "It's about time you learned that I'm more than a handsome face."

"Oh... I already knew that, I've just never seen you in action before."

The doors opened, and we cautiously stepped into the hallway. Finding it empty, we hurried to our hotel room and slipped inside, relieved to be alone.

Creed locked the door behind us and I let out a breath. Still reeling from what had just happened, I turned to Creed. "Did you know the media were going to be here?"

He shook his head. "No, but it wouldn't surprise me if my agent organized it."

"What are we going to do?"

Creed took my hands and squeezed them. "I know this seems overwhelming, but we can handle it. I'll talk to Rod and we'll get a story together that answers all the questions about us and our marriage. You know how the media is. Half the time the stuff they say is made up and everyone knows it." Noticing my shiver, he rubbed my bare arms.

"And the reporter who asked about me? Was that enough to stop her?"

"I'm sure we can find a way to discount that line of questioning. It's not believable, and we can spin it that way."

I wrapped my arms around his waist. "I hope you're right."

"I am. Trust me. We can handle this."

I nodded, letting out a long breath. "I can't believe everything that's happened tonight. It's a lot to take in."

"That's for sure... and you need to know... I never expected to get the part, let alone find out like this." He shook his head. "It's kind of mind-blowing."

I pulled away. "Your mom was sure excited."

"Yeah... I think she was more excited than me."

"Oh come on, I saw that look in your eyes. You may have been trying to act like it wasn't a big deal, but it is. It's huge." I twined my fingers through his. "I want to hear all about it."

"And I want to tell you. But first, I think you need to get out of that beautiful dress before it gets ruined."

"Why? You planning on tearing it off me?"

"I wouldn't go that far, but I've been imagining taking it off you all night."

"Hmm... then I won't argue with that." I kicked off my shoes and turned my back to him so he could get started.

Creed's hands brushed over my bare back before he began to push the zipper down. As the dress fell to the ground, a shiver ran over me. I stepped out of the dress and turned to face him.

His gaze roamed over my nearly naked body and his eyes darkened with desire. "Did I tell you how beautiful you looked today?"

"Maybe... but I won't stop you from telling me again."

He brought his lips down to nuzzle mine. "I'm the luckiest man in the world." His light touch on my mouth deepened, and I leaned into him, giving back all the passion he gave. I couldn't get enough of him and eagerly shoved his jacket off his shoulders. Unbuttoning his shirt took way too long, and my heart raced to feel his bare skin against mine.

Our discarded clothes lay in a heap on the floor, but neither of us cared. Creed kissed me with an urgency he'd never shown before, almost like it was a matter of life and death. Our lovemaking came hot and heavy, full of passion and an urgent need to blend our solitary lives into something bigger.

We both gave without holding back, lost in our shared feelings of love and commitment to each other. I hoped it was enough to sustain us, because, deep in my heart, I knew that, from this moment on, everything was about to change.

It wasn't until the next morning that Creed told me about the TV show. We'd just settled in to eat our complimentary breakfast in bed, and I asked him about it. As he began to explain, his eyes lit up with excitement.

"The show's about a couple of detectives. Peyton Lind plays the lead, and I'm her new partner. She can't stand me because I'm a little rough around the edges, and I don't always play by the rules... you know... that sort of thing."

"That sounds fun."

He grinned. "I really think it will be. I know the premise is something that's been done a lot, but there's a real twist with my character. I'm not exactly sure where they're going with it, but my character is not what he seems."

"Really? So he's not a real detective?"

Creed shrugged. "No, he's a detective, but there's something else going on. Probably something like... he's working undercover for the FBI to find a mole, or he's working for the mob as an informer, or... maybe he's a werewolf or something."

A laugh burst out of me. "Now that's something I'd like to see!"

"You would?"

The hope in his eyes sent my heart racing. He really wanted this. How could I stand in his way? "Yes. I really would."

He leaned over and kissed me, nearly knocking over the tray of food in the process. With a determined shake of his head, he picked up the tray and set it on the floor.

"Hey... I wasn't done with that."

He climbed into bed and pinned me beneath him. "Maybe, but I think you'll like this even more." He nuzzled my neck before smothering me with kisses. As his hands roved over me with expert finesse, I decided that he was right.

An hour later, it was time to pack up and leave. Before we left our room to check out, I gave John a call. He was heading back to New York, and I didn't want to miss saying goodbye.

"Ella, I was just thinking about you. I'm glad you called."

"Yeah... we're just getting ready to check out of the hotel. Are you still here?"

"Yes. I'm just leaving myself. Do you want to meet for lunch?"

"Yes. We would love that." It sounded perfect since we'd never gotten around to eating much of our breakfast.

"Great. I'll meet you in the lobby in a few minutes."

It didn't take long to meet up, and we decided to have lunch at the hotel restaurant. Because it was before noon, there was plenty of seating, and we snagged a table in a corner, away from prying eyes.

After our food arrived, John brought up the subject of Creed's offer. "I heard about the TV show," he began. "Everyone was pretty excited about it last night at the party."

"Yeah," Creed said. "It's a big deal."

John nodded. "I would imagine, but I don't think it's a good idea." At Creed's raised brows, John held up his hands. "I know that's not what you want to hear, but just give me a minute to explain. Ella needs anonymity, and having a well-known actor for a husband could backfire. It would put her in the spotlight, and that's not what she needs... now, or ever."

John was warming to his argument, so I put a hand on his arm to stop him. "I get that... we get that, but it's not that simple. This is Creed's career we're talking about. If he doesn't take the job, then what will he do? He can't put his life on hold because of me."

"Why not? Maybe that's what he's supposed to do, so he can help you whenever you need it."

"And maybe it's not."

Slack-jawed that I'd disagreed, he hesitated. "What do you mean?"

I sat back in my chair and glanced Creed's way. Wisely, he kept his mouth shut to let me explain, and I caught a glimpse of gratitude that I'd stood up for him. "We all know that Creed and I didn't meet by chance. If this is Creed's path, maybe that's the way it's supposed to be. How can you say it isn't?"

John's brows rose in surprise. "I guess I can't. But you still have to make choices. You can't leave everything to chance.

Just because one thing happened that way doesn't mean everything does."

"You're right," Creed said, joining in. "I'm not a firm believer in chance or fate, so I'm taking this seriously." He took my hand. "We'll figure it out. I don't want to do anything that isn't what's best for Ella, but I think there's more to it. Someone is already looking into the miracles at the hospital. Maybe if I'm in the limelight, I can spin it the right way and take the pressure off of Ella." He shrugged. "You never know... but it's something to consider."

John huffed out a breath. "It seems unlikely." He shook his head, glancing between us. "I guess it's up to you, but I'm just thinking about Ella's safety. Which brings us to something else I wanted to discuss."

He leaned forward. "After you left the party last night, Avery told Lauren and me about Dom Orlandi's visit." He turned his gaze to me. "Did he threaten you?"

"Not exactly." I explained what he'd said to me about Avery testifying, and that I'd told him to turn against Sonny and testify instead.

"He's not really going to do that, is he?"

"No," Creed said, firmly. "That will never happen."

"So what's to stop Dom from hurting Avery if she doesn't agree?"

I spoke up, knowing I needed to confess what I'd done, even though John wouldn't be happy about it. "I may have threatened to... send him straight to hell... if anything happened to her."

John's shoulders tightened. "What? By using your gift? You know that's going against St. John's wishes."

"You and I know that, but Dom doesn't. When I touched his hand, he about had a heart-attack."

John's brows drew together. "Ella—"

"I know... it wasn't very nice of me, but I couldn't help it." At his sigh, I continued. "Hey. Nobody said I had to be perfect. And, just so you know... I'm not." I didn't want to add that, if it came right down to it, I'd use my gift to save Avery. "Besides, St. John only said it would be best if I didn't use it that way, not that I couldn't."

John shook his head. "That's not what you told me."

"She's right," Creed said. "He didn't want her to use her power like that, but that's where I come in. I'm supposed to make sure she doesn't have to use it to kill anyone."

"And how do you do that?"

"I step in. If it comes down to him or her, I kill him first."

John threw his hands up. "I can't believe you're both talking about killing people. I'm sure St. John never intended you to go that far."

I caught Creed's gaze before glancing at John. "I think St. John meant that if my life was on the line, it could go that far. I've already died twice... I don't know if I'd come back a third time. I'd hope so, but I don't know. Maybe there's a limit? Besides, he called Creed my protector, and that was one of the reasons we were together."

I shrugged. "Maybe there's a bigger picture that we can't see right now, or maybe it's just a precaution, but it's not something I take lightly."

"And neither do I," Creed added, facing John.

"Well... I guess you have a point, which takes me back to this whole business of being a celebrity. I think Ella needs to stay out of the public eye, and maybe you do, too."

I let out a breath. "I don't know anything for sure. I don't even know if there is a right or wrong answer. We'll just have to do our best to figure it out."

"Yes," John agreed, letting out a sigh. "Which reminds me..." He pulled an envelope from his inner pocket and handed it to me. "This is everything you need to access the account I told you about."

I pulled the papers out and quickly skimmed over them. "Wait a minute. It says I gained control when I turned twenty-one." I caught his gaze. "So you haven't been able to touch it since then?"

"No."

I shook my head. "So how did you pay for the party last night? I thought you used this account."

"Not exactly. I received a small pension a long time ago and put it aside for you. That's where I got the money for the party."

I shook my head and continued reading but couldn't find any information about how much was in the fund. "It doesn't say how much is in there."

"You'll have to go to the bank that works with the brokerage firm to get all of that information. There's a branch here in L.A. You can visit them and set it up however you want. You could have them transfer a certain amount from the interest into your checking account every month, or just use it for special expenditures. It's totally up to you."

I was having trouble with the idea of having a lot of money stashed away for my use. And, even though John had kept it from me, I wasn't angry at him. In fact, I totally understood why he hadn't said anything until now.

I met John's gaze. "Now that I have plenty of money, I want to pay you back for the party. Please. Let me do this."

He shook his head. "That's not necessary. But if you ever need me to come for a visit, I'd happily accept airfare and accommodations. Wherever you are, I'll gladly come and help you however I can."

"Thanks John. That means a lot. But you have to promise me that if you ever need any money, you'll ask. It's only fair...

I mean... you raised me, and what am I going to do with all this money?"

He chuckled. "I'm sure you'll figure it out." His smile turned wistful. "I still consider myself your father. I'll always be here for you, Ella. Don't ever forget that."

My eyes got a little misty. "I won't."

"Good. Now... it's time for me to catch my flight, so I'll say goodbye."

"Can we take you to the airport?"

"No. You've got other things to do, and I can take an Uber. Lauren said you were meeting with your agent today to sign the contract, so you need to figure out what you're going to do." He shook his head. "I hope you won't rush into anything."

Creed nodded. "We won't. And, since it's Saturday, I'm pretty sure signing anything can wait until Monday, or even later if we need it to."

"Good. Take your time, and make it a matter of prayer."

I smiled. "Yes Father."

He grinned and bent to gather his bags. The concierge called an Uber for him, and we waited to say goodbye until it came. After he left, we headed to our car, and I took Creed's hand. "Shall we stop by the bank and see how much money is in my account?"

"I guess."

"What's wrong?"

"Nothing. I just don't want that money to determine what we do with our lives."

I nodded. "Yeah, I know what you mean, but I don't see how anything will change. I'm still going to work where I can do the most good, and you've got this amazing opportunity in front of you. Knowing how much money is in the account won't change that, but I'd like to have access to it, just the same."

"Sure. Let's do it."

We put our bags in the car and slipped inside. Before Creed started the car, his phone began to ring. He checked the caller ID. "It's my mom. I'd better take it." After he answered, his concerned gaze caught mine, and his brows knit together. "What? ... Yes ... Are you serious?" He rubbed his hand over his face. "Yes. Okay. We'll be right there." He disconnected, and my stomach tightened.

"What's going on? Is Avery okay?"

"Yes. But she just got a call from the prosecuting attorney in Las Vegas. They want to put her in witness protection, and someone is already on the way to pick her up."

CHAPTER SIX

We drove straight to Lauren's house and hurried inside.

"Aiden." Lauren rushed toward Creed, wringing her hands together. "Avery's packing a bag to leave, but I don't think she should testify anymore. What if something happens to her? I don't want to lose her again. Tell her she doesn't have to go. Make her stay."

Creed stepped past his mom and continued down the hall to Avery's room. As we all crowded inside, Avery stopped packing and threw her arms around Creed. "They said my life was in danger and I had to go."

"Who told you that?"

"The prosecuting attorney."

"Not Detective Nash?"

"No. Richard Martinez. He's the prosecuting attorney, and the one who told me to pack a bag. He said a couple of his men were coming to get me."

"But Nash is the person we've been talking to from the beginning. It should be coming from him, not the attorney." He shook his head. "You're not going anywhere until I call the detective."

Creed pulled out his phone. After finding the number, he held the phone to his ear. "Nash, this is Aiden Creed, Avery's brother. Avery just got a phone call from your prosecuting attorney, telling her to pack a bag. He said she's going into protective custody. What's going on?"

Creed listened, closing his eyes and pinching the bridge of his nose. "So it's a legitimate threat?" He let out a sigh before shaking his head. "I'm not sure I can do that." Listening, he frowned. "So you know who these guys are? You know them personally?"

He began to pace the length of the room. "But how do I know we can trust them?" He paused. "No. You need to do better than that. I'm not sending my sister off with a couple of strangers. Either you come with them, or the deal's off."

My brows rose, and I glanced at Avery. Her shoulders slumped with relief, and she sank onto the bed with a sigh.

"Yes," Creed said. "I'll be here." He pulled the phone away from his ear and disconnected. "Nash said he'd come. He's catching the next flight out. The others will be here soon, but you're not going anywhere until Nash gets here."

"So the threat's real?" I asked.

"Apparently." Shoving his phone into his pocket, he sat down on the bed beside Avery. "He said the trial is in two weeks. Did you know that?"

"Yeah. Owen... I mean... Detective Nash called and told me, but I didn't tell you because I didn't want to ruin your wedding. I thought there was plenty of time to figure out the details. Owen said that Martinez only needs me for one day." She glanced at Creed, then at me. "I was hoping you'd both come to Vegas with me."

"No," Lauren said. "It's too risky. I don't want any of you to go. Avery... they almost killed you. I know you want to testify, but what happens after that? Will they come after you anyway? It's too dangerous."

"I know Mama... but Owen said if I don't testify, Sonny will get away with it. I'm not sure I could live with that."

It almost sounded like she didn't want to let Owen down either, and I wondered how well they knew each other.

"She'll be okay with Nash," Creed said. "And once Sonny is behind bars, he won't be able to hurt anyone."

I knew Creed was trying to reassure his mother, but it sounded like he was trying to convince himself as well.

"And of course we'll be there with you at the trial," I said, sitting on the other side of Avery. "You won't be alone."

"Thanks."

Lauren shook her head. "I don't like this." She left the room in a huff, and Creed followed to console her.

I stayed beside Avery, listening to Creed as he did his best to reassure his mother. In a way, I didn't blame Lauren. Glancing at Avery, and knowing all she'd been through, doubt went through me as well. It wasn't fair that she had to put her life on the line to testify against such a terrible man.

I patted her hand. "I know this is hard, but hang in there. Maybe you won't have to testify after all."

She shook her head. "It's okay, Ella. I can do this. I've been through some hard things. I can handle it. I'm not going to let him ruin my life any more than he already has. I'll always be looking over my shoulder, whether I testify against him or not. That's the price I have to pay for getting involved with him and Dom in the first place."

She caught my gaze, and a small smile crossed her lips. "But at least you've given me the chance to have a good life, and I'm not going to waste it hiding or cowering."

Hearing raised voices in the other room, she shook her head. "I only wish this wasn't so hard on my mom."

"Just tell her what you told me. She may not like it, but I'm sure it will help her understand."

Avery nodded, and we both headed into the kitchen. Lauren leaned against the counter with her arms crossed and anguish filling her eyes. Taking one look at Avery, she crumpled and rushed to pull her into her arms.

After they broke apart, Avery told her everything she'd told me, and Lauren finally accepted it. She glanced at Creed. "How long before they get here?"

"I'm not sure. Nash is supposed to call me."

She looked back at Avery, resignation in her eyes. "Come on, sweetie. I'll help you pack."

They left, and I stepped to Creed's side. He wrapped his arms around me. "I wish you could tell the future," he said. "Like your friend, Shelby. Doesn't she get premonitions?"

I grinned. "Yeah... that would be a good thing to have right about now."

"I wonder if her uncle could help us?"

I shook my head. "We already owe him for getting us away from Sonny. I don't know what more he could do."

"He could get rid of him."

I pulled back with a gasp. "Creed—"

"I know, I know... not my finest thought, but it's not right that one man can hurt so many people."

"And that's exactly why Avery's going to testify."

His lips turned down, but he nodded anyway. His phone buzzed, and he pulled it out of his pocket. "It's Nash." Putting it to his ear, he answered.

They spoke for several minutes. By the time they were done, Avery and Lauren had joined us in the kitchen. Creed slipped his phone away and filled us in. "Here's the plan. Nash contacted Martinez and worked out that he would take charge of Avery on his own. He doesn't want to take a chance that her whereabouts would get leaked to Sonny's people, so it's just him and Avery."

"Is that wise?" Lauren asked. "Doesn't he need some kind of backup?"

Creed shook his head. "I think he's right. The fewer people who know where they are, the better." He turned to Avery. "What do you think? Are you okay with that?"

"Yeah. It makes sense."

"His flight will arrive in a couple of hours. Then he's planning to drive back to Las Vegas with you. Once you get to Vegas, he'll figure out a safe place for you to stay. Oh... and, in light of the threat, Martinez got the judge to move the trial up to next week."

Avery nodded. "That sounds good to me. The sooner, the better, right?"

We all agreed and settled in to wait for Nash's call. After Avery was packed and ready to go, we spent the next couple of hours playing a card game. It helped lighten the tense mood, but we were all sitting on pins and needles. Creed's phone rang and we all jumped, but it was his agent, and Creed managed to put off meeting with him about the contract until Monday.

"Are you going to take the part?" Avery asked.

"Of course he is," Lauren answered, her brows drawn together. "Why wouldn't he?" She glanced at me and then Creed, waiting for a response.

"That's the plan for now," Creed replied. "As long as we don't start shooting next week, since I'm going to be in Las Vegas."

Lauren waved her hand. "I'm sure they'll work with you. Besides, it usually takes a while to get everything settled before shooting begins, so you should be fine."

"Good to know." Creed sent me a tight smile of apology, and Lauren spoke about her experience on a couple of shows while we continued our game.

An hour later, Creed's phone rang again. This time it was Nash, and they made arrangements to meet at our apartment, rather than Lauren's house, just in case someone was watching.

To be on the safe side, we managed to sneak Avery and her luggage into the car, and she crouched down in the back seat all the way to our place. Dom had told me she'd be safe for a week, but now that the trial had been moved up, anything was possible. Creed and I both kept watch for anyone following, but neither of us saw anything out of the ordinary.

Our apartment was situated down a long driveway, with parking behind the garage, and Nash was already there waiting in his rental car. He stepped out to help Creed load Avery's bags into the trunk, and it surprised me to find him a lot younger than I'd supposed.

Of average height, he had the broad shoulders of someone who regularly worked out. His intense, dark eyes, short cropped hair, and square jaw, along with his confident swagger, made him stand out as someone you wouldn't want to mess with.

Avery stepped from the car and Nash froze, his jaw dropping open. As she moved toward him, he shook his head. "I heard you'd recovered enough to testify, but... I didn't expect to see you like this. You're walking... on your own. How?"

Avery glanced my way before lowering her eyes. "I can't explain it... but I'm certainly grateful."

Nash let out a long breath. "I remember after the accident... you were in really bad shape. I was there, and it was awful. Now look at you." He motioned toward her. "You look great."

Avery's lips twisted into a shy smile. "Thanks. Should we get going?"

That snapped Nash out of it, and he straightened. "Yes, of course." He turned to Creed before glancing my way.

Creed motioned to me. "Nash. This is my wife, Ella."

"Your wife? Wow... a lot's happened around here. Uh... sorry. Nice to meet you, Ella." He extended his hand, and I shook it.

"Likewise."

"We're both coming to the trial," Creed said. "And I'd like regular updates from you so I know Avery's okay."

"Of course." Nash glanced at Avery. "I'm sorry, but you'll have to leave your phone here. I don't want to worry about anyone tracking it. I've got a couple of burner phones we'll be using."

"Sure." Avery handed her phone to Creed. "I'll call you every night."

Creed nodded. "You'd better." He turned to Nash, worry tightening his brow. "There's something you need to know. Dom Orlandi was here yesterday, and he told Ella that Sonny might have asked for help from someone." He glanced at me. "What was his name?"

"Gage Rathmore," I answered. "Do you know him?"

Nash's eyes widened, and his expression turned bleak. "Yeah... I know him. Thanks for letting me know."

His worry was hard to miss, and my stomach tightened. "Does this change anything?"

He shook his head, and his lips thinned. "No."

Creed's brows drew together. He'd seen Nash's expression, and he couldn't keep the worry from showing. "Nash, promise me that you'll protect Avery with your life, otherwise, she's not going."

Nash's brows rose slightly, and he almost seemed offended. "I will, Creed. She'll be fine with me, I promise."

"Good." Creed turned to Avery and caught her up in a hug. "I love you little sis. Call me tonight... and be sure and call Mom too."

She sent him an annoyed smile. "I will."

He released her, and she gave me a quick hug before slipping into the car. Nash nodded our way and slid behind the wheel. As he backed out of the driveway, we gave Avery one last wave, and they were gone.

We stood there for several seconds before Creed wrapped his arm around my waist and pulled me against him.

"She'll be okay," I said, hoping that saying it meant it was true.

Creed nodded, and we climbed the stairs to our apartment.

Monday rolled around as a day off for me. So far, Avery had reported that she was safe and sound, and I hoped she'd stay that way. The trial was now slated to begin a week from today, which meant I'd need to ask for some time off.

We sat at the kitchen counter, finishing up our breakfast. Creed's appointment to meet with his agent wasn't for a couple of hours, but we both knew he was going to take the job.

"Are you sure you're okay with it?" he asked me again.

"Yes. I'm sure. I know how much this means to you. But just remember what you told me about actors."

His brow puckered. "What was that?"

"You said you were glad you weren't famous because those guys were jerks."

"I did?"

"Well... maybe not in so many words... but it was something like that. I also distinctly remember you saying that you couldn't act. So I don't get it. Do they just want you for your pretty face, or can you act after all?"

His lips twisted at my backhanded compliment. "Oh... I'm sure my pretty face has something to do with it, but... there was something different about my audition this time. I can't explain it, but it's like I had... something more... it was a feeling deep down inside of me, and I drew on that for the audition." He met my gaze. "I think it's all because of you."

At my raised brows, he continued, "I'd never known real fear until you nearly died. When you took that bullet meant for me..." His breath whooshed out. "It changed me. To be honest, I don't know if being an actor is the right thing to do, but I don't know how to do anything else.

"Part of me wants to take the job because of my mom and how hard she pushed me in that direction. I don't want to let her down, so... maybe I need to take the job to prove to her, and to myself, that I can do it. But is that a good enough reason? I don't know."

I placed my hand over his. "I think it's the right reason for now. Would you regret not taking the part?"

"Yes."

I smiled. "You didn't even have to think about it, so I guess that's your answer."

Creed leaned close enough to kiss my forehead. "You're the most amazing person I've ever known. Whether it's acting or doing something else, I want to be a better person because of your trust in me." His lips met mine in a sweet, tender kiss. "I love you, Angel."

"I love you, too." It was moments like this that made all the hard times worth it. To have him beside me gave me hope that, whatever happened, we'd be all right because we had each other. "Want to head to the bank before your meeting?"

"Oh yeah... we never got around to that. Sure... that's a good idea."

I took the papers John left for me, along with my driver's license and birth certificate, to the bank. After we arrived, it didn't take long to get it all sorted out.

The bank manager left us alone to discuss the best way to manage and disperse the funds, but the shock of finding out I was a millionaire left me speechless. Glancing at Creed, I shook my head. "Eight million dollars? That's insane. I don't need that much money." I sighed. "What should we do?"

Creed was at a loss for words too. "I don't know, but it makes me a little worried. I mean… if St. John had something to do with it… does that mean hard times are ahead, or did he just want you to do your job without worrying about getting paid? Or are you supposed to travel all over the world to help people?"

Hearing it like that, a heavy weight fell over my shoulders. "I don't know. I can't think about all of this at once, it's too overwhelming."

Creed took my hand. "Then let's just take it a day at a time. Why don't we set up a fund with a certain amount of money that you can have access to as you need it, and just leave the rest as it's been?"

I nodded. "That sounds good, as long as you have access to it too."

"Sure. That makes sense. We could start with a hundred grand. When that gets low, you can just add to it as we need."

My breath whooshed out of me. "That seems like a lot… but okay. Let's set up something like that."

The bank manager was more than willing to help with my wishes. He had several recommendations that I followed, and I was grateful to have an expert help me take care of everything.

He advised me about taxes and all the other details about accessing the account. Soon, it was all set up, and we had plenty of money to draw on and a debit card with which to do so, along with all the proper security codes in place.

We left the bank in a daze, and only a few minutes before Creed's appointment with his agent. He talked me into going to the office with him, even though I was a little uncomfortable, and we soon sat across from Rod at his desk.

Rod placed the contract in front of Creed and went over the details. While they spoke about the terms, I glanced around the room, taking in the framed photos of famous actors standing next to Rod. Most of them were signed, and there were only a few actors I didn't recognize.

They came to the end of the contract and the amount of money Creed would be paid. My eyes widened at how much he'd make, and I finally understood why Creed had said I wouldn't have to work if he got a full-time gig. Of course, it was just for one season, with the option for residual payments, but the amount still astonished me.

Rod went on to discuss how many episodes were scheduled for the first season. It surprised me to find that the show was on a streaming service, rather than a regular broadcast television channel, and the first season only had eight episodes.

Rod explained that the contract was for the first season and included an option for a second season if the first did well.

"Shooting starts in three weeks, and there's a six-week time frame to film the episodes, so it's going to move fast. I assured them that you're up to the task, but it's going to take up all of your spare time."

Rod glanced at me, and his brows drew together. "I hope you know that you may not see much of your husband while they're shooting. Is that going to be a problem?"

His question caught me off-guard. "Uh... no. It's fine."

Rod turned back to Creed, mentioning that this was a great beginning to all kinds of opportunities for Creed's career. He spoke about health and accident insurance, along with the fee he would take, before finally pointing to the line where Creed needed to sign.

He handed Creed a pen, but, instead of signing, Creed glanced my way. "Rod, could you give us a minute?"

Rod's eyes widened. He glanced at me with a frown before pushing away from his desk and leaving the room.

"Why did you do that?" I asked Creed. "He's going to have a heart attack."

Creed snickered. "He'll get over it. Besides, he's making a killing off me, so don't feel too bad for him." He turned to face me. "Now that you've heard it all, I just wanted to make sure you're still okay. It's a huge commitment, not just for the six weeks we'll be shooting, but for the series if it gets picked up."

I nodded. "I understand, but we have to see where this takes us. Who knows? It might only last one season, but it's a place to start, right?"

He swallowed. "Yes."

"Then let's do it."

Creed nodded and pulled the door open, finding Rod pacing up and down the hallway. "We're ready."

Rod smiled, but it was more of a grimace, and I tried to hold back a smirk. As Rod sat down behind his desk, Creed held the pen above the line for a few seconds before signing it.

Rod let out a relieved breath and came around his desk to shake Creed's hand and pound him on the back. "Congratulations. You won't regret this."

"Thanks."

They spoke a little longer about the details, and we finally left the office. As we walked to our car, I turned to Creed and threw my arms around him. "You did it!"

He picked me up and twirled me around. "We need to celebrate."

"You know it. After you tell your mom, let's call your friends and meet at a fancy restaurant for dinner."

That night, we met several of his friends to celebrate. It was so fun to talk to everyone and feel part of the group. Thank goodness I'd switched to the day shift so I could stay to enjoy it.

At nine-thirty, Creed's phone rang with the expected update from Avery. He quickly answered, holding the phone close to his ear and ready to share his news. "Hey Avery, how are you doing?" With all the noise in the restaurant, he excused himself and hurried outside.

Since I wanted to talk to her, I told everyone it was his sister, and I'd be right back. I followed him out and listened while he told her the good news. As soon as he was done, he handed the phone to me.

"Hey Avery. How's it going?"

"It's going okay. I'm a little bored since Owen won't let me go out or do much, but I can't complain."

"So... how is Owen anyway?"

She sighed. "He's fine."

My brows rose. "Fine... as in, damn girl, he's so fine... or he's barely tolerable fine?"

"Ella."

"Wait... he's not married, is he?"

"No."

That came out pretty fast, and I grinned. "Oh... that's good. He seems like a nice guy. Maybe someone you might like to get to know better?"

"Yeah..." She lowered her voice. "I guess you could say that."

"Nice. So... maybe when this is all over you could— "

"Uh… you know what? I've got to go, but it's been great chatting. Tell Creed I'm thrilled for him, and I'll call again tomorrow night. Okay?"

"Sure."

"Great. Talk then." She disconnected, and I couldn't help the grin that settled across my face. She liked Owen… and now they were spending all their time together. Hmm… there might be a silver lining to this situation after all.

The next morning, I left Creed sound asleep in bed and got ready for work. We'd stayed up way too late celebrating, but I didn't mind. For the first time, I felt like I could fit in with his friends.

At work, I met a whole new group of people and looked forward to a fresh start. After introductions were made, one of the nurses eyes widened in recognition, "Oh yeah… I've heard of you. You're that nurse everyone's talking about." She held up her hands. "With the healing hands, right?"

I froze, unsure of what to say. "Uh… I guess."

"I'm Stacy." She sent me a little wave. "And I'm thrilled to have you on our shift. I think we'll get along great."

"It's good to meet you. Thanks."

I caught sight of Cody from the night shift, waiting to speak to me. "Excuse me." I stepped to Cody's side and raised a brow.

"Hey Ella," he began. "I was wondering… uh… before you get started here, could you check in on someone?" At my blank expression, he quickly continued. "A sixteen-year-old girl was brought in during the night. She just got out of surgery, and it's not looking good."

"What happened to her?"

He lowered his voice. "She was in a boating accident. They're trying to stabilize her arm, but it looks like they might have to amputate it. Would you mind just taking a look? She's on the fifth floor. I'll take you up."

Before I could answer, he told one of the other nurses that I'd be right back and rushed to the elevator. Heaving out a breath, I followed him, surprised that he was so concerned about a patient. "Do you know her family from somewhere?"

"Uh... no, but I just couldn't stop thinking about her, and so I thought of you and your... uh... touch. Thanks for doing this. You don't have to, and I know there might be nothing you can do, but it doesn't hurt to take a look, right?"

"Yes... of course."

He took me down the hall to her room and opened the door. The girl's mother sat beside the bed, holding the girl's hand. She saw Cody, and relief changed her face from grief to hope.

"Are you Ella?" she asked, her dark eyes intense. At my nod, she continued. "Cody said he'd bring you up if he could. If there's anything you can do to help my sweet Gracie, we'd be so grateful. The doctors said if things don't improve in the next few hours, they'll have to amputate." She stifled a cry and held her hand to her mouth. "She's only sixteen... just a baby."

I glanced at the bed, finding a beautiful caramel-skinned young woman with her long dark hair in cornrows across her head. Her eyes were closed, and her right arm was bandaged and resting on top of a cushioned stand. "Is she sedated?"

The mother nodded. "Yes... the pain meds knock her out, so she's finally getting some relief."

"I don't know if there's anything I can do, but I'll take a look."

I sent Cody a pointed nod, and he pulled the mother toward the door. "Let's give Ella some space. Now might be a good time to grab some coffee or something." With reluctance, the mother agreed and slipped out the door with him, leaving me alone with Gracie.

I quickly brushed my fingers across Gracie's swollen hand. I knew immediately that the blood wasn't circulating correctly, and she was on the brink of losing her arm. Concentrating my healing energy, I pushed it through her hand and found the damage to her arm just above her elbow.

Her arm must have been caught in the propeller. The doctors had reattached it, but it didn't look like it was going to take. I sent my energy to the wound and found the severed blood vessels and muscle tissue the surgeons had done their best to reattach.

Focusing on establishing a bigger connection between them, I closed my eyes and sent a pulse of heat. I kept the flow of energy going until I felt the change. It was like a river that had been blocked down to a trickle, was now surging back into its normal course.

With the connection re-established, the blood began to flow back into her arm, giving it the nourishment it needed to survive. I sent another wave of energy into her arm to help revitalize the damaged muscles and swollen tissue.

That done, I pulled away, knowing she'd be okay. It might take her some time and therapy to regain the use of her hand and fingers, but now she could get better.

Totally drained, I took several deep breaths until I felt steady enough to walk. I turned to leave, and the door opened. Gracie's mother came in, her eyes bright with hope. "How is she?"

I sent her a smile. "I think she has a good chance of keeping her arm. Only time will tell, but don't lose hope."

She clasped my hands. "Thank you." Stepping toward her daughter, she sat down and took Gracie's hand, immediately noticing how much better it looked. Gasping, her wide-eyed gaze found mine, but I slipped out of the room before she could say anything.

Cody was nowhere to be found, so I took the elevator back to the main floor. Back in the ER, I grabbed a granola bar and quickly scarfed it down. I looked for Cody, and someone told me he'd left. It surprised me that he hadn't waited to speak to me, but maybe he had somewhere to be.

Feeling a little better, I went about my duties. The rest of the day continued without a lot of drama, and I was grateful. While nothing drastic came into the ER, it was easy to only use my touch when absolutely necessary and let nature work as it should the rest of the time.

Still, by the end of my shift, I was ready to go home and recuperate. It helped to know that I'd get to spend the evening with Creed. I found it easy to admit that working days certainly had its advantages, and I was more than grateful for the change.

Before leaving, I decided to find Reyna and tell her it was nice to see her at the wedding. I felt a little guilty that I'd left her to fend for herself and hoped to rectify that. She wasn't with the others who'd arrived for the night shift, so I asked them if they knew where she was. They thought it might be her day off, so I gathered my things to go home, sorry I'd missed her.

As I walked out to my car, I caught sight of the reporter who'd accosted Creed and me at the hotel. She waited just outside the doors and spotted me as I passed by. I kept my head down, but she'd already seen me and hurried to my side. Panicked, I picked up my pace and began to sprint to my car.

"Ella! Wait. Please."

Unlike the other night, her voice had a desperate edge to it. I slowed and turned to face her, noting her flushed face and determined gaze. She closed the distance between us, and I took a step back, not wanting to be so close.

Noticing my hesitation, she halted in her tracks and raised her hands in surrender. "Ella, I'm sorry. You must think I'm crazy, but I needed to talk to you." She folded her arms across her chest and began to rub them like she'd taken a chill.

"Something's happened..." Her eyes filled with tears, and she took a deep breath to get under control. "It's my husband... he's really sick, and yesterday he took a turn for the worse. He's the reason I've been so focused on you. When I heard about the boy who'd been miraculously healed at the hospital, I did some digging into the patients you helped. They seemed to think you played a part in their miraculous recoveries, and it gave me hope that maybe you could help my husband."

She shook her head and looked down at her feet. "I didn't mean to intimidate you, but I wanted to be sure." Her desperate gaze caught mine. "None of it was for a story. That's just a cover for why I was asking questions about you. Please believe me... I would never tell anyone if it's true. Please, Ella. Can you help my husband?"

The pleading in her eyes overwhelmed me. "I... I honestly don't know." All the work she'd gone through to ask me for help finally made sense. But I couldn't promise anything. "Why don't you tell me what's going on?"

Her shoulders slumped with relief, and she nodded. "Oliver's got a rare form of cancer. They managed to slow it down, and we thought he was out of the woods, but yesterday they told us it had spread to his liver and his stomach. He's in a lot of pain, and they said there was nothing more they could do. Will you at least come and see him?"

"Sure. But..." I shook my head. "I can't promise anything." I knew I could heal him, but I wasn't sure I could trust her to keep quiet about it. "I don't even know your name."

"Oh... sorry... I'm Georgia. Georgia Donlon."

"Is he here? At the hospital?"

"No." She shook her head. "There's nothing they can do for him here, so he wanted to go home. We talked about putting him on hospice." Her voice broke. "But I wanted to talk to you first."

I nodded. "I'm just a nurse. You know that, right?" At her nod, I continued. "Okay. I'll see him, but I can't promise anything."

"I know. Thank you so much." Even with my warning, hope infused her voice.

"Give me your address, and I'll follow you home."

Half an hour later, I pulled up in front of a red brick duplex. Georgia waited for me on the porch, and I followed her inside. We found her husband lying down on the couch, watching TV. His pinched face spoke of incredible pain that he tried to smooth away as soon as we entered the room.

His eyes turned wary when he saw me, and he struggled to sit up. Georgia hurried to his side to help him. "Oliver, this is Ella. She's the nurse I told you about."

"Georgia," Oliver scolded. "I told you not to bother her." He sent me an apologetic smile. "I'm sorry she brought you all the way out here."

"It's okay... I don't mind."

He shook his head. "I know this has been hard on Georgia." He sucked in a breath, clearly in pain. "I wish I could change it for her." He spoke to me, but his gaze rested on her face. "I think it's harder on the people you leave behind, and I'm sorry for that."

Georgia stroked his back. "Don't worry about that right now. Just let Ella have a look at you."

At his reluctant nod, Georgia helped Oliver ease back against the pillows. She glanced my way, her eyes anxious. "What do you need? Can I help you with anything?"

I scrambled for a reason to touch him. "Oliver, you look like you're in a lot of pain. Do you have any medication to take for that?"

"Yes, but it makes me groggy, so I haven't had anything for a while. I wanted to be able to talk to Georgia when she got home."

I nodded. "Sometimes I can help with the pain by applying pressure to certain pressure points in the neck and back. It's a little like a massage. Would it be okay to try something like that?"

"Sure."

"Okay. I just need you to turn to your side, facing away from me, and I'll get started." I knelt beside the couch and gently ran my fingers over his shoulders to his neck and back. I used gentle pressure to massage the area and connect to him.

As I worked, I concentrated on finding the source of his pain. My awareness was drawn to his stomach and the pain centered there. I reached for my power to send it into him, and a sharp, burning sensation stopped me.

Surprised, I pulled back. This had never happened before, and unease tightened my chest. I massaged Oliver's shoulders again and tried to push my power into him. The burning came again, stopping me in my tracks. What did it mean?

I knew I could push past the heat and heal him, but the feeling of wrongness persisted, leaving me panicked. Did this mean I wasn't supposed to heal him? But... if I didn't help him, he would die. How could this be right?

St. John's voice flashed into my mind, and I remembered his story that he'd wanted to heal my mother, but he'd been forbidden. Was this how he knew, and now it was happening to me? I could still feel Oliver's pain through my touch, and my heart ached.

With sudden clarity, I knew I wasn't supposed to heal him. Deep sorrow lanced through my chest, and I closed my eyes to deal with the pain. This was so unfair. This young man didn't deserve to die, and what about Georgia? The horrible sorrow she'd have to bear at such a young age wasn't fair.

I tried once again, not willing to accept it, but the burning sensation was so strong, I had to pull my hands away from his skin.

"Is something wrong?" Georgia asked.

My heart raced, and I struggled to reassure her. "I'm not sure. Let me try again." What was I going to do? I couldn't leave him like this... but if I couldn't heal him, what else was there?

I sucked in a breath. If I couldn't heal him, maybe I could help ease his pain. Once again, I placed my hands on his neck. Drawing from my power, I connected to Oliver, this time concentrating on his pain. The burning sensation didn't come, so I sent a soothing pulse of power into his stomach. It didn't heal him, but it took enough of the pain from him that he could breathe evenly.

I pulled my hands away, and his whole body relaxed. He eased onto his back and glanced up at me with wonder. "It doesn't hurt so badly anymore. Thank you."

Georgia gasped, her eyes filling with hope. "Does this mean he's going to get better?"

I couldn't meet her gaze. "I... I've done what I could to ease his pain, but I don't think his condition has changed. I'm sorry, but I can only do so much... and he's..." I swallowed. The lump in my throat blocked any words of comfort I wanted to give her.

"It's okay, Ella," Oliver said. "Whatever you did made a big difference. I've heard about pressure points and pain, and what you did helped a lot. It's such a relief to have that pain gone without all the drugs. I can't tell you how grateful I am."

His sincerity eased some of my guilt, but the pain etched into Georgia's face brought tears to my eyes. She'd been so convinced that I could help him, and I'd failed. I caught her gaze, and anguish filled my heart. "I'm sorry I couldn't do more."

Her lips trembled, but she managed to nod. "It was probably crazy of me to ask, but I needed to try. You know?"

"Of course."

"How long will it last?" Oliver asked.

I shrugged. "I don't know. Hopefully a few days, but I can come back if the pain starts up again."

"That sounds wonderful." Oliver glanced at Georgia. Seeing her sorrow brought tears to his eyes. He tugged at her hand. "Hey Babe... I'm still here. Let's make the most of the time we have left, okay? No more looking for cures. With my pain more manageable, I think I could make it to the beach. We could spend the whole day there and eat fried food and watch the sun set like we used to. Remember?" He tucked a finger under her chin, and she raised her gaze to meet his. "What do you say?"

She nodded. "Yes. Let's go tomorrow, and as many days after that as we can."

"That's right... we can do that." He glanced my way. "Thanks so much. I don't know how much time I have left, but you've made it easier. I don't know why, but I feel lighter, like something dark has been lifted from my heart."

He glanced at Georgia and smiled. It transformed his features into something beautiful. His body was still the same, but his spirit was buoyant and strong.

"I'll see myself out." I hurried away, shutting the door softly behind me. Inside my car, the tears began to flow. I wiped them away and sat for a minute to get under control.

On the drive home, I managed to keep my feelings at bay, concentrating on the road and making sure I obeyed all the traffic lights. I finally pulled into our driveway, relieved to find the lights on in the apartment. A swell of emotion that Creed was there, waiting for me, quickened my pace.

CHAPTER SEVEN

I hurried up the stairs to the apartment and opened the door. Creed sat on the couch in front of the TV and glanced up. Taking one look at my face, he jumped to his feet and rushed toward me. "What's wrong?"

I threw my arms around him and let the tears flow. "You know that reporter?" He nodded, and I continued, telling him the whole story. Sometime during my explanation, he led me to the couch and held me close, listening while I rambled on about how unfair it was.

"I'm sorry you went through that," he said, rubbing my arm. "But maybe it was just for today. Maybe tomorrow you could do more?"

I shook my head. "I don't think so. That burning... it was like a warning. I think I might have been able to push through it and heal him anyway, but I knew it was wrong."

"I'm glad you didn't. Who knows what would have happened then."

"But don't you see? I couldn't heal someone who deserved it. How is that right? A few months ago, I was punished for not helping a known killer who ended up dying, and now... I was stopped from healing someone who deserved to live. Now he'll die... and his wife... she loves him so much. It's going to devastate her. Maybe this power isn't so great after all."

"Don't say that." Creed's brows tightened. "You were given these powers for a reason. I believe that. You still helped ease his pain. Maybe it's his time to go."

I sighed. "Yeah, I understand all that, but I can't help thinking that maybe it's my fault."

Creed's brows dipped. "How could it be your fault?"

"Because I went in there with the idea that I could save him... me... like this power is mine alone, and I have the right to decide who lives. It's not like that at all, and maybe God was trying to teach me a lesson."

Creed shook his head. "I don't know. I guess we can talk all we want and still never know the real reason for anything. But I do know that you were given this ability for a special purpose. For now, maybe that's enough."

Totally exhausted, I nodded and burrowed into his side. "Yes... maybe you're right. I did help a sixteen-year-old girl today, and that was rewarding." I explained what had happened, and my sadness over Oliver lessened.

Feeling better, I sat up to catch his gaze. "So... enough about me. Tell me about your day."

He chuckled. "Well, if you'll notice, I have a script." He bent down to pick the papers up off the floor. "I've got the first three episodes right here in my hands, and I've been going over them." He shook his head. "This is not at all what I thought."

"What do you mean?"

"You know how I told you that I'm a detective with an unusual twist?"

"Yeah."

"So get this... my unusual twist is that I can read minds."

"Seriously?"

"Yup. And I don't want anyone to know, so I have to be creative about how I help my partner. The first episode is all about my reactions to people's thoughts, and how hard I have to work at keeping my cool."

"Does the audience know?"

"Not at this point."

I snickered. "Oooo, I bet that's going to be fun."

"Yeah... but now I think the main reason I got the part was because of my poker face. I thought it was because I was learning how to act, but I really think it's because I don't show a lot of emotion on my face."

"Hmm... maybe so. But I think it sounds like a great premise for a show. Maybe not quite as serious as you'd imagined though, right?"

He shook his head. "Yeah... I mean when they said there was a twist to my character, I thought maybe it was because I worked for the mob or something... but reading minds is a lot further off the beaten path than that."

"Yeah." I shrugged. "But... there's all kinds of shows out there... like those about angels and demons, or the vampire series that's gone on for years. Maybe this one will too. You never know, right?"

"Well... at least I'm guaranteed one season. So I can't complain."

My stomach growled, and Creed's brows rose. "Whoa. Someone needs food. Good thing I've got dinner ready."

"You do?"

He grinned. "I've got to do something to keep my woman happy."

"What did you make?"

"Well... I wouldn't go that far. But I picked up something from that noodle place you like. And I made sure to get plenty of vegetables in that good sauce you love to go with it." We stood up, and he swatted my butt. "Why don't you change out of those scrubs while I warm it up?"

"If I wasn't so hungry right now, you'd pay for that."

His sexy grin sent my heart pounding. Since I couldn't resist teasing him, I made it all the way to the partition between the room and our bed before I pulled off my scrub top and threw it at him.

He immediately came after me, and I tried to hold him off. "No... food first." His arms came around me, and I struggled against him. Laughing, we fell onto the bed, and he began to tickle me. I shrieked and fought back, but it was only half-hearted, mostly because he started kissing me.

My need for his touch outweighed my need for anything else, and I kissed him back with an abandon that took him by surprise. Our lovemaking was fast and furious, with each of us taking as much as we gave. The intimacy we shared loosened the tight bands of all my worries and fears. This moment with the man I loved strengthened and fortified me beyond reason, sending me into a place of deep contentment and well-being.

Lying together on our bed, each of us spent and breathing heavily, I caught his gaze and smiled. "Hmm... that was amazing... if I could live off your love, I'd never need to eat anything ever again."

My stomach chose that moment to gurgle, and Creed laughed.

By the time we finished eating dinner, it was after nine-thirty. At ten, we both realized Avery hadn't called, and panic began to set in. I met Creed's gaze. "Maybe she just got distracted."

"Yeah," he agreed, but his heart wasn't in it. "I'd call her if I could, but Nash keeps changing her burner phone." He let out a breath. "I'm sure she'll call. She's just late, that's all."

"Right."

After we tidied up the kitchen, the phone rang. Creed sent me a smile of relief and quickly answered. His face paled, and his brows wrinkled. "What? Avery... slow down. I can't understand you."

His panicked gaze caught mine, and my heart picked up speed.

"But you're okay? You're not hurt?" He paused to listen. "Where are you now?... Okay, that's good." Another long pause. "Yes, I know where that is, but it's going to take us a while to get there. Are you sure he'll be okay until then?... Yes, I'm bringing Ella... Okay, but why don't you talk to her? She can tell you what to do."

Creed held out the phone to me. "We've got to go. Talk to her while I get dressed."

I nodded and held the phone to my ear. "Avery? It's me. What's going on?"

"It's Owen," she sobbed. "He's been shot."

"Where?"

"I didn't even know... he kept driving until he nearly passed out."

I spoke louder. "Where is the wound?"

"His side. We're at a motel right now, and I've wrapped him up the best I could. I think the bleeding's stopped, but he's sweating and pale. Is there something else I should do before you get here?"

"If the bleeding's stopped, that's good. I think you just need to keep him lying down. Don't let him get up for anything. If he can drink some water, just give him little sips."

"Okay."

I hurried into the bedroom and frantically searched through my drawers for my medical bag. "We're on our way. Call me if anything changes."

"I will." She hung up, and I handed the phone back to Creed. He was dressed and slipping on his shoes.

"So where is she?" I rummaged through my clothes and began to get dressed.

"They're in a motel just off I-15 in Victorville. It will take us a little over an hour to get there if we're lucky. Bring a change of clothes and whatever else you need. I don't know what to expect, but we might be awhile."

I nodded and grabbed a few other things, slipping them into a small travel bag I kept on the shelf. "I'll bring my medical bag. I sure hope I can heal him once we get there." I'd never worried about that before, but what if I couldn't?

"You can... it will be all right. I just hope they weren't followed. Avery said that Nash wouldn't let her call anyone else for help, so someone must have found out where they were."

I zipped up my bag. "Okay, I've got everything. Let's go."

We jumped into the car, and Creed backed out of the driveway, turning toward the freeway.

"Did Avery tell you what happened?"

He nodded. "Yeah, but she wasn't real clear. It sounded like they'd just checked out of their motel when someone took a shot at them. They jumped into their car and got away. Nash kept driving without letting on that he'd been shot until a little while ago. After they checked into a motel, he collapsed. He told Avery she was not to call anyone except for us, and not to take him to the hospital. That's all I know."

I nodded, but fear tightened my chest. Sonny's men must have found them. We got on the freeway, and Creed hit the gas. He tried to stay below eighty-five. At least the traffic wasn't too bad since it was so late, but it still seemed like a long way to go.

We took the San Bernardino Freeway for the first hour until it merged with I-15. I spoke with Avery a few more times, and it sounded like Nash was keeping calm, although he was in a lot of pain. As we drew closer, she told us the name of the motel, and we found the directions on our phone's map.

At midnight, we finally pulled into the parking lot and drove around to Nash's car on the far side of the building. I sent a text to Avery, and she opened the door, falling into my arms and ushering us inside.

Nash lay on the bed, his face gray and his breathing raspy. "He's taken a turn for the worse," Avery said, wringing her hands. "I did the best I could, but he's in bad shape. I think the bullet went all the way through, but he lost so much blood."

"It's okay Avery," I told her. "I'm here now. I'll take care of him." I set my bag on the floor and touched his forehead, finding it hot and clammy. I pulled the blanket away from his bare chest and found his side bound in a towel, with more towels beneath him.

With his chest exposed to the air, he shivered and moaned.

"Nash? Can you hear me? It's Ella. Creed and I are here. You're going to be fine."

"Av..Avery?"

"I'm here," she answered.

"They found us," he rasped out. "I don't know... how..."

"It's okay," I said. "We're here now. I'm going to take a look at your wound and see if I can patch you up."

The tension drained from his brow, and he let out a labored breath. "Guard the... door. My gun... it's... in my... jacket."

"I've got it," Creed said, finding the jacket and pulling the gun out. "I won't let anything happen to Avery."

"Good." Nash closed his eyes, and his breathing slowed, almost like he'd only been holding on to life until we got there.

"Nash!" I said, shaking him. "Don't quit on me now. We've still got to get Avery to safety." His eyes blinked open and he took a deep breath.

"Good. Now hold on while I take a look at your wound."

I unwrapped the towel from around his torso, pulling it away from the wound. Blood seeped from the hole in his side, and I turned him slightly to see the exit wound in his lower back.

The bullet had probably done some damage to his kidney and stomach, and I knew he wouldn't last much longer without my help. I wiped the blood away from his side with a wet washcloth before sterilizing it with some alcohol. "This might sting a little. Try and hold still."

Nash gasped as I wiped down the entry and exit points the bullet had taken. Finished, I held the washcloth to his side and placed my hand just above the wound. Taking a breath, I closed my eyes and drew on my healing power.

Pushing my fear away, I sent the power into him and held my breath. The power flowed sweetly, without a hint of heat, and I exhaled with relief, sending it deeper into his wounded flesh.

Nash groaned before passing out, and I concentrated on repairing the damaged internal organs, keeping the flow of energy steady and even. The damage was extensive, but I kept my focus sharp, sending as much energy into him as I could.

The swelling began to go down, and his internal organs knit back together and slowly resumed their normal function. With the worst of it healed, I changed my focus to the entry and exit wounds. With slow and complex weaving, the tissue began to come back together.

At the last moment, I pulled my power away, knowing I needed to leave something there so he wouldn't be too suspicious. I could stitch the remaining skin together with the needle and thread in my medical bag. It would leave a scar, but that was better than trying to explain where his wound had gone.

I lifted my hands from his side and glanced up, finding that Nash's cheeks had taken on a ruddy hue, and his face no longer held the strain of pain from before. Creed and Avery spoke quietly near the window, occasionally glancing my way to check Nash's progress.

I pulled what I needed from my medical bag and quickly stitched Nash up. Luckily, he was still half out of it and hardly noticed. I skipped the stitches on his back, since the wound had already closed up, and bandaged it with gauze and tape, hoping he wouldn't be able to see it.

Placing my hand on his forehead, I could feel that his body had been in a state of shock and was now working hard to recover. Sleep was the best thing for him, especially since he'd lost a copious amount of blood. After cleaning up, I pulled the blanket over him and sat down on the floor, resting my back against the bed. Healing him had taken a lot out of me, and I wasn't sure I had the strength to stand.

"How is he?" Avery stepped to the bed, touching her fingers to his forehead.

"He'll recover. Right now, he needs to get some sleep, and he'll be a little weak for a couple of days, but he'll be fine."

Avery dropped to the floor beside me. "Thanks Ella." She gave me a quick hug. "I thought he was going to die."

I nodded. "Yeah... I'll bet, but it wasn't as bad as that."

Creed sat down on my other side and pulled me into his arms. "How are you doing?"

"Honestly, I'm tired. That took a lot out of me, especially after the day I've had."

Creed nodded. "We've been trying to decide what to do. Is Nash well enough to leave?"

"Don't you think it's safe here?"

"Not really. I'd feel better somewhere else. They found Avery once. They could find her again."

I nodded. "That's true. But where should we go? Back home?"

He shook his head. "I don't know. Vegas is only about three hours from here, so we could drive in that direction and maybe stop at another motel for the rest of the night. I think if we leave Nash's car here, it will throw off whoever is after Avery, and she'll be safe."

"Yeah... that should work."

"Will Nash be feeling better in the morning?" Avery asked.

"Yes. Much better."

"Good," Creed said. "Then he can help us figure out what to do." He glanced at Avery. "I thought you'd be in Las Vegas by now. What's going on?"

"Nash had problems getting a safe house, so we've been taking our time."

"Oh... that makes sense. You okay with leaving now?"

"Sure. Let's do it."

Creed and Avery loaded up our car, giving me a little more time to get my strength back. Creed left the keys to the room on the coffee table, along with a couple of twenty dollar bills to pay for the blood-stained towels and the pillow we took for Nash.

Avery sat in the back seat and we half-dragged Nash into the seat beside her, careful of his stitches. With the pillow on her lap, she got him settled and absently played with his hair. From the way she fussed over him, I knew her feelings were more than friendly, and I hoped it wouldn't make things more complicated than they already were.

Once Nash was situated as comfortably as possible, I slid into the passenger seat beside Creed, and we drove away. After we got on the freeway, he took my hand with a tight squeeze. "I've got this. Go ahead and close your eyes. I'll probably stop in an hour and get us a room somewhere, but until then you might as well rest."

Since my eyes kept drooping shut, I agreed. He handed me his sweatshirt to use as a pillow, and I rested my head against the door. I fell asleep, grateful that I'd been able to heal Nash. Avery was safe for now, but how had they found her? Was there a mole in the police department?

Someone had figured it out, which meant that, even though Nash had taken Avery to safety this time, they were still after her, and now Creed and I were right in the middle of it. Hopefully Nash would have an idea about what was going on in the morning.

Sometime later, Creed jostled me awake, and I blinked to get my bearings. We were parked in front of a motel, and the door to a room stood open. I managed to get out of the car and shuffle into the room.

Nash was already inside, asleep on one of the double beds, with Avery hovering beside him. While Creed bolted the door behind me, I ambled to the other bed and barely managed to get my shoes off before climbing under the covers and promptly fell asleep.

CHAPTER EIGHT

I woke to the sound of voices and sat up, rubbing the sleep from my eyes. Creed and Nash sat talking at a small table at the far end of the motel room, and I could hear the shower running.

They both glanced my way, and relief washed over me to find Nash with some color in his face and looking so much better. "You're awake," Creed said. "We were just trying to figure out what to do next."

I stood up and stretched before shuffling over to sit on the bed beside them. "How are you feeling?" I asked Nash.

"I'm still a little weak, but I'm doing a lot better. I don't know why... but I thought I was hit worse." He scratched his head. "I thought I was dying. Anyway, thanks for coming to patch me up."

"Of course. I'm glad you're feeling better. Do you know how they found you?"

He shook his head. "Creed and I were just talking about that. Unless someone hired an investigator to find me, I don't know how it could have happened. All of our communications have been through burner phones."

"Could someone be tracking your cell phone?"

"No. I switched it to Airplane Mode. That makes it untraceable."

"Oh... I didn't know that."

"The only thing that makes sense is that someone figured it out through my rental car. They must have found out what company I rented it from and then hacked into it to find us."

I nodded. "Well... at least they can't do that now. So what's the plan?"

"I want to continue on to Las Vegas. I've already got a secure place to stay that no one knows about, and I'm sure I can keep Avery safe there. With the trial coming up in a few days, I don't want to take a chance that we don't show up in time."

The shower turned off, and I checked my watch, finding it just after seven a.m. "Oh crap. I need to call the hospital and tell them I'm not coming in." I found my phone and quickly called, explaining that I had a family emergency and might be out for a few days. My supervisor sounded understanding, so I hoped it wouldn't get me fired.

Finished, I turned to Creed. "What about you? Are they expecting you to come in today?"

"No. I took care of most everything they needed yesterday, and I don't need to go in again until the end of next week."

I let out a relieved breath. "That's good."

Nash felt along his stomach where I'd stitched him up and grimaced. "Is it all right if I take a shower?"

With his wound so shallow, I knew he wouldn't run any risk of infection. And he was still in the clothes he'd worn when he got shot, so he probably needed it. "Normally... I'd say no, but since I'm here to check the wound, it should be okay."

The tension left his shoulders, and his eyes brightened. "Really? Great. As soon as Avery comes out, I'm going in."

"Sure. But I'll need to bandage you back up when you're done."

He nodded before leaning over his luggage to find something clean to wear. Creed pulled me against his side and spoke softly. "How are you doing? Feeling any better?"

"Yes... much better."

"Good. Why don't you and I get us all some breakfast while these guys finish getting ready?"

Since I was starving, he didn't need to ask me twice.

We made it to Las Vegas by noon. Creed followed Nash's directions to an Airbnb that he'd reserved a couple of days earlier.

"You're sure it's safe?" Creed asked him.

"Yes. It's totally off the grid and has nothing to do with the police department or the prosecuting attorney's office. The house is in a gated community, and I don't see how anyone could find us there."

Creed wasn't convinced. "But could someone trace your credit card?"

"No. I've been using a pre-paid credit card that I set up before going to L.A. It's not traceable."

Impressed, I glanced at Nash in the backseat. "So the only way Sonny could have found you and Avery at the motel was through your rental car, like we thought?"

He let out a breath. "I don't know, but that's the only thing I can think of."

I nodded, sending a smile Avery's way. Sitting in the back seat, next to Nash, she leaned toward him like he was a magnet, and I knew it was hard for her to be so close and not touch him.

He still had dark circles under his eyes, and he'd need another day or two to rebuild his blood supply, but at least he wasn't dead. I could probably help him with the blood problem, but I didn't want to be so obvious. At least he didn't remember anything about last night, so he believed that he wasn't hurt as badly as he'd thought.

We pulled up to the gated community and stopped to push in the code Nash had been given. The gate slowly opened, and we drove inside. From there, the house was down the street and around a corner. Finding it, we pulled into the driveway.

The Spanish style house had a stucco exterior, a clay-tile roof, and an arch around an entry walkway. The front yard was made up of light-colored rocks and landscaped with a couple of palm trees and several bushes.

Getting out of the car, Nash put a code into the garage-door panel, and it opened. We pulled inside and found the keys to the house and instructions on the door. Nash unlocked the door, and we headed inside before unpacking our luggage.

We stepped into a big kitchen with dark wooden cabinets and granite countertops. A table that seated six took up the far end of the room, and a set of double-doors opened into the back yard, with the same kind of landscaping as the front, except for the pool in the center of the yard taking up most of the space.

The living room area had a vaulted ceiling that spanned both floors. The walls were painted a soft cream color with cream colored carpet and furniture that made the space open and airy. Prints of famous paintings hung on the walls, and a tall, green plant stood in the corner. A gas-powered fireplace was centered on the inside wall with a floral painting above the mantelpiece and red crystal vases on either side.

The lower part of the two-story window had blinds across it, and dark red drapes hanging from the top of the window were tied back out of the way. Off to the side of the fireplace, we found a carpeted staircase that led up to the second story with three bedrooms and a separate bath.

The large master bedroom sported a queen-sized bed and was painted in the same shades of cream. It had a walk-in closet and a large bathroom attached that included a Jacuzzi bathtub. The other two bedrooms also contained queen-sized beds and shared another bathroom between them.

"This is nice," Avery said, eyeing the bathtub with longing.

"It sure is," I agreed, wondering how much this was costing Nash. Of course, maybe he was getting reimbursed, so it wasn't a big deal.

Back downstairs, Creed and Nash got our bags out of the car, while Avery and I checked out the kitchen cupboards and the refrigerator. The cabinets held dishes and everything needed to cook a meal, and the fridge held several bottles of water and a few soft drinks along with some condiments.

After bringing in the luggage, Creed and Nash joined us at the table.

"So, what's the plan?" I asked. "I think it would be a good idea if Creed and I stayed with you guys until the trial." I wasn't sure my supervisor would be happy about that. But, on the other hand, I didn't need the money, so maybe it didn't matter.

"As much as I'd like that," Nash said. "I don't think it's a good idea."

"Why not?"

Nash shook his head. "I don't want to have to worry about protecting both of you as well as Avery. If something were to happen, my first priority would be Avery, and I'd hate for you to become collateral damage."

"I guess you have a point."

"What about a car?" Creed asked. "How are you going to get around if we leave?"

"I can get another one easy enough, but I might need your help with that. If we could find one this afternoon, and pick up enough groceries to last until the trial is over, we'd be set."

"Are you feeling strong enough for that?" I asked.

He nodded. "Yes... I mean... I'm not a hundred percent yet, but I'm doing better than you'd think after getting shot." His brows drew together, and he shook his head. "I still can't figure it out. It seemed so much worse... but I'm not going to complain."

"I'll go with you to get a car," Creed said. "And then maybe Ella and I can go to the grocery store for you." He glanced at Avery. "Why don't you write up a list while we're gone?" She nodded, and he continued. "We could stay here tonight and leave sometime tomorrow. Would that be okay?"

"Yeah, that should work," Nash agreed.

"All right. Let's go."

Nash turned to Avery. "Keep the doors locked, and stay away from the windows. If something seems off, you know the drill."

Avery nodded. "Yeah, I got it."

"Good. We won't be long."

We followed them to the door, and Avery locked it up after they left. She turned to me and frowned.

"What's the drill?" I asked.

"He wants me to run." At my raised brows, she continued. "I need to go through the house and plan out all the ways I could escape. Then I'm supposed to stay out of sight and keep the burner phone on me at all times."

She shook her head. "It's funny that, even though I've been doing that all along, the only time we were attacked was when we were leaving the motel. It's lucky that we got away. If I'd known Owen had been shot, I would have been more scared, but he didn't let on until we'd been driving for about half an hour. Even then, he kept driving longer than he should have. I finally pointed out that if he passed out and wrecked the car, I'd be a sitting duck."

She threw her hands up. "He didn't even consider letting me drive. I could have patched him up before he lost so much blood and kept driving. But did he even think of that? No." She shook her head again. "Sorry. I'm still a little rattled by everything."

"Makes sense to me. I'm sure it scared you to death."

"Yeah. It did. I guess Dom couldn't stop Sonny from trying to kill me. After what you said to him, a small part of me hoped he'd have a change of heart and consider turning against Sonny. I mean... I once thought he loved me. But he chose Sonny over me. How does someone do that?"

"I think it's a matter of surviving. We both know Sonny would kill him for that."

"Yeah... I guess so." She sighed. "Well, Dom can rot in hell for all I care."

I found the disgust in her tone totally understandable, but quickly changed the subject, since there was nothing either of us could do about it. "So... it looks like you and Nash are getting along rather well. You seemed pretty worried about him."

"Oh..." Her cheeks flushed. "We're just friends. If I thought he really cared about me, it would be different, but he's just doing his job."

"What do you know about him?"

Her eyes narrowed. "He's in a relationship at the moment, and this is just a job for him. No matter what you may think, he doesn't have feelings for me, so I'm keeping my distance."

At my widened eyes, she shook her head. "All right... it's true. I like him, but I'm pretty sure he doesn't return the feeling. He's keeping everything strictly professional. Besides, now's hardly the time to begin a relationship."

"Yeah... I can see that, but you may be wrong about his feelings. I've seen the way he looks at you. I think you're more than just a job to him." She opened her mouth to refute my claim, but I raised my hands to cut her off. "But now's not the time... like you said."

"Exactly." She let out a deep breath. "I'd better get started on that grocery list."

We had the list done by the time Creed and Nash returned. They came inside and explained that Nash had borrowed a car from a friend, so he wouldn't be leaving a trail behind that an investigator could pick up.

Before Creed and I left to get the groceries, Nash put in a call to his boss. He explained what had happened, leaving out the part where he'd been shot, and let him know that he and Avery were back in Las Vegas.

"Are there any new developments we should know about?" Nash asked. "Is the trial still set for Monday?" After listening, he nodded. "Sure. I'll check in with you in a couple of days. Make sure Martinez knows there's been an attempt on Avery's life. He needs to make sure no one knows we're here." He paused. "Yeah... I know, but someone found out, and I don't want to take any chances."

A moment later, he disconnected and glanced at us. "Everything's still on, so now we just need to wait." He shook his head. "But I'm not sure how long we'll stay here." He held Avery's gaze. "I thought a gated community would offer some protection, but now I'm not sure. Maybe we'll only stay a couple of days and find another random place after that. Would you mind?"

"No... not at all. Anything to keep them from finding us sounds good to me."

"Are you having second thoughts?"

Avery took a breath. "I'd be lying if I said I wasn't. You came so close to dying. It scared me."

"I get it, but it wasn't that bad... right? I'm feeling pretty good for getting shot. So please don't let that stop you from testifying."

"I'm still going through with it." Avery licked her lips. "But now it seems like the stakes have gone up, so it makes me nervous."

"Let's re-evaluate our situation in the morning and see what we can do to make you feel safe, okay?" At her nod, he glanced at Creed. "I guess we need some food for tonight. You still want to get it?"

"Sure."

We discussed getting take-out, along with a few things that would tide us over, and headed out to the grocery store.

By the time we got back it was early evening, and everyone was starving. After eating, Creed pulled out a deck of cards, and we played a little poker. The tension eased as the evening wore on, but we still noticed every little sound, and, more than once, Avery asked what a certain noise was.

I didn't think any of us would sleep well, so we all agreed to take turns staying awake through the night. Nash slept first, since he was still recovering, and took the bedroom with the window overlooking the street, setting his phone to wake him at two in the morning.

The rest of us weren't sleepy enough to go to bed, but Avery wanted to take a bath in the master bedroom, and I couldn't blame her. She deserved some time to relax after the last couple of days.

After she left, Creed and I settled down on the couch. He turned on the TV, and we watched a sports channel with the sound turned down low. It wasn't long before I fell asleep, and I didn't wake up until Nash spelled us off.

I took some time to wash my face and brush my teeth before joining Creed in our room. It had been a long day for him, and he was sound asleep. I snuggled next to him, but it took me a little longer to drift off.

I couldn't stop thinking about Sonny and how much I hated him for what he was doing to Avery. I could hardly wait until this was over and he was put away for good. Even then, I wasn't sure that was enough. Part of me wanted him dead, so he couldn't ever threaten Avery again.

The next morning, I had a hard time getting out of bed, so Creed let me sleep a little longer. By the time I got up, it was ten o'clock, and I could hear voices downstairs. I took a quick shower and hurried down for something to eat.

Creed and Avery sat at the table, their heads close together, and they both glanced up as I entered. "Hey beautiful," Creed said, standing up to give me a hug. "How did you sleep?"

"Pretty good. How about you?"

"I slept like the dead." He chuckled, and I shook my head.

"How about you, Avery?" I asked.

"I slept better than I thought I would," she admitted. "It must have been the bath. That was amazing. And it didn't hurt that you guys were here. There's just something about having my family close that makes everything better, you know?"

"I wish we could stay here with you," I said. "With the trial in three days, there's no point for us to go back home before that."

"Yeah," Avery agreed. "There's plenty of room here, but I guess Nash has a point about not staying too long in one place."

"I have an idea... if you guys have to leave today or tomorrow, we'll just stay here." I turned to Creed. "What do you think about that?"

He nodded. "That's a great idea."

I sent him a smile and glanced into the living room. "Where's Nash?"

"He's resting in his room," Creed answered. "He told me to wake him in half an hour. He was pretty tired from being up most of the night."

I grabbed some cereal and milk for breakfast. Creed stepped into the living room to update his new boss for the show, and it reminded me that I needed to call the hospital. After cleaning up my breakfast dishes, I put the call through.

My supervisor wasn't too happy with me, but, after thoroughly explaining what had happened, and the trial being moved up, she understood. "I won't be back until after the trial ,so if that's a deal breaker, I get it."

She huffed. "Not for me. We want you back. You're irreplaceable... at least in my book. Just let me know when you get back to L.A., and we'll work it out. Good luck with everything."

"Thanks."

It wasn't long before Nash joined us. He'd showered and looked better than he had yesterday. Catching my gaze, he motioned toward his bandage. "Can you look at this for me? I'm afraid I got it wet, but I didn't know whether to take it off or not."

He followed me back upstairs to the bathroom where I decided to take the stitches out since the wound was practically healed. He got his first good look at it and shook his head. "That's weird. From where it hit me, it looks like the damage should have been a lot worse."

"I guess you were lucky. It missed all of your vital organs." That was a whopping lie, but I didn't have a choice.

"Yeah. But… I don't know how that—" His phone began to ring, and he pulled it out of his pocket. "Yes?" He listened for a few seconds. "I guess. No… it's not that. I know you want to put him away as much as I do." He nodded. "Okay. Sure. I'll be there soon."

His lips twisted, and he shook his head. "That was Richard Martinez. He's the prosecuting attorney. He needs to go over Avery's testimony with her."

"Is that normal?"

"Yeah. I trust him. He's one of the good guys."

Reassured, I followed Nash out of the bathroom and down the stairs so he could tell Avery and Creed what was going on. "Richard Martinez wants to prepare Avery for the trial, so I'm going to pick him up and bring him here. Are you all okay with that? I know it's a risk, but I trust him. He wants to put Sonny away more than anyone."

We all agreed, and he left, but I couldn't help the worry that tightened my stomach. Forty minutes later, Nash brought Martinez in through the garage and introduced all of us. In his mid-forties, with dark hair and a burning intensity in his dark eyes, he looked ready to take Sonny on.

He wore a suit and tie and brought a laptop and a briefcase with all his notes. There was a small office just off the kitchen, and he and Avery got set up in there. While they went over everything, I asked Nash what he thought about Creed and me staying in the house.

"I know you were thinking about taking Avery somewhere else, but we thought we'd stay since we're planning on coming to the trial. How long is the reservation? We'd be happy to pay for the extra days."

Nash shrugged. "I paid for two weeks. It was cheaper that way, so… yeah. It's fine if you want to stay here." He rubbed the back of his neck. "I was thinking of leaving tonight, but tomorrow is probably soon enough."

Creed called his mom to update her on everything, and I found a good book to read on my phone's Kindle app. I couldn't remember the last time I'd had a chance to relax like this, and I actually started to enjoy it.

I glanced longingly at the pool and decided that, after Avery and Nash left, I'd take Creed shopping with me to get a swimming suit and some nicer clothes to wear to the trial. We'd left in such a hurry that we only had one change of clothes each. Plus, using the pool would be a nice diversion from all the worry and drama of the last few weeks.

Avery and Richard spent the rest of the day in the office, only coming out for food, bathroom breaks, and snacks. Nash took him back to their rendezvous point just after six, and promised to pick up some dinner on the way back. While he was gone, Avery told us about the case and how important her testimony was in putting Sonny away.

"After the accident, I forgot how much I saw. It was kind of weird how it all came back to me. No wonder Sonny wanted me dead." She shivered. "I remember seeing the headlights rushing toward me and the sheer panic of knowing there was nothing I could do. I didn't remember any of that until now." She shook her head. "I almost wish I didn't."

"You're okay now," Creed said, slipping an arm around her. "Concentrate on that."

She glanced at me and tried to smile. "Because of Ella. Will you tell me how you managed to heal me, and now Nash? I know you don't want to talk about it, so if you can't, I get it. I just... I'd like to understand."

I met Creed's gaze. I couldn't mistake the yearning in his eyes to tell Avery the truth, but I didn't know if it would become a burden for her. "You know I was raised by a priest after my mother died when I was born. There are some things that I've discovered about my life that defy normal explanations. I wish it was easier to understand, but there are times when I don't understand it myself."

Avery nodded, her face relaxing. "It's okay, Ella. I trust that it came from a higher power. That's all I need to know right now."

We all heard the garage door opening and a car pulling in. The door opened, and Nash stepped inside with our dinner. "I decided to go big tonight, since Avery and I will be leaving in the morning." He set a couple of large brown bags full of food on the counter.

"What did you get?" Avery asked, her eyes bright.

"You told me you loved sushi, so I got several sushi rolls, some fried rice, tempura vegetables, some egg rolls and won tons... the works."

Avery's smile lit up the room. "Yay! Thanks so much."

We enjoyed the food, hardly sparing a thought for the predicament we were in, and the evening flew by. Before we knew it, it was time for bed. We took the same precautions as the night before, with Creed and me taking the first watch, and Nash spelling us off at two in the morning.

Avery decided to enjoy another bath while she could, and we settled in to watch a show on TV. After binge-watching several episodes of a supernatural TV show, I wasn't sure I'd be able to fall asleep. But around midnight Creed changed to a sports channel, and I nodded off on the couch beside him.

After Nash spelled us off, I was more than happy to snuggle beside Creed in bed and finish the rest of the night in comfort and peace.

Loud pounding on our bedroom door jolted me awake, and I sat up with a start.

"Creed! Ella! Avery's gone. Is she in there with you?" Nash's frantic voice sent panic through my heart. Creed scrambled to the door and pulled it open. Nash rushed inside, searching our room for any sign of her.

Creed bolted to the master bedroom and I followed. The bed sheets were a rumpled mess, but there was no sign of a struggle. The French doors that led onto the veranda stood ajar, and I followed Creed outside. The veranda curved around the corner of the house and the master suite. On the far side, adjacent to the bathroom, a stone pathway led down to the backyard and the pool.

Taking the pathway, we followed it down to the yard and around to the fence. At the side of the garage, a gate to the street opened with a simple tug. In the predawn light, there was no sign of activity on the street. Whoever had taken Avery was long gone.

Back inside the house, we found Nash shouting into his phone, calling for backup. I hurried into our bedroom to get dressed. Creed followed me inside and shut the door. Our gazes met, and the panic in his eyes chilled my heart.

"I can't believe she's gone," he said. "You don't think she just left, do you?"

"No. She wouldn't have done that. Someone took her."

"But... why? How did they find us?" Creed's face tightened with worry, and he sank onto the bed. "How could this happen? We were right here." His brow puckered, and he caught my gaze. "Why was she taken... instead of..." He couldn't finish.

I swallowed. "Killed? I don't know."

"I should have stayed in her room with her. I don't know why I didn't think of that."

"If you had, you might be dead." I sat beside him and took his hand. "We'll find her. We can call Dom and work something out." Hearing sirens, I glanced out the window.

The flash of red-and-blue lights came closer. "We'll do it without involving Nash or any of the police. It's obvious we can't trust them."

"I agree." His determined gaze caught mine. "If she's alive, we can still make a deal with Sonny."

"Exactly." I nodded. "Let's get dressed."

Knowing we had a plan made it a lot easier to cope with Avery's disappearance. Still, it took nearly two hours before we had some privacy. The police had gone over Avery's room for fingerprints and any kind of trace that the kidnapper could have left, leaving it messier than when they'd started.

By the time they'd done all they could, Nash turned to us, his eyes haunted and his face pale. "I'm so sorry. I don't know how they found us, but I take full responsibility. I promise to do everything I can to find her. The fact that they didn't kill her..." He shook his head. "I don't understand it, but it gives me hope. There must be some reason they need her alive. I'll use every resource I have available. I'll find her, I promise."

Creed's jaw clenched, and he struggled to keep his frustration in check. "Let me know the minute you hear anything."

"I will. You can stay here as long as you need."

He left, taking the last of the police officers with him. In their absence, the silence fell over us like a heavy blanket.

Avery was gone.

"I'm calling Dom." Creed pulled out his phone and made the call. "It went to voice mail." He called again, repeating the process two more times while he paced back and forth across the room. On his next try, Dom picked up, and Creed jerked to a stop. "Dom, it's Creed. Where's Avery? I swear if you hurt her, I will kill you."

I held my breath, not sure that Dom would help us.

Creed shook his head. "Don't play stupid with me. Someone took Avery from the safe house, and I want to know where she is." Listening, Creed shoved his hand through his hair. "Wait! We'll make the deal. Tell Sonny that she won't testify against him. I just want her back alive, okay?" He paused. "Sure... just... call me back the minute you know anything."

Creed sank onto the couch, dropping his head, and I sat beside him. "What did he say?"

"He didn't know. He doesn't know anything. He didn't even know she was here in Las Vegas."

"How is that possible?"

He shook his head. "Maybe he's not in Sonny's inner circle anymore."

"Maybe not, but he should be able to find out something."

Creed rubbed his hands over his face. "I don't get it. How did Sonny know where we were? Nash called his police chief, but I find it hard to believe that he's on the take. The only other person is Richard Martinez, but that makes no sense. He wants Sonny to go down. He wouldn't give up his star witness."

I squeezed his hand. "Dom will know something. We just have to wait for him to call us back."

Creed's shoulders fell, and he shook his head. "We have to find her. If they kill her..." He swallowed and closed his eyes. "I feel so helpless. Nash never should have spoken to anyone."

Huffing out a breath, Creed jumped to his feet, his barely controlled anger giving way to agitation. "I shouldn't have let her testify. Not after Dom's warning. I should have known this would blow up in our faces."

I could see that he wanted to punch something, and I wasn't sure how to comfort him, not when I felt the same way. I couldn't imagine losing Avery, not after everything she'd been through. How had this happened?

Creed's phone rang, and he jerked it to his ear. "Hello?" He listened before nodding. "Yes. Okay." He glanced my way. "Yes. Ella's here, and she's coming with me." His lips turned down, and he let out a sigh. "I know. I'm not involving the police. I don't trust them." Another pause. "Okay, we'll be there in about twenty minutes."

He put his phone away. "Dom wants us to meet him at that restaurant just off the strip. The one where we had that meeting with your friend, Shelby, and her uncle."

"Does Dom know where Avery is?"

"He didn't say. All he said was that he had some information for us."

"Okay. Let's go." We grabbed our things and locked up before heading out. My stomach tightened, and I glanced at Creed. "You don't think it's a trap, do you?"

"No. He's just as clueless as we are."

"Maybe... but don't forget that he knows what I can do. He's seen it. That's dangerous all by itself."

Creed pursed his lips and nodded. "You're right. I forgot about that. We'll have to be extra careful."

With the morning traffic, it took us twenty-five minutes before we pulled into the restaurant parking lot. I couldn't help the shiver that ran down my spine. The last time we'd been there, I'd thought we were safe. Instead, I'd ended up getting shot and had nearly died.

Inside, we found Dom sitting in a corner booth, waiting for us. The grim set of his jaw put me on edge. Whatever he had to say wasn't going to be good.

We slid into the bench across from him, and he nodded a greeting. A server came over with water and our menus, telling us about the breakfast special. After pouring coffee all around, she left us.

"What's going on?" Creed asked. "Where's Avery?"

Dom took a breath. His deep-set eyes were rimmed with fatigue. "Sonny didn't take her."

Creed straightened. "How do you know?"

"Because he didn't know Avery was in town. When I told him Avery had been taken from the police, he had a fit."

"But that doesn't make sense. Who else would take her?"

Dom licked his lips. "We have a pretty good idea."

"Who?" Creed slapped his hands on the table, making the silverware jump.

"Calm down." Dom shook his head, glancing around the restaurant. "The only other person with something to gain, and now Sonny's furious with me."

Before he could explain, the server came back for our orders. I didn't have much of an appetite, but I ordered some pancakes anyway.

After she left, Creed rounded on Dom with clenched teeth. "Who is it?"

Dom leaned forward and lowered his voice. "I told Ella that Sonny had made a deal with Gage Rathmore. Sonny owes him a huge debt. After Sonny lost the poker tournament, he tried to settle his debt with other promises, but it didn't go over well. You might know Rathmore as The Debt Collector."

Creed's brows rose. "That's him? Gage Rathmore?" Creed swore under his breath. "I've heard plenty about The Debt Collector, but I didn't know his name." He shook his head and sighed. "He's a dangerous man. Why would Sonny ever get involved with him?"

"He was stupid. He thought he was smart enough to play Rathmore's game. Ever since Sonny lost the tournament, Rathmore's been trying to collect the debt, but Sonny's put him off. He's handed over small payments to keep Rathmore off his back, while he's been working to get the money together another way.

"But then Sonny made the mistake of telling Rathmore about his upcoming trial, and how nice it would be if Avery disappeared." Dom shook his head. "I think Sonny was trying to make a case for himself—help me out and you'll get your money—that sort of thing. Instead, Rathmore must have seen an opportunity to bring Sonny down, and now I think he's taken it."

Dread filled my heart. "What do you mean?"

"I don't know for sure, but if Rathmore has Avery, he can use her to make Sonny do whatever the hell he wants. I don't know what he has in mind, but if I were him, I'd make the most of it."

Dom leaned closer to us. "Just think of it this way... he could tell Sonny to sign over his hotel and casino to pay off his debt, and he'd give him Avery. But if Sonny won't go through with it, he'll make sure Avery testifies against him and he goes to jail."

Creed's brow quirked. "Do you think Sonny would actually give up his hotel and casino?"

"I don't know." Dom sighed. "He might want to take his chances with a jury, but it's hard to say."

Creed let out a breath. "How well do you know Rathmore?"

Dom lowered his eyes and began to shred his napkin, a clear sign that he was uncomfortable. "Mostly by his reputation, but I have met him a few times, and let me put it this way... there's nothing soft about him. He's hard and cold. Worse than any mob boss you've ever known."

That didn't sound good, and my dread deepened, sending a shiver down my spine.

"If Rathmore has Avery..." Creed shook his head. "Do you think he'll hand her over to Sonny if he agrees to his demands?"

Dom shrugged. "Probably. He won't want to dirty his hands by killing her himself."

The server brought out our platters of food, and we all straightened in our seats. She set them down in front of us with a smile and left. My golden pancakes might have looked good on another day, but now I had no appetite.

Creed and Dom dug in like this might be their last meal, so I tried to eat as well. I got a couple of bites down, but that was all I could manage. I wiped my lips with my napkin and glanced up at Dom. "Did Sonny say anything else when you talked to him?"

"Yeah, but you're not going to like it." He finished up the last few bites of his food before continuing. "I told him about Creed's offer to keep Avery from testifying, but, since Sonny doesn't have her, it's not like it matters. I just know that Sonny wants her dead."

He shook his head. "It all depends on what Rathmore wants in return for Avery. Since he hasn't reached out to Sonny yet, this is all speculation. I think we need to wait and see what his demands are."

"And you're sure he has Avery?" I asked.

Dom sighed. "If he doesn't, then I have no idea what happened to her. Look... I don't think Sonny's in any hurry to make a deal. The trial's still three days away, so we need to have some patience and see where this is all headed. I just wanted you to know what I thought was happening."

Dom glanced between us, and his eyes filled with remorse, something I hadn't seen before. "Look... I'm really sorry about Avery. I'll help however I can. It's my fault that she's in this mess, so I need to make it right."

My brows rose. If I hadn't seen that flicker of guilt in his eyes, I might not have believed him. "Do you really mean that?"

"Yes."

Creed shook his head. "Our only chance to help Avery might be getting her away from Rathmore before he turns her over to Sonny."

"But we don't know if Sonny will go along with his scheme," Dom said. "I mean... if he even has her, Rathmore is protecting Avery from Sonny right now, so that's working in our favor."

Creed leaned back against the booth. "This is crazy."

"I know. Why don't you come back to my place? We can talk over our options there, and when Rathmore calls Sonny, we'll know what to do."

"Fine," Creed said. "We'll work with you, but the minute anything goes sideways... whatever this is..." He motioned between us and Dom. "It's over. I don't trust you, Dom, and I'm not sure I ever will."

CHAPTER NINE

W e followed Dom to his apartment. As we drove, Creed glanced my way. "Do you think Dom is really going to help us?"

"He seems sincere, but that could change in a heartbeat. Still, I don't think we have a choice. It's the only way we'll know what happened to Avery."

He nodded, and I understood his worry. Working with Dom was like heading into the wolf's den. With Sonny, and now Rathmore, we were getting in deep with some bad people who had no morals. But we wanted to get Avery back, so what choice did we have?

Dom lived in a condo just off the Strip. We followed him into the underground garage and parked in a visitor's parking space. At the elevator, he pushed the button for the fifth floor.

Exiting the elevator, we followed him to the end of the hall, where he paused to unlock his door. Inside, the layout was roomy, with large windows overlooking the street in the main room. A kitchen took up one end, with two bedrooms beside it. The place was clean and tidy, which kind of surprised me.

If someone had told me a week ago that I'd be here in Dom's apartment, I never would have believed it. Taking a look around, I noticed the place was austere and impersonal. There were no pictures of his family, and the prints hanging on the walls were those you'd find in a hotel. "Is this building part of Sonny's empire?"

My question caught Dom off guard, and he stuttered an answer. "Uh... not exactly, although he does have a financial investment in the property."

I wasn't sure if that was a yes or a no, not that it mattered in the long run.

Dom shrugged out of his jacket and motioned us to the table in the kitchen. We sat down and spoke for the next several minutes about what could happen if Sonny gave in to Rathmore's demands, and what we could do about it if Sonny got a hold of Avery.

"Do you think he'd want you to kill her?" Creed asked.

Dom shook his head. "If I'm being honest, I don't think Sonny would trust me to do the job. He'll ask someone else and leave me out of it. I probably won't even know when the exchange takes place."

Creed blew out a breath and closed his eyes. "Then we'll have to deal with Rathmore."

I nodded. "Yeah. Maybe we can convince Rathmore that he has more to gain if Avery testifies than he has to lose."

"Maybe," Creed said. "Or he might even agree to double-cross Sonny. Once Sonny gives in, he could just keep Avery for insurance that Sonny stays in line until after the trial."

Dom shook his head. "I don't think Rathmore would do that without our guarantee that she doesn't testify."

I huffed. "I would think Rathmore would be happy if Sonny went to jail."

"Maybe." Dom tilted his head. "But if he gave Sonny his word that Avery wouldn't testify, I don't see him going back on that."

"Why not? I thought you said he was ruthless."

"Okay, I probably said that wrong. He might do that to Sonny, but there would be a price. There's always a price. And it would be you and Creed who'd have to pay."

"But he doesn't know either of us, and we have nothing he wants besides Avery."

Dom's lips thinned. "You should never underestimate Gage Rathmore. He's already ten steps ahead of us. You have no idea what he might want from you."

A cold chill ran down my spine. If I thought he was bad before, he'd just gotten ten times worse.

"So we just have to wait?" Creed stood and began to pace across the room before coming to a stop in front of Dom. "Do you know anyone on Rathmore's side you can call? Someone who would tell you if he has her?"

Dom leaned back in his chair. "There's a guy I know who might tell me. It's a long-shot, but he owes me a favor. I'll give him a call." He pulled out his phone and punched in the number.

"Hey Ty, it's Dom. My boss is losing his mind. He wants me to find out if the girl you guys took from the police is dead or alive. Can you help me out?"

He listened for a few seconds. "Sure... sure... I get it. Yeah? So she's alive? Okay. Thanks. I owe you one." He disconnected. "Well... now we know he has her."

Creed bowed his head and let out a breath. "That's something. Maybe I should set up a meeting with Rathmore before he talks to Sonny."

"How is that going to help?" I asked.

Creed shook his head. "I don't know. At least it would give him another option that might keep Avery alive."

"No," I said. "We need to wait. I know that's not what you want to hear, but we shouldn't talk to Rathmore unless we absolutely have to. He's too dangerous."

Creed heaved a sigh. "You're right. I'm just... I hate waiting around." Creed's phone rang, and he cursed under his breath. "It's my mom. What should I do?"

I shook my head, unsure of anything. "I don't know. Let it go to voice mail?"

"She'll just keep calling." Resigned, he answered the phone and began to pace across the room. "Hey Mom, now's not a good time, can I call you back a little later?" He listened for a few seconds. "Yeah. We're staying here until after the trial. I called my boss, so you don't need to worry." He paused. "You did? What did she get?" His face brightened. "Wow. Uh... sure, I'll let you tell her but... Mom, I'm sorry... I really have to go. I'll call you back in a bit."

He disconnected and sank down into his chair. "I hate lying to my mom. I probably should have told her... but I just couldn't do it."

"What did she want?"

"She wanted to tell Avery about her test scores. I guess she took the SAT test again, and the results came in." He rested his elbows on the table and dropped his head. "Mom opened it up and looked at the results."

"How did Avery do?"

He met my gaze. "She got a 1600. That's a perfect score."

My breath caught. "Oh wow."

"Is it because of..." He trailed off, suddenly realizing Dom was listening.

I glanced Dom's way and found him staring at me. He hadn't moved this whole time, almost like he'd been hoping we'd forget he was even there. Now his eyes held mine with both fear and awe in their depths.

"Who are you?" he whispered.

Creed shoved his chair back and moved like a viper, putting himself between me and Dom. With fire in his eyes, he glared down at him. "What Ella does is not your concern. Understand? You don't know anything about her. Not a thing."

His harsh tone put Dom on the defense, and he stood to face Creed. "Hey... I can't help it if I was there. I know something miraculous happened." He motioned to me. "Ella should be dead, but she's not. Then, at that rehab place, it was like she pulled the life right out of me. It's not something I can forget. Ever."

Creed shoved Dom back against the wall and grabbed his shirt with both hands. "You don't know the first thing about it, so stay out of it. If you breathe a word of this to anyone, I swear I'll kill you myself."

They stood toe-to-toe, and Dom's face turned to granite. He spoke between clenched teeth. "I said I'd help Avery, and I will, whatever it takes. And you might remember that I'm the only reason you know where Avery is. So don't threaten me."

I stepped beside them, tugging Creed's arm to pull him away. It didn't do any good. "Creed. That's enough. We're all a little upset, so take a minute to cool off." With a huff, Creed released Dom, and they stepped apart.

I caught Dom's gaze. "Do you have any pain reliever? I'm starting to get a headache."

The fight went out of Dom and he nodded. I followed him to the kitchen sink, and he took a bottle of pills from the cupboard above. He handed it over and grabbed a bottle of water from the fridge.

"Thanks." I took a couple of pills and drank most of the water. Creed stood frozen for a moment longer before sitting back down at the table. His anger had cooled, but he wasn't over it yet.

I handed the pill bottle back to Dom and sat down at the table beside Creed. Dom grabbed another bottle of water and offered it to Creed. He took it grudgingly and twisted the lid open. Dom got some water for himself, but he stayed near the fridge to drink it.

Before he'd finished, his phone started to ring, causing my heart to race, and I automatically reached for Creed's hand.

"Hello?" Dom's jaw tightened, and he listened for several seconds. "Yes sir." He checked his watch. "Yes. I can take you." He nodded. "I'll come over now."

Putting his phone away, he reached for his keys. "That was Sonny. He's supposed to meet with Rathmore in an hour, and he wants me to go with him."

The tension left my shoulders. "That's good. Now we'll know what Rathmore wants."

Creed jumped to his feet and stepped in front of Dom. "Get all the information about Avery that you can. Like where he's keeping her and if she's okay. Anything that will help us figure out what to do."

Dom raised a brow and stepped around Creed. "I know what I'm doing. You can stay here or go back to your place. I'll call once I know something." He grabbed his jacket and strode out the door.

Once again, we were left alone to wait. I stepped to Creed's side and wrapped my arms around his waist. He pulled me close, and I felt the stress radiating off him. I held him a few seconds longer before pulling away. "I think we should stay here. Then he can't ignore us." Creed's lips twisted, and I continued. "Why don't you call your mom, and I'll call Nash."

He groaned. "What am I going to tell her?"

"Tell her that there was another threat, so Avery was moved to a safe house where no one will find her until after the trial. Say that, because they've limited any kind of access to her, she'll be out of contact until after she testifies. It's close enough to the truth, and your mom won't be expecting to talk to her. That way she won't worry."

He made a sound in the back of his throat. "That's a pretty creative way to put it, but it seems kind of wrong for someone raised by a priest to tell me to lie."

"Hey... I'm not all goodness and light. As a kid, I had to learn ways to stretch the truth in order to have any kind of fun at all."

"I can see that." His amusement turned to ice. "What are you going to tell Nash?"

"I don't know. I think I'll just start out by asking him if they've learned anything and go from there."

"Okay. Let's do it." Creed stepped into the kitchen to make his call, and I sank down on the couch.

Nash picked right up, so I didn't waste any time. "Have you learned anything new?"

"Yeah. From the house security cameras, we have a video of a person dressed in black entering the house through the balcony doors in Avery's room. A few minutes later, it shows him leaving and carrying Avery over his shoulder, so he must have drugged her. We lost him after that. There was no trace of a car, so we don't know how he left the gated community. He just disappeared."

"How did he get in? I thought the house security system was armed?"

"Yeah, it was, but I think the balcony door was ajar. Since it wasn't closed all the way, it didn't trigger the alarm."

"How did that happen?"

He sighed. "I don't know. I can't imagine that Avery left it open, unless she stepped out and didn't notice that it wasn't completely closed when she came back in. But that's not like her."

"No it's not."

"I've been going over everything, and I haven't found a thing. It's like she disappeared into thin air. Whoever took her was a professional."

"Did you reach out to Sonny?"

"He was the first person we visited. I thought he'd be elated that she was missing, but he didn't seem so thrilled. In fact, based on the information that she was taken alive, I'd say he wasn't behind it."

"Then who do you think is?"

"I'm working on that. Are you guys okay?" From his quick change of subject, I figured he wasn't telling me everything.

"Yeah. Creed's talking to his mom. He's only telling her that Avery's someplace safe for the moment, but she's out of reach. Hopefully that will keep her from worrying too much."

Nash might not want to share everything he knew with me, but I wanted him to know as much as possible about what was going on. "Have you considered that Gage Rathmore might be involved somehow? Didn't I tell you that Sonny was working with him?"

Nash sighed. "Yes, you told me Dom Orlandi mentioned it. You haven't seen him lately, have you?"

"We have."

From Nash's sharp intake of breath, I must have surprised him. "What did he say?"

"Just that Sonny wasn't behind it. We weren't sure we could believe him, but, from what you've told me, Dom must have been telling the truth."

"Yes... apparently. So why did Rathmore do it?" he asked.

"I have no idea."

"If Dom gets in touch with you again, I'd like to know what he has to say."

"Sure... and if you find out anything about Avery, please call me. Oh... and one more thing... I think you have a leak in your department. It's the only way they could have known where Avery was."

"I know," he growled. "And I plan to get to the bottom of it."

"Good." We said our goodbyes and disconnected. Creed was still talking to his mom, so I took a moment to freshen up in the bathroom. I'd barely had time to wash my face this morning.

After washing up and combing through my hair, I felt much better and joined Creed in the living room. "How's your mom?"

"She's good. I just hope she doesn't get too mad at me when she finds out I lied to her."

"Once we get Avery back, it won't matter."

"True. So what did Nash say?"

"Nothing we don't already know. I admitted that we'd talked to Dom, and Nash didn't seem surprised. As far as Rathmore's involvement is concerned, that was news to him. So I guess we know more than he does."

Creed nodded and let out a sigh. "I don't trust Dom. He knows too much about you, and I hate to think of him telling Rathmore."

"You really think he'd do that?"

"With the right motivation, he would."

I shook my head. "Maybe if his life was on the line, but I don't see it coming to that. It seems like he's trying to help us, and I think he feels bad about Avery. Maybe if he knew where my power came from, it would give him a reason to keep his mouth shut. You know... the fear of God and all that."

Creed huffed out a breath. "Listen, I've known Dom for a long time, and, based on where we are today, I don't think that would stop him."

I sighed. "You're probably right."

An hour and a half later, the door opened, and Dom stepped inside. He barely glanced our way before heading into the kitchen. We followed him in and sat down at the table, while he got a bottle of beer from the fridge.

"Rathmore made his offer." Dom brought his bottle to the table and sat down, looking haggard and tired. "He told Sonny that he'd hand Avery over if Sonny gave up his hotel and casino. He even had the papers drawn up and ready for Sonny to sign. Sonny barely held it together. When he could talk, he told Rathmore he'd rather take his chances with a jury. Rathmore didn't seem surprised. He just smiled and told Sonny that the offer would stand until the jury came back with a guilty verdict. After that, it would be too late."

Dom shook his head. "We left right after that. I went back to Sonny's office, and he made me a proposition." He caught Creed's gaze. "If you can believe it, he asked me to kill Rathmore."

"Are you kidding me?" Creed said.

"Nope." He sniffed. "And he thinks you'll help me."

"Why would I do that?"

"Because, if you do, he'll make sure you get Avery back alive. You still have to agree that she won't testify, but he won't kill her."

Creed huffed. "That makes no sense. How stupid does he think I am?"

"He wanted me to talk you into believing that Rathmore plans to kill Avery, since they're business partners now." Dom took a long pull of his beer. "But I don't see Sonny signing away his property, so unless something happens to change things, Rathmore will make sure that Avery testifies."

"Then I guess Avery's safe for now. You'll let us know if Sonny changes his mind?"

"Sure."

"Do you have any idea where Avery is?"

Dom nodded and grabbed his laptop from the kitchen counter. He sat back down at the table and booted it up. "I can show you where Rathmore's offices are, and the other properties he owns, but I don't think he'd keep Avery here in the city. He has a ranch just outside of town, and it makes more sense to keep her there." He shook his head. "But seriously, he's got so many properties, she could be anywhere."

He pulled up the map of Las Vegas and pointed out an area west and south of the city. "He's built a ranch out here at Blue Diamond in the Red Rock Canyon area. If he wanted to keep her secluded, that would be the place, and it's only about half an hour away from the city."

"Have you ever been there?" Creed asked.

"Yeah, once. From what I know, Rathmore spends a lot of time there, but he has a penthouse on the Strip as well. His corporate offices are here." He pointed to another area, closer to the Strip. "But my money's on the ranch."

"Okay, thanks. That's helpful. We might want to drive by, just to see what it's like."

Dom shook his head. "Rathmore's ranch is at the edge of Cottonwood Creek. It's a small community in Blue Diamond, and his house is at the end of a street nestled into the top of a hill, so you can't just drive by."

"We can still drive up there. I just want to see where it is."

Dom huffed out a breath. "Fine. Just don't linger." He grabbed a paper and pencil from the counter. "I'm sure he has surveillance cameras all over the place, and you don't want to catch his attention." He handed Creed the paper. "Here's the address."

Creed took it and stood. "I guess we'll be going." He caught Dom's gaze, and his lips twisted. With a sigh of reluctance, he spoke. "Call me if you hear anything."

Dom's brows rose. "Sure. I'll be in touch."

We left the condo, and Creed took my hand. As we rode down the elevator, I leaned against him. "Do you want to drive out to the ranch now?"

"I don't know. It doesn't sound like it will do us any good."

"Maybe we should tell Nash what's going on."

Creed shook his head. "Maybe, but I find it hard to trust him right now. I mean... someone found us, and it's because of him."

Glancing toward our car, my step faltered, and I grabbed Creed's arm. "What's that?" A paper was tucked under the windshield wiper. Creed pulled it out and examined it. "It says Rathmore Enterprises, LLC, with an address and a phone number. That's it."

My heart began to race, and I glanced around the garage. Seeing no one, I edged closer to Creed. "What should we do?"

Creed pursed his lips and stared at the card. "It's obviously a message. I'm going to call."

He dug out his phone and made the call. "This is Aiden Creed. I'm calling for Gage Rathmore." He listened for a few seconds. "Where?" He glanced at the business card. "Sure." His brows rose, and his gaze cut to mine. "Yes, she is." He listened before replying. "All right, we'll be there."

He slipped the phone away and let out a breath. "Gage Rathmore wants to meet with us." He glanced at his watch. "At four, which is in a couple of hours."

My heart pounded. "Why?"

He shook his head. "His secretary didn't say. But we're supposed to meet with him in his corporate offices."

"How does he even know about us?"

He shrugged. "I don't know. Maybe Avery told him something?"

"Let's go back and talk to Dom. I want to know what to expect."

A minute later, we stood in front of Dom's door. He pulled it open, and his brows arched in surprise. "What's going on?"

"Rathmore," Creed said. "He wants to see us." Dom stepped back to let us in, and Creed explained the business card and the phone call. "Did you or Sonny tell him we were here?"

"No." Dom shook his head. "But I'm not sure you should go. You don't know what he wants from you. As long as Sonny doesn't sign over his assets, Avery is safe. Meeting with Rathmore is more dangerous than you know."

"We have nothing he wants."

Dom glanced my way, and Creed drew in a breath. "Did you tell him about Ella—about what she can do?" Creed crowded into Dom's space, and Dom raised his hands.

"No! No... I swear. I didn't say a word."

From Dom's quick denial, I had a feeling he was lying. "What did you tell him?"

"Nothing... he asked about Avery's sudden recovery from the accident, that's all. He knows you and Creed went to visit her, but I didn't tell him you had anything to do with it. I swear."

Creed let out a breath and rubbed the back of his neck. "Dammit. Do you think he suspects something?"

Dom backed away. "I don't know. Go ahead and go. Just don't blame me if it doesn't turn out the way you want."

I sank down on the couch. This just went from bad to worse. "I don't think we have a choice. We're supposed to meet him at his corporate offices. Is there anything we should know?"

Dom's gaze traveled over us, and he frowned with distaste. "Yeah. You should buy some better clothes."

I glanced at my t-shirt and jeans, surprised at his disgust. "Okay. We can do that. Anything else?"

He shook his head. "Yeah. Don't go."

"That's not an option." Creed said.

"Fine. Then there's nothing else I can tell you."

With a heavy heart, I followed Creed to the door. Before stepping out, I glanced at him over my shoulder. "We'll be in touch."

CHAPTER TEN

A s we drove to Rathmore's corporate offices, my stomach got tighter with each passing minute. We'd taken Dom's advice and had found some nicer clothes at a trendy department store. For the first time in my life, I wasn't worried about spending money, so we just bought what we liked, which ended up saving us a lot of time.

Back at the house, we showered before slipping on our new clothes.

I'd opted for a black pant set with a cropped, double-breasted blazer that looked amazing on me. In fact, with the pleated, high-waisted pants and tortoiseshell buckle on the belt, I looked more polished than ever, especially with the white, square-neck tank top underneath. The black pumps I got to go with it were expensive, but I'd hardly batted an eye at the price, grateful they were so comfortable.

After applying a fair amount of makeup, and styling my light blond hair in wispy waves, I had more confidence to meet a man whose reputation was so forbidding. I knew I wasn't in the same league as him, but at least I had more confidence in these clothes.

Creed had gone more casual with a grey, tweedy sports jacket over a black, untucked t-shirt with dark, slim-cut jeans. He'd also needed new shoes, and had opted for a black leather half-boot style.

With his scruffy beard, tousled dark hair, and deep blue eyes, he looked so good he could have been a model... or a movie star. I shook my head. If we survived, he would soon be on a hot, new TV show, and I wasn't sure I liked it much. All the women would be crushing on him, and I'd have to be okay with that.

Still, I'd be okay with anything, as long as we got out of this mess with Avery alive.

We pulled into the parking lot, and Creed gave my hand a reassuring squeeze. "We can do this." His eyes shone with intensity, and he leaned in close for a kiss. "Whatever happens, we stick together."

I nodded and kissed him back, loving the way his mouth felt on mine. I inhaled his clean, fresh scent and tried to memorize this moment. Leaning my forehead against his, I sighed. "Are you sure this is the right thing to do?" I hated to ask, but, after Dom's warning, I couldn't help the worry that knotted my stomach.

"Angel... I don't know anything for sure. But I want to know Avery's okay."

I let out a breath. "I know... we need to see this through."

We got out of the car and entered the impressive, glass-encased building, both of us walking tall and straight and presenting a united front. Inside, the walls were painted white, with lovely blue accents, ranging from turquoise to a light, sky-blue color.

The receptionist examined us, her gaze lingering longer on Creed than I liked. "Please have a seat. I'll let Mr. Rathmore know you're here."

We sat on the white leather couch near the window, with an oblong, glass coffee table in front of us, and a deep-blue glass sculpture of a seashell sitting on top. The decor was not what I'd expected.

The desert theme of tan stucco and Spanish arches were nowhere to be found. Instead, this space reminded me of a cool seaside resort. The tiled floors resembled sand, and blue-green vases filled with bright flowers. Large pots containing green plants were spread throughout the space, giving it a light, airy feel.

The receptionist motioned to us. "Mr. Rathmore will see you now. Please follow me."

She took us through a security gate, where a guard checked us for weapons and allowed us through. At a bank of elevators, the receptionist swiped her security card over the box, and the elevator doors opened.

Inside, she pushed the button for the thirteenth floor, and the doors closed. Creed's eyes widened and he caught my gaze. "Thirteenth floor, huh?" He shook his head. "Figures."

The receptionist ignored him. When the doors opened again, we followed her into a wide-open office suite, decorated in the same bright theme as the lobby. A woman sat at another desk and thanked the receptionist for bringing us up.

The receptionist left, and the secretary looked down her nose at us like we were gnats under her thumb. I took an instant dislike to her. She wore an impeccable navy suit, and her deep red hair was cut in a perfectly styled bob, reaching just below her chin. Her slim figure and upright posture spoke of money, making her seem cold and aloof.

"Follow me." With a haughty twist of her head, she led us down a short hall to a double door and knocked before entering the room. Holding the door open, she motioned us inside.

A tall, commanding man stood from behind a beautiful oak-wood desk. His wavy, dark hair flowed away from his face, accenting his golden-olive skin tones. With a jutting forehead, his dark brows accented his eyes, bringing out their hazel color of green and brown, flecked with gold, making him seem soulful and mysterious.

His bearing reminded me of a modern Arabian sheik, without the beard and head covering. He was also much younger than I'd imagined. Even though he had a few silver strands of hair at his temples, he still looked like he was in his late forties or early fifties. He wore a gray-brown herringbone suit and a white shirt without a tie.

The tilt to his head, and the intense gleam in his eyes made him both imposing and imperious. With a flick of his hand, he gestured toward the chairs in front of his desk. "Please… have a seat."

His deep, domineering voice sent a shiver down my spine. After we sat, he took his chair and studied us with narrowed eyes. His gaze lingered on me, studying me like he'd found something exotic, and I tried not to fidget. From behind his desk, it seemed impossible that he could loom over us, but I felt his intimidation falling over me like a dark shadow.

He shifted his gaze to Creed and began. "So… you're Aiden Creed." He examined Creed with a raised brow. "I remember you from Sonny's poker tournament. You were one of Sonny's players. You outlasted all of the card sharks he hired and made it to the final round, where you lost spectacularly. Tell me… did you do it on purpose?"

Creed's mouth twitched. "Of course not. I play to win."

Rathmore's brows rose, and he turned his focus to me. "And you… I remember you as well, but I don't remember your name."

"It's Ella. Ella St. John."

"Yes… that's right. It was your connection with the woman who won the tournament that saved your skin. Shelby Nichols, right? What can you tell me about her? I've heard rumors that she's a psychic of some kind. Is it true?"

I tried not to show that he'd hit a nerve. "I don't really know her that well."

When I didn't elaborate, he leaned forward. "I'd say you know her well enough. After all, she and her uncle, Joe Manetto, got you off the hook with Sonny. From what I know, it seems to me like they're very good friends to have, or you might not be sitting here in my office today."

I stiffened. How did he know so much about us? "I met Shelby several months ago in New York, but that was the first time I'd ever met her uncle. I'd say she's more like an acquaintance than a friend."

"And what about her psychic abilities?"

I squirmed under his intense gaze. "I think she has premonitions about things. But that's all I know."

Creed leaned forward, impatient with Rathmore's line of questioning. "Look… we're here because you have my sister, and I want her back, unharmed."

Rathmore returned his focus to Creed. "I find it interesting that you're asking about your sister, when the reason she's in this position is because of you. If you had won the tournament, Sonny would have paid me. But now, I think I'm doing you a favor by keeping your sister out of his reach."

I glanced at Creed, wanting to tell him not to agree to anything Rathmore said. This man was an expert who could twist any circumstance to his benefit, and I didn't want to fall into his trap.

Creed gave no indication that Rathmore had upset him. "You have it wrong. She was safe from Sonny until you interfered. But that's beside the point. If Sonny owes you money, there are easier ways to get it from him than by kidnapping my sister."

"I'm not so sure about that," Rathmore countered. "I don't know if Sonny will go for the deal I offered him. Which I'm sure you know all about, since you and Dom are old friends. But it's a chance I couldn't pass up. If Sonny doesn't take my offer, Avery will testify. I can't say that her testimony will be enough to put Sonny in jail, but it's a strong motivator for the moment, and I enjoy seeing Sonny squirm."

His satisfied grin, and the wicked gleam in his eyes, left no doubt that he was telling the truth.

"So what do you want with us?" I asked him.

"A better question to ask is how can you ensure Avery's safety."

"What's that supposed to mean?" Creed asked, his voice low. "Are you threatening to hurt her?"

"Not at all. In fact, I'm keeping her safe. But what happens if Sonny takes the deal?" He shrugged. "I'd have to turn your sister over to him before the trial. You think he'd let her live?"

Neither of us said anything, so he continued. "I suppose you could make Sonny an offer, but I doubt that he'd care now. You have nothing to offer him that he'd want. That's where our paths differ. You have something I'm willing to bargain for."

"What's that?" Creed asked.

"Shelby Nichols." Rathmore focused on me. "As we already discussed, you both have a connection to her. I could use someone with her particular skills for a venture I'm looking into. So far, I've not been able to get past her uncle, but she might be willing to help you if she knows what's at stake."

My heart began to race. Was he really going there? I tried not to let him see my disgust, but I wasn't sure I could mask it.

Creed shook his head. "No. We already owe Manetto for helping us with Sonny. Going against him could get us killed."

Rathmore's lips thinned. "Not even for your sister's life?"

"What do you mean?" I asked. "You need her alive to testify against Sonny."

He waved his hand dismissively. "I don't really care if she testifies against him or not. Her life means nothing to me except as a means to an end. If Sonny doesn't take the deal I offered, I will make him pay one way or another. This just makes it easier. And I don't expect that he will go to jail anyway, because how can he settle his debt to me if he's behind bars?"

"Are you saying the trial's rigged?" Creed asked.

Rathmore's brows rose. "Of course not, but there's no guarantee he'll be found guilty. Now... will you do it or not?"

"What if Shelby won't agree?" I asked. "Like I said, we're not that close. She doesn't owe me anything. She'd probably turn me down. What happens then?"

Rathmore's lips tightened, and his brows dipped. "Ella. You surprise me. With Avery's life on the line, I'd think that's motivation enough to persuade her. From what I witnessed, she seems like the helpful sort. You could play on her sense of duty."

"I need to think about it." I glanced at Creed. "We need to think about it."

He looked between us, and his lips thinned. "I suppose that's understandable. But fair warning... don't wait too long. Avery won't live past the trial, whether she testifies or not. Call when you're ready to make the deal."

Creed's jaw clenched and he stood. There was nothing more to say, so we made our way toward the door. Before Creed could pull it open, Rathmore stopped us. "One more thing."

We turned to face him. "If you think about it, I'm not asking that much. You must know I'd never harm Shelby. I just need her help for this particular job. Just this one time... and that would be the end of it. There are worse things I could ask of you. So remember that while you're considering Avery's life."

Anger and helplessness burned in my chest. As we headed down the hall to the elevators, dread descended over my shoulders like a heavy weight. How had it come to this? Now we were in a fight for Avery's life. All because Rathmore wanted Shelby Nichols.

Sure, he'd wanted us to think it wasn't a big deal, but that wasn't true. He'd said it was just one job for Shelby, but he didn't mean it. How could he? Once he sank his teeth into someone, he wouldn't let go, especially someone special, like her.

There had to be another way out of this. But what that was, I had no idea.

With nothing else we could do, we began the drive back to our rental house. It was frustrating that things just seemed to get worse, no matter how hard we tried to solve the problem. "I can't believe it." I finally said. "He was at the tournament, and we had no idea."

"Yeah. I don't remember seeing him there, but I was a little preoccupied. Still, how did he know we were here in Vegas with Avery? I don't think Sonny or Dom would have told him, but his card was on the car at Dom's place, so he knew where we were."

"You're right. It's like he knows our every move." I shuddered. "How do we fight against someone like that?"

"I don't know." Creed sighed. "I don't know how we're going to save Avery without doing what he wants."

"I know, but at least we have time to think about it."

We pulled into the garage and unlocked the house to step inside. Just yesterday, Avery and Nash had both been here. Now, it seemed too quiet. After changing out of our new clothes, it was nice to put on something comforting and familiar.

"I'm going to pack up Avery's stuff. I want to make sure it's all there."

I caught the flash of pain in Creed's eyes before he nodded. "I'll see what I can scrounge up for dinner."

Avery's luggage bag sat opened, with her clothes spilling out in a jumbled mess on the floor. I moved it to the bed and began straightening it up. Next, I checked all the drawers, gathering her things and folding them up.

It gave me something to do while I processed what had happened. The trial was to begin on Monday. That meant we had two days to figure things out. It didn't seem like enough time, but it was better than nothing.

By the time I finished, I had a few ideas about how to proceed and hurried downstairs to talk them over with Creed. The smell of peppers and onions hit me first, and my stomach gurgled with hunger since I'd barely eaten a thing all day. It still surprised me that Creed liked to cook, and I was learning that cooking relaxed him. As he added several eggs to the pan, he glanced my way.

"Want to make some toast?"

"Sure." After loading the toaster, I watched Creed add a few spices and top his creation off with shredded cheese. My mouth watered in anticipation, and when the toast popped up, I quickly buttered it.

Soon we had a delicious meal on our plates, and we sat down to devour it. "This is so good." I told him. "Thanks. I haven't been this hungry in a long time."

He sent me a smile, and we finished eating. After cleaning up and stacking the dishes in the dishwasher, we settled in the living room on the couch. Creed pulled me against him, and I closed my eyes.

He kissed the top of my head. "You're going to have to call Shelby. You know that, right?"

"Yeah. I know. But first, I thought it wouldn't hurt to tell Dom what Rathmore said about the trial. If Sonny knows it's rigged, he won't sign anything, and that should buy us some time."

"True."

"And what do you think about Nash?" I straightened. "I thought maybe he should know too."

"Yeah... but I'm pretty sure he might already know. Someone in his department is talking with Rathmore, and maybe even taking orders from him. How else would Rathmore know about us and that we were here in the city?"

He sighed and shook his head. "So much for Avery being safe with the police. It makes me mad that she ever agreed to testify. None of this is worth it. Mom was right." He closed his eyes. "And now what am I going to tell her?"

"Nothing yet. We've still got time. Let's put our heads together and see what we can come up with."

We spent the next couple of hours going over everything we knew and tried to figure out a way to get Avery back that didn't involve Shelby.

"I could talk to Dom about taking Sonny up on his proposal to kill Rathmore," Creed said. "Other than that, I've got nothing."

"That's the last thing you should do. I'd happily call Shelby before I ever let you do that."

"Let me?" Creed raised his brows. "I don't think it's such a bad idea. Maybe if we got close enough to him, you could do it." At my widened eyes, he quickly continued. "But only as a last resort. I know you're not supposed to use your power like that, but if things go sideways... we should at least consider it."

Before I could respond, my phone rang. Glancing at the caller ID, I quickly answered. "Hi Nash. Find anything?"

"I have an idea I'd like to pass by you and Creed. Are you at the house?"

"Yes."

"Good. I'll be there in a few minutes."

The line disconnected, and I turned to Creed. "Nash is on his way. What do we tell him?"

"Let's see what he has to say first."

Ten minutes later, a knock sounded at the door. Creed pulled it open, and Nash stepped inside, still wearing the clothes he'd had on this morning. His eyes were bloodshot, with heavy bags beneath them, and his jaw was dark with stubble. His clothes hung on him, rumpled and askew, and his hair stood on end in a few places, like he'd been pulling it out.

The transformation shocked me, and I immediately motioned him toward the kitchen. "Have you had anything to eat?"

His brows drew together like that was a stupid question. "Uh... I don't remember."

"Come on. We've got plenty of milk, and I'll make you a PB & J sandwich." As I prodded him in that direction, Creed followed, and they both sat down at the counter while I got busy.

Creed asked him about Avery. "What's going on? Any news?"

"We scoured through all the security cameras around here and found a van that was parked a couple of streets over. We caught the kidnapper getting inside with Avery and driving away. Naturally, there were no plates on the van, but we managed to keep up with it on the street cameras until it turned off the main road and into the Rancho Charleston neighborhood."

Creed stiffened, and I glanced his way. "What's wrong?"

"It's one of the worst parts of town."

"That's right," Nash continued. "It's full of gangs. Everyone who lives in Vegas knows to stay away from there because of the violence and murders that are a daily occurrence. We spent the last few hours driving around the neighborhood, hoping to find the van, but we couldn't see it anywhere."

A prickle of unease ran down my spine. "She can't be there."

"How do you know?"

"Because Rathmore has her. He wouldn't be holding her in the worst part of town." But did I know that? Had either of us asked for proof that Avery was alive and safe? Why hadn't we done that? We had no idea where she was or how she was doing.

"How do you know he has Avery?"

I quickly explained that we'd found his card on the windshield of our car and had called him. "We met with him at his corporate offices." I left out the detail that we had been at Dom's condo at the time, since Nash wouldn't appreciate it.

"Rathmore seemed to think that, even if Avery testified, Sonny wouldn't be convicted. Does he have that much power here?"

Nash shook his head, still trying to take it all in. "Rathmore has a great deal of power in this city, and it just keeps growing. Three years ago, no one knew who he was. Now he's got his fingers in everything. He's like a virus that just keeps spreading, and now he's got his hooks in you. What did he want?"

I glanced away. "I know someone he wants to meet with. In exchange for setting that up, he'll return Avery safe and sound."

"What about the trial?"

I shook my head. "He's got something on Sonny, so he'll see that she testifies. But, like I said, he mentioned that Sonny won't be convicted."

"He might have the power to do that." Nash's brows dipped. "But I just don't know. I'd better tell Richard Martinez to make sure he has no loopholes in his case against Sonny. It's a good thing he went over all of this with Avery before she got taken." He glanced at me. "Are you sure she'll be released to testify?"

"It sounded like it."

"But what about your deal? Will that change anything?"

"No. I don't think so."

"So... you're telling me that somehow Rathmore will get Avery to the courthouse to testify and then spirit her away when she's done if you don't agree to his terms? That sounds like poor planning on his side. Unless you agree to his terms first and he can just let her go."

I shrugged. "I know, but that sounds about right."

"Who does he want to meet with?"

"A friend of mine. That's all I want to say for now."

"Okay." He shook his head. "Then it looks like we may have an opportunity to get Avery away from Rathmore during the trial. Are you going to agree to his terms?"

"I'd rather not," I said. "But I will if I have to."

"Why don't you hold off until after her testimony? I'll figure out a plan to surround her after she's dismissed and get her away from him. In a courtroom full of people, I think we can pull it off. What do you say?"

"I say that sounds great. What about you, Creed?" He'd been silent during our exchange and I had no idea why.

"Sure."

"Okay." Nash stood and his eyes filled with hope. "This is a good plan. I'll have to tell Martinez all about your bargain with Rathmore, but at least he'll be relieved that he can go ahead with the trial."

"How is that going to work? I mean... won't you have to coordinate with Rathmore to get her to the courthouse?"

Nash rubbed his neck. "Let Martinez and me worry about that."

He didn't elaborate, so I shrugged. "Okay. Just make sure you have a plan to get her away from him once she's done."

"I'll take care of it." Nash hurried out the door, but stopped to glance over his shoulder. "Be sure to call me if you hear anything new."

I nodded, and closed the door behind him. "You were awfully quiet. What's wrong?"

Creed shook his head. "I don't know. Something about this seems off, and I'm not sure who we can trust anymore." He sighed. "I feel like I've let Avery down. We should have made sure she was alive and well when we were in Rathmore's office. Now it's too late."

"We'll get her back, even if we need to call Shelby. I'm sure it will all work out."

Creed raised a brow. "I wish I had your optimism."

"Come on. We could both use a good night's sleep. Things will look better in the morning."

I wrapped an arm around his waist and we climbed the stairs to our bedroom. It seemed almost wrong to find comfort in Creed's arms when Avery was in trouble, but we needed each other now more than ever. Knowing we were in this together strengthened and comforted us both. For this small moment in time, we could find peace in our union, and forget our troubles.

Tomorrow would come soon enough.

The next day, we woke to a ringing phone. Creed quickly answered it, while I blinked the sleep away from my eyes. I didn't hear what he said, but the call ended quickly. Coming back to bed, he sat down. "That was Dom. Sonny wants to meet."

"Why?"

"I don't know for sure, but Dom thought Sonny wanted to make a deal with me."

"You mean the deal about you and Dom killing Rathmore?"

"That's what Dom thinks."

I sighed. "Okay... I'll have to get ready."

"He just wants me."

I froze. "What? No. I should come with you."

Creed took my hands in his. "Ella, please. I want to know what he has to say, so I have to go without you."

"Seriously? You can't trust him. How do you know you'll be okay?"

"Because he wants something from me, and I want to know what it is. If I can use it to get Avery away from Rathmore, then I have to go. Don't worry, I'll be careful."

I wasn't convinced talking to Sonny was worth it, but it wasn't like I could stop him. If it meant helping his sister, he'd take the chance. "Okay... fine. But I don't like it."

"I know... I don't either." He stripped off his clothes and padded into the shower.

Hearing the water turn on, I slipped downstairs to make some breakfast. I knew it wouldn't be as good as Creed's cooking, but I needed to do something normal to keep my worry under control.

After Creed left, I took my time getting ready for the day. I considered calling Rathmore to ask if Avery was okay, but decided against it. I had to trust that Creed's instincts were better than mine.

At least the trial would begin tomorrow. I suddenly realized that I had no idea where the trial would be held, or even what time it would start. With that in mind, I put a call through to Nash. He told me all the details and assured me that they would be ready to take Avery into their custody. I sure hoped he'd come through so this nightmare would be over.

Creed returned an hour later, and I could finally breathe again. "So what's going on?"

He shook his head and sat down on the couch. "Dom was right. Sonny wants us to get close to Rathmore and take him out. He decided not to sign any kind of deal with Rathmore, so we don't have to worry about that.

"I also told Sonny that I spoke with Rathmore and what he'd said about Sonny not being convicted if he gave the word. It surprised me that Sonny was so easy to convince, but I guess he thinks Rathmore has enough clout to pull it off."

"What about his offer? What did you tell him?"

He shrugged. "Dom and I agreed to come up with a plan." At my gasp, he continued. "That doesn't mean we'll do it, but at least it's enough to satisfy Sonny for now, especially since he knows that Rathmore is threatening me."

My stomach dropped. "Did you tell him why?"

"No... I didn't tell him anything about Shelby. I just told Sonny that I tried to bargain with Rathmore for Avery's life, and it didn't go so well."

"But what if word gets back to Rathmore? Seriously, I don't think there's much he doesn't know."

"I don't know, but it can't be worse than it is now."

I wasn't sure I agreed with that, but I kept my opinion to myself. "I called Nash to find out about the trial. They've already selected a jury, so the trial's ready to start at nine tomorrow morning."

Creed blew out a breath. "It can't come fast enough for me. As long as Nash can come through for us, this nightmare could be over by tomorrow afternoon."

I nodded, but couldn't help the shiver of doubt that ran over me. Nash's plan seemed too easy, but since it was just about the only way out of this mess, I had to hope that he could pull it off.

CHAPTER ELEVEN

We arrived at the courthouse at eight-thirty the next morning. My stomach was a jumble of nerves, and I felt a little sick. Several people had already crowded into the room, and we found some seats near the back.

Close to the front, behind the defense table, I spotted Dom sitting next to Grant Ellingson. Grant was one of Sonny's enforcers, so it didn't surprise me to see him. But it still unnerved me to see Dom so entrenched on Sonny's side.

We'd spoken with Nash earlier, and he told us that Richard Martinez had taken care of everything, and we didn't need to worry. For some reason, that didn't help us feel any better. Sonny and his two lawyers came in to sit at the defense table, but the prosecuting attorneys had yet to arrive.

With five minutes to spare, Richard Martinez rushed into the courtroom followed by another attorney. They quickly took several folders from their briefcases and arranged them on the table.

A moment later, the bailiff asked everyone to rise while the honorable Judge Blomquist took his seat. He called everyone to order and spoke to the jury about what to expect before telling Richard Martinez to begin with his opening statement.

With great somberness, Martinez rose to his feet and addressed the jury, telling them that he would prove without a doubt that Sonny Dixon killed Shannon Guy in cold blood.

The defense attorney, Paul Burke, countered by telling the jury that Sonny Dixon was an innocent and upstanding businessman who didn't deserve to have his name dragged through the mud. He told the jury that the court system was set up to make sure innocent men like his client were able to defend themselves against lies and false accusations.

"Mr. Guy's body was found in the parking lot of the Palomino Club, nowhere near Sonny Dixon's casino. We will prove that these accusations are false and that my client had nothing to do with Shannon Guy's death."

After he finished, the judge nodded to Martinez. "You may call your first witness."

Martinez stood. "Your honor, we call Avery Creed to the stand."

My breath caught. I hadn't expected Avery to be called so fast. All eyes turned to the double doors where a court-appointed officer stood. He pulled one of the doors open and motioned to someone in the hall.

Two men wearing suits, white shirts, and ties stepped into the courtroom. Behind them, Avery followed. Her step faltered, and she glanced around the courtroom with wide eyes. Her gaze met Creed's and she instantly relaxed, drawing strength from his presence. Meeting my gaze, her lips quirked up in a tight smile, and I sent her an encouraging nod.

Taking a fortifying breath, she held her head high and continued to the witness box. She wore an expensive pant suit of somber gray, which made her look professional and confident. Her dark, short hair was artfully tousled to frame her heart-shaped face, making her beautiful blue eyes seem even larger than normal. Two more men, wearing dark suits, followed in her wake.

Stepping into the witness box, she raised her right hand and the bailiff swore her in. As she took her seat, her gaze landed on Sonny Dixon, then behind him to Dom. She stiffened slightly and quickly pulled her gaze away to concentrate on the questions Richard Martinez began to ask. Raising her voice, she answered succinctly for all to hear, just like they'd practiced a few days ago.

She answered his introductory questions by stating her name and her relationship to the defendant, Sonny Dixon. Once that was established, Martinez got down to business.

"Were you working for Sonny Dixon at the Mojave Desert Casino on the night of August seventeenth?

"Yes."

"What was your job?"

"I served drinks in the casino, and I also served drinks at Mr. Dixon's private parties and business meetings."

"Can you tell us what happened on the night of August seventeenth?"

Avery licked her lips and nodded. "Yes. It was my night to serve Mr. Dixon's guests in his private business room. I was on my way there when I heard him yelling at someone. The door was ajar, and I glanced inside. That's when I saw his guest, Shannon Guy, bleeding out on the floor. His neck was slit, and he wasn't breathing. Sonny was upset and yelling at Grant Ellingson."

"Did you see Mr. Dixon kill Shannon Guy?"

"No, but I heard him tell Grant Ellingson that he'd killed the man."

"Objection!" Paul Burke jumped to his feet. "This is hearsay evidence and should not be allowed."

Judge Blomquist leaned back in his chair. "Under an admission of a party opponent, I will allow." He nodded at Martinez. "Overruled."

Martinez continued. "What were his exact words?"

"Sonny said, 'This piece of shit has been cheating me out of my money for years. He had to die for that.'" Avery swallowed, and her lips tightened. "He was pretty upset."

"What happened after that?"

"I backed away and ran down the hall."

"Did anyone see you?"

"Not that I knew of. The hall was empty, and I didn't look back."

"What did you do then?"

"I went back to my station." Avery's voice began to shake. "But once I got there, I ran to the bathroom to throw up. When I came out, Grant Ellingson was waiting at the bar. He asked me where I'd been, and I told him I'd been in the bathroom with a stomach bug."

Her face had gone pale, and her shoulders were rigid. "I could tell he was suspicious of me, so I told him I was sorry for not making it to Sonny's private room, and I could go now if he wanted. He told me not to bother and said I should go home if I was sick. I told him I was feeling better, but he insisted that I leave. I thanked him for understanding and left."

"Did you mention what you'd seen to anyone?"

"Not then. I saw my brother on the way out, and I told him I might have seen something I shouldn't have. He encouraged me to talk to the police, but I put him off. I was too scared. My boyfriend worked for Sonny, so I thought if I kept my mouth shut, he'd make sure nothing happened to me."

"Who was your boyfriend?"

"Dom Orlandi."

"Is he here?"

Avery glanced toward the defense's table. "Yes. He's sitting behind Mr. Dixon, next to Grant Ellingson."

"Did you tell Dom Orlandi what you'd seen?"

"Yes."

I gasped. So Dom had known all along? I glanced at Creed. His jaw was clenched and his face tight. Unleashed anger radiated off of him in waves, all directed at his so-called friend.

Martinez continued. "What did he tell you to do?"

"He told me to keep quiet about it, and he'd make sure nothing happened to me." She took a breath and continued more loudly. "But he lied, because a couple of days later, someone ran me down with their car and nearly killed me."

Amid gasps from the spectators, the defense attorney jumped to his feet. "Objection! This is a different matter and has nothing to do with Shannon Guy's death."

"Overruled." The judge banged his gavel to get everyone to stop talking. "Counselor, I'd like to know where you're going with this. You may continue."

Martinez picked up a folder and took out a police report. "Let the record show that Ms. Creed was involved in a hit-and-run accident that left her in a coma just days after Shannon Guy's murder." He handed the report to the judge and a copy to the defense attorney.

"Please tell us about your injuries."

"I nearly died that night," Avery began. She explained her long recovery and the brain trauma she'd experienced. Since she looked completely healed, it didn't seem to have a big impact on the jury.

Martinez continued. "Have there been any more attempts on your life?"

"Yes."

"Objection!" The defense attorney jumped to his feet again, cutting Avery off.

The judge frowned. "Sustained." He glanced at the jury. "Please disregard the question. Counselor, you will refrain from this line of questioning and keep your comments to this case only."

Martinez nodded, but held his head high, knowing he'd made his point. "Ms. Creed, is the man who killed Shannon Guy in this room?" At her nod, he continued. "Could you point him out?"

"Yes." She pointed to the defense table. "That's him, Sonny Dixon."

"Thank you." He turned to Sonny's attorney. "Your witness."

Sonny's attorney stood for the cross-examination. He stepped closer to Avery than was necessary, and his lips pursed into a frown. "Ms. Creed, how old are you?"

Her jaw dropped open, but she quickly shut it. "I'm twenty."

"Did you know the legal age for serving drinks in Nevada is twenty-one?"

Avery's eyes widened, and she nodded.

"A yes or no, please."

"Yes."

"Did you lie on your application for the job?" At her hesitation, he continued. "A simple yes or no will suffice."

"Yes, but I'll be—"

"A yes is all we need. Have you ever been arrested?"

Avery's face paled, and she glanced Creed's way. "I... I wasn't ever charged with anything."

"Please answer the question. Yes or no."

"Objection!" Martinez stood. "This has no bearing on the case."

Burke turned to the judge. "Your honor, I'm establishing the witness's character."

Judge Blomquist shook his head. "Sustained. Please disregard the question."

Thwarted, Burke blew out a breath. "I have no further questions at this time, but reserve the right to recall the witness if needed."

Judge Blomquist nodded and turned to Avery. "You are dismissed until further notice."

Everyone watched as Avery left the witness stand. The men who'd accompanied her inside quickly positioned themselves around her and ushered her out. I glanced to the back of the room for Nash, but he wasn't there.

Creed jumped to his feet to follow them, and I hurried behind him.

"Avery!" He called. "Wait."

Without slowing, the men hustled her outside the building and down the steps. One of them took her arm and pulled her toward the curb where a limo waited. As she disappeared inside the limo, Creed rushed to the car. He reached it, but one of the guards grabbed him from behind to hold him back. Creed shoved at the man, but the car took off before he could do anything more to stop it.

Creed let out a frustrated growl. "Where are you taking her? She's my sister." Without answering, the man climbed into another waiting vehicle and drove away.

"Where the hell is Nash?" Creed asked.

I scanned the street, but found no sign of him. "I don't know."

Shaking his head, Creed grabbed my hand. "Come on. Let's follow them."

We ran to the parking lot by the side of the building and jumped into our car. Creed pulled onto the street, turning in the same direction we'd seen them go. Scouting ahead, I could see no sign of the limo or the other car.

Creed smacked the steering wheel with the palm of his hand. "Dammit. We lost them. It doesn't make sense that they'd go far. It sounded like they might question her again."

"I know. I'm surprised they left the building."

Creed continued down the street, but no sign of them remained. "Let's drive to Rathmore's ranch. Maybe they took her there. I think I put the address in my phone."

As he dug into his pocket, I shook my head. "But we'll miss the trial."

"I don't care. We need to find Avery."

Creed handed me his phone, and I searched through his notes. "Here it is. Nineteen-twenty Montana Court in Blue Diamond." I found the map app and entered the address. The directions took us out of the city toward a small western mountain range.

"It says our estimated arrival is in twenty minutes. You still want to go that far?"

Creed let out a frustrated breath. "I don't know. They took her somewhere, so we might as well try it. I don't think we'll miss much of the trial, and it might be worth it."

"Okay. Let's hope we can find her before she's called back to the courthouse."

"I doubt that they'll need her again today. We'll be fine."

I hoped he was right. "I wonder what happened to Nash. I thought he and his men were going to surround her."

"Something must have happened. It's hard to believe that he'd let her go without a fight."

"I know. I thought we could count on him." Everything was falling apart. How were we ever going to get Avery away from those guards? I shook my head. "So it looks like Dom knew Avery was in danger from the beginning. It's hard to believe. He seemed so clueless."

Creed's hands tightened on the wheel. "Yeah. I guess all that time he thought nothing would happen to her since he had an in with Sonny. Arrogant bastard."

"Yeah, but it explains his change of heart... if he meant what he said."

Creed snorted. "I highly doubt it."

I had to agree. Dom had some explaining to do, but I wasn't sure it mattered now. Rathmore had Avery, and, somehow, he'd gotten her to the trial just in time to testify. Did that mean he was working with the police? If that were the case, it meant that Nash didn't stand a chance of getting Avery away from him.

Maybe it was time to consider calling Shelby Nichols, and hope she'd help us out, because that might be the only way we'd ever get Avery out of this alive.

Twenty minutes later, we turned off the highway to enter the small Blue Diamond development.

We wound through a few streets before coming to the one we wanted, which took us deeper into the hillside. In this small community, the neighborhood streets had little or no traffic on them.

Turning onto Montana Court, we followed the road all the way to the top where it dead-ended next to a large, gated home that sat below the street, overlooking the valley. A high, rock wall followed the edge of the property, with a closed gate blocking the driveway.

Creed turned the car around and pulled to the side of the street, facing the way we'd come. I got out of the car and followed Creed to the gate, hoping to find a way inside. A large pedestal with a side panel containing buttons for a code, stood next to the gate.

I looked past the gate into the yard, hoping to see any evidence of the limo or the car from the courthouse. The driveway sat empty, but the cars could have pulled into the garage, so they might still be here.

"Over here," Creed said. I stepped to the side of the rock wall where Creed had discovered an opening. Above the small nook was a sign that read, "Deliveries." Inside the nook sat a speaker with a button. Creed pushed the button, and we both heard the faint buzzing of a bell.

The speaker clicked, and a man spoke. "Yes?"

Creed glanced at me, and his eyes widened. "Uh... we need to talk to Mr. Rathmore."

"He's only available with an appointment."

"Wait. I want to see my sister, Avery. I know she's in there. I want to make sure she's okay."

The speaker clicked, but there was no response. Creed pushed the button several more times, still getting no response. "Dammit." Creed stepped back to look up at the gate. "I think I can climb over it."

"Creed... wait." Ignoring me, he reached up and pulled himself to the top of the iron bars. Before he could swing a leg over the top, a man holding a shotgun strode down the driveway.

"That's far enough. Get back down or I'll shoot. See that sign? It says no trespassing. I'll be within my rights to put a bullet through your head."

With the shotgun trained on him, Creed lowered himself back to the ground. "I just want to see my sister."

The man shook his head. "You'll have to make an appointment with Mr. Rathmore."

"Fine. I'll call him right now." Creed pulled out his phone and pushed in the number for Rathmore's office. He waited while it rang, then went still. "This is Aiden Creed. I need to speak with Mr. Rathmore." He waited until Rathmore picked up. "I'm outside your house on Montana Court. I want to see my sister."

Creed caught my gaze, his face tight. "Yes. Ella's here." He paused. "We need proof that Avery's okay first." He closed his eyes. "... yes, we saw her, but..." He shook his head before letting out a sigh. "Yes. I understand but..." he pulled the phone away from his ear. "He hung up on me."

"What did he say?"

"He said he'd talk to us after you've made contact with Shelby." Creed shook his head. "He's given us until the end of the trial."

"I wonder how long that will be."

"I don't know." Creed shook his head. "I guess we might as well head back to the courthouse."

The man holding the gun watched us walk to our car, not letting us out of his sight until we drove away.

"I'm going to call Nash and find out what happened." I pulled out my phone and put the call through. It rang several times before Nash picked up. I didn't waste any words. "What happened? Why did you let Avery go?"

Instead of answering, he asked. "Where are you?"

"On our way back to the courthouse. We tried to follow Avery, but we lost her. What's going on?"

He huffed out a breath. "Look... I can't talk about it now. I'll explain when you get here." He disconnected, and I let out a frustrated breath.

"Someone in the department must have waylaid Nash." I glanced Creed's way, taking in his flat lips and narrowed eyes. I rubbed his arm, hoping to calm him down. "At least we know she's okay. She didn't look scared, and she kicked butt on the witness stand. If Sonny gets off, it won't be because of her."

Creed's shoulders relaxed. "You're right. We'll figure this out, but I sure hope you have Shelby's number. I think that's the only way out of this mess."

"Yeah... I think you might be right, but let's see what Nash has to say for himself first."

Several minutes later, we pulled into the parking lot and made our way back into the courthouse. Seeing no sign of Nash, we slipped inside the courtroom to find him standing just inside the door. He motioned us back into the hall, and we followed him outside the building.

Once we were in the clear, he turned to face us, his lips turned down and his gaze stormy. "Those men with Avery were part of a personal protection team put in place by Richard Martinez." He let out a breath. "At least that's what he told me. But now I know he was behind Avery's abduction."

Creed's face turned to stone. "What? Martinez?"

"Yeah. He's working with Rathmore."

My eyes widened. "So he's the one who told Rathmore where Avery was? Why would he do that?"

"Probably to keep Avery alive and safe from Sonny. Rathmore must have convinced Martinez that he could do a better job than me."

"So when Martinez came over to help prepare Avery for the trial, he was also making it easier for her to get captured by Rathmore's people?" I threw up my hands. "Unbelievable. He must have unlocked her balcony door and given them the layout of the house."

"It looks that way." Nash ground his teeth. "And once they don't need her testimony, Martinez couldn't care less about what happens to her."

Anger and astonishment swept over me. We knew there was a leak in Nash's department, but to have it be the prosecuting attorney was almost more than I could take. I tried to relax my clenched jaw and took a couple of breaths to calm down. "Now what? How much longer will the trial last?"

Nash shook his head. "Martinez just called the coroner to the stand to confirm the cause of death. We might as well go back inside. We can talk later about what to do next."

Back in the courtroom, it was hard to look at Martinez, knowing he was such a two-faced traitor, who didn't give a fig about Avery. I wanted to go yell at him, and I could feel the same anger coming from Creed, although, from his narrowed eyes and the set of his jaw, I was sure he'd rather beat him to a bloody pulp. How had we ever thought Martinez was on our side?

We spent the rest of the day in court, where Martinez established that the victim had been killed somewhere else before his body was dumped in the parking lot of the club. He didn't have as much luck showing evidence of the man's blood in Sonny's private office. Apparently, the carpet had been removed, and they couldn't get a good enough sample of the victim's blood.

From what I could gather, I didn't think they'd need Avery again. The judge called for a recess until the next day. Martinez would finish up with his witnesses, and, after that, the defense team would present their case. Once that was done, the trial would be over, and the jury would decide the outcome.

As Martinez started down the aisle to the doors, Creed stood in his way with his fists clenched and his narrowed gaze trained on the man. Martinez came to an abrupt stop and his co-chair bumped into him from behind. As his eyes filled with panic, Martinez pivoted around and rushed out the side door.

"Coward," Creed muttered. He turned to rush out the doors and track him down, but I snagged his arm.

"Creed... don't."

He jerked his arm away, but his gaze caught mine. Whatever he saw in my eyes brought him back, and he heaved a deep breath. Swallowing, he nodded. "Let's get out of here."

I took his hand, and we left the courtroom and headed back to our rental house. Neither of us was hungry, but we fixed a couple of sandwiches and settled down to eat. When we finished, I met Creed's gaze. "I'm going to call Shelby."

He closed his eyes and nodded. "We have no choice."

Licking my lips, I put the call through. Shelby answered with a pert hello, bringing a smile to my lips. "Hey Shelby, this is Ella. How are you? It's been a while."

"Ella! It's so good to hear from you. I've been wondering how you were doing. Did you ever make it back to New York?"

"Yeah, I did."

"And what about Creed?"

"Well, that's another story. We're married."

"What?"

I couldn't help chuckling. "Yeah. It's kind of a long story."

"That's okay. I've got time."

"If you're sure." She assured me that she had plenty of time, so I told her the whole story, only leaving out the parts I couldn't share. I made sure to include Avery's part in Sonny's upcoming trial, and why Creed had been coerced into playing poker in the first place.

She wanted to know all the details about our marriage, and it took a lot longer to explain that part, since I had to gloss over the bits about St. John's visit and my enhanced healing abilities. I finally got to our second wedding in Los Angeles, and how awesome that had been. "But Dom showed up at the wedding reception and kind of ruined it."

"He did? Holy hell. What did he want?"

"That's the reason for my call." I explained that Avery was well enough to testify at Sonny's trial, which was happening now, and that we were in Las Vegas. I then filled her in about the attempt on Avery's life, and her eventual abduction by Gage Rathmore.

Shelby got real quiet after I mentioned his name, and my brows puckered. "Do you know him?"

She sighed before answering. "Uh... I haven't met him, but yeah... I've heard of him. Why does he have Avery?"

"Well, it turns out that Sonny owes a lot of money to Rathmore. We know Rathmore took Avery to put the pressure on Sonny to sign over his hotel and casino to pay his debt. In return, Rathmore said he'd hand Avery over to Sonny so she wouldn't testify against him. But that didn't work. Sonny refused to sign anything, and now Avery is testifying against Sonny. The trial started today."

"Wait. I don't get it. Rathmore will lose if she testifies. Does he still have her?"

"That's the thing." I sighed. "Creed and I went to see him to bargain for Avery's release. He's a powerful man. Besides owning most of the city, he's got his fingers in the police department and probably the state government too.

"It sounded like the charges against Sonny wouldn't stick if he didn't want them to, but he still wouldn't give up Avery. He's holding her hostage for another reason now." The line was silent, and I wasn't sure Shelby was still there.

She finally spoke, but it was hardly above a whisper. "What does he want?"

I hated to tell her. She'd never want to talk to me again. All I ever did was bring trouble to her door. "I'm so sorry Shelby." I glanced at Creed and caught his encouraging nod. "He wants me to set up a meeting with you."

Shelby made a low sound in her throat, so I quickly continued. "I guess he's been trying to work something out with your uncle, but he hasn't had any luck. Somehow, he found out about our connection, and now he's threatening Avery if I don't set something up."

"Did he say what he wanted?"

"Yes. He was at the poker tournament and saw you play. He promised that he just needed you for a one-time thing, and then you'd be done. It's a meeting of some kind that he wants you to attend. That's all I know."

She sighed. "Well damn."

"I'm sorry to ask, but he promised that if you came to this meeting, he'd release Avery to us, and you'd never have to help him again."

She laughed, but it was humorless. "Right. I've heard that before."

My chest ached with remorse. "I'm so sorry. I had no idea this would involve you. We have until the trial is over to give him an answer, so I can still try to figure out another way to get Avery away from him. But if I can't... I don't know what else to do."

"What's going on with the trial?"

I told her everything that had happened so far. "I'm not sure if Avery's testimony is enough to convict him or not, but I'm sure he's guilty."

"Did Rathmore really say he could get Sonny off?"

"It sure sounded that way."

"Okay... let me see what I can do. Maybe you could tell Rathmore that I'll come, but only if Sonny goes to jail. That way at least something good will come out of it. But I have to be honest. Uncle Joey won't want me to come, even with Avery's life on the line.

"Rathmore's dangerous. More dangerous than you know, and Uncle Joey won't want me anywhere near him. That means I'll have to go behind his back, and that scares the crap out of me."

I didn't know what to say. She was right. This whole business was a nightmare. "I'll come with you. I'll make sure nothing happens to you. Creed and I can both—"

"No. That's not necessary. I might be able to get Ramos to come with me. You remember him? He's great in a fight, and I'm not so bad, either. Besides, it won't come to that. If Rathmore just wants me to use my premonitions in a meeting... that's not such a big deal, right? It will take what...

an hour? That's a piece of cake. And then Avery will be fine. It'll all work out."

I knew she was just trying to make the best of it. That was something I'd learned about Shelby. She always tried to look on the bright side of every situation. It reminded me of St. John's warning. He'd told me that because I'd refused to help Tony Bilotti, I'd put someone else's life in danger. I was pretty sure he was talking about Shelby.

Now here I was, doing the exact same thing. Maybe I shouldn't have called her. "Look. We'll see if we can figure something else out. We have until the trial's over. Let me see what I can do before you worry about coming."

"Ella... I know you wouldn't have called if there was any other way. This isn't your fault. Tell Rathmore I'll agree to come, and then let me know what he says. In the meantime, I'll figure things out on my end and see if Ramos will come with me."

I let out a relieved breath. "I'm so sorry to ask this. I just don't know what else to do."

"I know. It's okay."

"Thanks Shelby. I'll call you soon."

We disconnected, and I laid my forehead on the table. What had I just done? It felt wrong to ask her, but I didn't have a choice. Now I just had to make sure she survived. At least that was something I knew I could do, and just knowing that made all the difference.

CHAPTER TWELVE

C reed and I arrived at the courthouse the next morning, ready for anything. We'd decided to hold off telling Rathmore that Shelby had agreed to his demands until we'd exhausted all of our options.

Before going to bed the night before, Creed had spent nearly an hour on the phone with Nash, trying to cook up a plan for getting Avery out of Rathmore's hands. Nash said he'd do everything he could to make sure Martinez called Avery back to the stand at some point.

That way he'd be ready to grab Avery before she left. If just one of us could pull her aside before she left the courtroom, we might have a chance. Nash promised to talk to Martinez about keeping Avery at the courthouse once she was done, but I didn't hold out much hope that would happen.

As we settled into our seats near the back of the courtroom, Nash stepped inside the doors and gave us a nod. I hoped that meant he had everything under control and was ready to grab Avery.

A few seconds later, Sonny, along with his lawyers, took their places at the defense table. He glanced over his shoulder to nod at both Dom and Grant, who were once again sitting right behind him. Just getting a glimpse of Sonny's face turned my stomach, and Dom sitting behind him like a willing participant didn't help much either.

Martinez and his co-counsel marched into the courtroom, and the trial quickly resumed. Martinez didn't waste any time, calling Grant Ellingson to the witness stand. After he was sworn in, Martinez began his questioning, establishing Grant's identity and that he worked for Sonny Dixon.

"Were you working for Mr. Dixon on the night of August seventeenth?"

"Yes."

"Did Sonny Dixon kill Shannon Guy and ask you to take care of the body?"

"Of course not. Sonny didn't even know the guy." He smirked at his pun. "Get it? Guy?"

Martinez pursed his lips. "On the night in question, did you speak to Avery Creed?"

"I don't remember. I saw her around, so if she was working, I probably spoke to her."

Martinez asked a few more questions, but he didn't get anywhere, and I worried that questioning Grant could backfire.

Burke cross-examined Grant and made him out to be nothing more than a wonderful employee. "How well did you know Avery Creed?"

Grant shrugged. "Not that well, but she did a good job serving our customers. Then she was in that accident, and I never saw her again."

Burke smiled at Grant. "Thank you. I have no further questions."

Martinez blew out a breath and called his next witness, who turned out to be one of Avery's co-workers. He asked questions about Avery, and if the co-worker remembered the day of the murder, but she didn't seem to remember a thing. At least she told the court that Avery was a good person, so that helped.

Martinez looked disappointed, so she must have changed her story and didn't help him a bit. The next witness he called surprised me.

"We call Dom Orlandi to the stand."

I straightened and shifted to the edge of my seat. Would Dom deny everything Avery had told him, too? After he was sworn in, Martinez established who Dom was and that he'd worked for Sonny Dixon for a couple of years.

That done, he began with his questions. "Avery Creed mentioned that you were her boyfriend at the time of the murder. Is this correct?"

"Yes."

"Was she living with you at the time?"

"Yes."

"So you were in a close relationship?"

Dom huffed out a breath. "Yes."

"On the night of August seventeenth, did she tell you what she saw in Sonny Dixon's private meeting room?"

"No. I didn't see her that night."

Martinez stiffened. "Where were you?"

"I spent the evening with friends, and I didn't get back to my condo until the next day."

"Did she talk to you then?"

Dom raised a brow. "No. I had to go to work, so it wasn't until later that night that I spoke to her."

"Did she tell you about the murder?"

"No. She told me she wasn't happy working at the casino, but I figured it was because she was having second thoughts about us. Her brother had shown up, and he was putting a lot of pressure on her to go back home. It made her question everything, but it had nothing to do with Sonny."

I sucked in a breath. All hope that Dom would come clean and do the right thing vanished, replaced by a wave of disgust. I'd thought there was a chance for him, and I hated that I was wrong.

Martinez didn't seem too fazed by Dom's testimony, and he was dismissed without cross-examination by Burke. Next, Martinez continued by turning his attention to the victim, Shannon Guy. He presented information about him and his ties to Sonny, showing that they were business associates.

Burke objected, saying that Guy's ties to Sonny were through a separate investment company, and that they only knew each other as investors. He claimed that Martinez was misrepresenting their relationship.

Martinez countered that he had several witnesses who would corroborate the relationship, and Burke asked for a recess, claiming that he knew nothing about the witnesses and this line of questioning.

The judge granted them a two-hour recess, since it was time for a lunch break, and court was adjourned.

We stood as the judge left and people began to file out. Sonny left through another door, beckoning Dom and Grant to follow him. Creed watched them go and turned to me. "I'm so pissed at Dom right now. He's been lying to us this whole time. He knew exactly what Avery had seen, and he didn't do anything about it. He could have protected her, and all he cared about was himself."

"Yeah... well... we pretty much knew that. I'd hoped that maybe he'd changed, but after his testimony, and seeing him with Sonny... I guess it was foolish to think so."

Creed let out a big sigh. "Come on, let's get out of here."

After grabbing a sandwich at a nearby deli, we found a round table outside and took our time to eat. As we finished up, Creed's mom called for an update, so I left him there to take a walk. I knew how much he hated lying to her, but at least he could tell her he'd seen Avery and she was okay.

Soon, the recess was over, and we arrived at the courthouse. We sat down in time to watch Sonny and his lawyers take their places, with Dom and Grant following closely behind. Dom glanced our way, and a flash of regret washed over his face before he pulled his gaze away.

At least he felt guilty, but it was a little late for that.

The trial resumed, and Martinez called his next witness. We all waited for the man to take the stand, but he never appeared. Martinez searched the crowd before sending his second-chair attorney out to look for him. He apologized to the court and called the next person on his list.

This person was a no-show as well, and Martinez began to sweat. "Your honor, may I approach the bench?"

They spoke quietly for a few minutes before a commotion at the doors broke them apart. The second-chair attorney called Martinez to the door, and he hurried out. He came back in with another man who wore a rumpled suit and walked with hunched shoulders. The man's hair stood up in a few places, and his face was pinched with worry.

The man was introduced as the witness they'd been waiting for, and Martinez began to question him, stating that he was a forensic bookkeeper who had been working on Sonny's bank accounts, looking for suspicious money transfers.

"Please tell the court what you found."

The man rubbed his hands on his pants and chewed on his bottom lip. He took so long to answer that the judge finally told him to answer the question. After swallowing, the man began. "I found several money transfers that seemed suspicious, which I confirmed with Mr. Martinez. But, after studying them again this morning, I came to the conclusion that I made a mistake. The transfers never went to Shannon Guy as I first suspected, but rather to another company."

Martinez froze. "But the company belonged to Shannon Guy. Isn't that right?"

The bookkeeper swallowed and glanced at his hands. "No. I thought it belonged to Mr. Guy, but I made a mistake. I'm sorry, but I was wrong."

Martinez huffed out a breath, thoroughly frustrated. "You know you're under oath?"

"Of course, that's why I had to admit to my mistake."

After asking several more questions and getting nowhere, Martinez dismissed the witness and asked the next witness on his list to take the stand. This man had worked for Sonny in the past, but had recently been fired. Martinez questioned the man about what he'd seen, and he answered him each time with "I don't recall."

The next witness did the same, and Martinez finally asked for another recess. The judge granted it, saying that the trial would resume the next day, and the prosecution had better get their act together by then.

My stomach sinking, I shared a glance with Creed. It was obvious something had happened. "He got to them, didn't he?"

Creed nodded. "But was it Sonny or Rathmore?"

Martinez rushed out of the courtroom, his face a mask of rage. He brushed past Nash, who grabbed his arm to stop him. They spoke for a moment before Martinez jerked his arm away.

We stepped to Nash's side just as Martinez left the building. "What was that all about?" Creed asked.

Nash's eyes held worry. "Nothing good. I'm afraid Rathmore just pulled some strings. I'll see what more I can find out from Martinez, but you need to get Avery out of this. Whatever it was that Rathmore asked of you... you need to do it—now."

Without waiting for a response, he followed Martinez out the door.

Creed glanced at the people around us. "We need to find Dom. He'll know what happened." He surged down the hall toward the doorway Sonny usually used. Instead of following, I went the other way, hoping to spot Dom outside the building.

After several minutes of searching, with no luck, I turned back to the doors and found Creed coming toward me. "Did you find him?"

"No."

"He's not answering his phone either. Let's see if we can track him down at his condo."

It didn't take us long to pull into Dom's parking garage. His car wasn't in his usual spot, so we waited for him to show up. After calling with no answer, Creed sent him a text, telling him we were waiting at his condo.

This time he got a response. "He's on his way."

A few minutes later, Dom pulled in. We met him as he climbed out. "What happened?" Creed asked.

"Let's go inside," Dom said, glancing behind us. Another tenant had pulled in and was walking toward the elevators. We shared the elevator with the woman until she got off on the third floor.

After she left, Dom pushed the button for the fifth floor. "Sonny made the deal."

The doors swished open, and we followed Dom to his apartment door. Unlocking it, he ushered us inside.

"He signed over the casino and hotel?" Creed asked.

Dom nodded and stalked into the kitchen. Taking out a bottle and glass, he poured some amber liquid into the glass and swallowed it down. "You saw how the trial was going. Sonny knew from his lawyers that Martinez had subpoenaed his bank accounts. He knew a good accountant would find the money linking him to Shannon Guy. Combined with Avery's testimony, he couldn't take the risk, so he called Rathmore. That's where we were during the break. Sonny signed over his casino and hotel. They belong to Rathmore now."

"So Rathmore got what he wanted," I said.

"That's right," Dom said. "He always does." He offered the bottle to us, but we both declined. "Sonny begged Rathmore to let him run the hotel and casino. I can't believe that Rathmore agreed, but there were stipulations. Sonny won't have access to the accounts, and he has to follow Rathmore's orders on everything, or he's out."

"What about Avery?" I asked. "Sonny didn't ask about her did he? I could just see him wanting to kill her just for spite."

Dom snorted. "You got that right, but Rathmore told him he had something better in mind than letting Sonny take her. It just about killed Sonny. In fact, all the way back to the trial, he kept saying how much he wanted Rathmore dead."

"I don't feel sorry for him," Creed said. "In fact, I'm glad he's lost everything. I just wish Avery didn't have to pay for it." Creed turned to me, "We have no choice. We have to bargain with Rathmore."

"What did he want?" Dom asked me.

"I have to arrange a meeting with Shelby Nichols."

Dom froze. "Good luck with that. Manetto will never allow it."

"I'm not asking Manetto."

Dom huffed out a breath. "Whatever works. Just don't underestimate Rathmore. He's got me under his thumb now, which will last as long as I'm useful. I don't know how long Grant or Sonny will stay on his good side. We're all running on borrowed time."

Dom finished off his drink and poured another. "Once you get Avery out of this mess, stay away from him... stay as far away as you can."

"We'd better go," Creed said. "If you hear anything that will help us, will you let us know?"

"Sure."

With his mind centered on his own survival, I didn't think Dom would help us, but I was still glad that Creed had asked.

We left the condo and drove back to the rental house, both of us lost in our thoughts. As we pulled into the driveway, I turned to Creed. "I'll make the call to Rathmore and work it out with Shelby."

Creed nodded, his lips turning down. "I don't think we have a choice."

He was right. As much as I didn't want to, it was time to make a deal with the devil.

After changing my clothes, I put the call through. The secretary sent me straight to Rathmore's office and he picked right up. "Ella. It's good to hear from you. I was getting worried."

Not wanting to engage in small talk, I got right to the point. "I talked to Shelby. She said she'd do it, but she might have to be secretive since her uncle would object."

"Excellent. I'm sure I can assist her with that. Will you relay the information about the meeting and transportation to her?"

"Yes... and... I want to be there for the meeting."

"You do? That surprises me. Why would you want to do that?"

"Just to make sure she's okay."

He sniffed. "Fine. Then, after she's met with me, I'll release Avery to you. It will work out smoothly, and everyone will get what they want. Tell Shelby I'll have a plane ready to bring her here tomorrow morning. Once she's done, I'll fly her straight home. You'll get Avery, and our business will be concluded. I'll send you a text with all the information."

"Okay."

"And Ella... make sure Shelby comes through."

"She will."

"Good." He hung up, and I sagged against the back of the couch. Creed sat beside me, and I explained everything he'd said. A second later, my phone dinged with a text.

"That must be his demands." I read through the text, finding that Rathmore had outlined everything, from the time Shelby would board the plane to the time of her meeting in his corporate offices. I was invited to meet her at his building when she arrived. After she left, he'd release Avery to me. It all looked so simple on my phone, but I didn't trust it for a minute.

"I'm coming to the meeting with you," Creed said, annoyance flashing over his handsome face.

"Of course you are, but Rathmore doesn't need to know that. After the meeting is over, we'll get Avery. It will all work out."

"Yeah... as long as Shelby comes through."

"I'd better call her." Shelby picked up after the second ring. I explained Rathmore's demands and sent her a copy of the text with all the details. "Can you do it on such short notice?"

"Yes. I have a plan. Don't worry, I'll be there tomorrow. Did he say any more about what I can expect?"

"Sorry... no. Do you want me to call him back?"

"No... it's fine. I'll see you tomorrow."

I thanked her and disconnected. Relief and worry flowed over me at the same time. "She's in, but she didn't sound very happy. Do you think it will work out? I guess I could have told Rathmore that I wanted Avery before Shelby met with him, but I needed to make sure Shelby got out of there safely. She didn't say anything about Ramos coming. Do you think he will?"

Creed nodded. "If he's anything like I remember, he'll be there."

"You're right. I just feel so... guilty."

"It will work out. There's no reason to think Rathmore won't want it to."

"Yeah... until the next time he wants something."

"There's not going to be a next time. Once we get Avery back, this is over for all of us."

Creed's phone rang, and he checked the caller ID. "It's the producer for the show. I'd better take this." After answering, he wandered into the kitchen, and then outside.

It was hard to believe we all had our normal lives to get back to once this was over. But, if all went as planned tomorrow, it could happen, and this whole mess would be over. I sure hoped so, but a part of me couldn't stop the fear that something even worse was just around the corner.

Later that night, Nash stopped by with an update about the trial. We sat at the table, and he began to explain what he knew. "Martinez is furious, but he has no one to blame but himself. None of the witnesses are talking, and he knows Rathmore is behind it. He wanted to call Avery to the stand again, but the men holding her wouldn't let him in. He's tried, but he hasn't been able to talk to her on the phone, either."

Creed huffed out a breath. "Serves him right. Is he even worried about her?"

Nash shook his head. "Maybe now he is, but he's not going to admit it. I had to work hard to get him to admit that much.

I hope you have a plan, because it doesn't look like she's coming back to the courthouse."

"Yeah... we do." Creed didn't say another word, and Nash raised his brows.

"Are you going to tell me?"

"I don't think so." Creed studied Nash. "Don't take it personally, but we don't exactly trust the police right now. Since you're part of that, you don't get to know what we're doing."

"I could help, you know."

"Yeah... but we've got it covered."

Nash heaved a sigh. "I won't tell anyone at the precinct. Just let me help you. I know she's at the house." Neither one of us responded, so he continued. "At least tell me you'll call if you get into trouble."

"Sure," Creed said. "We'll call."

Nash twisted his lips. "Okay. I'd better get going." He stepped to the door and glanced over his shoulder. "Are you coming to the trial in the morning?"

I exchanged a glance with Creed and shook my head. "Probably not. It's pretty obvious that Sonny's not going to jail, even with Avery's testimony. There's too much doubt, and no jury will convict Sonny—unless you're planning on a miracle."

"No... no such luck."

"Be sure to call us as soon as it's over," I added. "We still want to know the verdict."

"Sure. As long as you call me once you have Avery."

"It's a deal."

We spent the next morning packing up our stuff. Once we had Avery, we planned to drive straight to L.A. and leave this desert city in the dust. Shelby wasn't due to arrive at Rathmore's corporate office until one in the afternoon, and we'd decided to skip the trial. Neither one of us could stomach the idea of Sonny getting away with murder.

I put on my black suit again, but wore it over a blue tank instead of the white one. The morning crawled by, but, when the time to leave came around, my dread was so strong, it was hard to walk out the door. Did that mean something bad was going to happen?

We arrived at Rathmore's office building ten minutes early and had to wait in the main lobby for Shelby. By the time I caught a glimpse of Shelby, my stomach was a bundle of nerves. I jumped up as she came inside, relief pouring out of me in waves.

"You made it." I gave her a quick hug, hoping to convey how much I appreciated her. "I'm so glad to see you. Thanks for doing this." She nodded, but she wasn't her usual, bubbly self. I sent a nod to Ramos, grateful to see him. "How did your Uncle take it? Are you in trouble?"

"Let's just say that I will be."

I gasped. "He doesn't know?"

"Oh yeah... he knows. But I kind of put off telling him until we landed, twenty minutes ago." She glanced at Ramos, who didn't seem too happy about it either.

"I'm glad you came with her." I told him.

His lips flattened. "Yeah, well... it was a last minute thing for me too."

I glanced back at Shelby. "How much trouble are you in?"

A mirthless chuckle popped out of her. "Oh... some... but not too much. We'll see how bad it is when I get back."

Ramos shook his head, and she swatted his arm. "It was the only way. You know that."

I glanced between them, sure I'd missed something.

Creed stood beside me and thanked them for coming. "We're in your debt. If there's ever anything you need from us, we'll do it. No questions asked."

Ramos lifted a brow before nodding. He still had that whole dangerous vibe coming off him. Before, it had always made me nervous, but today, I was grateful for his intimidating presence.

"Ella St. John?" The receptionist called. "I'll take your group up now."

I sent her a nod, and we all started toward the bank of elevators. We had to pass through security, and Ramos ended up leaving a knife behind. Shelby's purse didn't make it through either. The security man pawed through her bag and pulled out a small, pink flashlight.

"What's this?" He pushed one of the buttons, and an electric charge arced between two metal points, making a buzzing sound that made everyone flinch. He sent a frown Shelby's way, and her lips turned up into a dazzling smile.

"A woman's got to have some protection, right? Especially here... in Las Vegas."

His lips twisted, and he set the flashlight down by Ramos's knife. "You can pick it up on your way out."

"Oh... okay." She shrugged like it didn't matter, but I could tell it vexed her. As we stepped into the elevator, she leaned toward me. "No one's ever done that before. Usually they let me keep it."

Ramos gave a mirthless laugh. "No one's ever pushed the button before either. Just hearing the sound is enough to scare someone off."

"That's true," she agreed.

The receptionist swiped her key card and pushed the button for the thirteenth floor. With her there, none of us spoke, and nervous tension filled the space. It was a relief when the doors opened and we could step out.

The woman led us down the hall to a set of double doors and pushed them open to the same plush elegance I remembered from the last time I'd been there. Rathmore's secretary jumped up from her chair, and the receptionist left us in her care.

"Please take a seat. Mr. Rathmore is running a little late, but he'll be with you shortly."

"How late?" Ramos stepped closer to the secretary, and she took a step back.

"Uh… like fifteen minutes or so. Please, make yourselves comfortable."

It did me good to see her squirm, and I glanced at Ramos with new appreciation. He sent me a quick nod and sat down next to Shelby on the couch. I sat on the other side of Shelby, and Creed took the wingback chair next to me.

Shelby looked professional in a navy dress-and-jacket ensemble. It made the beautiful golden necklace, with a teardrop stone of white-and-gold quartz, stand out. Ramos was dressed more casually, but still looked intimidating in his black shirt and jacket, with deep indigo jeans.

The hard cushions on the couch were uncomfortable, and Shelby straightened her dress before glancing my way. "So, tell me about Rathmore. What's he like? Older? Like Uncle Joey?"

"No," I answered. "He's got to be in his late forties or early fifties, but it's hard to tell. He's kind of got this whole intimidation thing going for him, but don't let him get to you."

"I'm not planning on it." She let out a breath and tried to relax.

The doors to the office opened, and the receptionist from downstairs ushered three men and a woman inside. Two of the older men were dressed in suits, while the younger man wore a jacket over a dress shirt without a tie. The woman wore a power-red jacket over a white blouse and black pencil skirt, with red pumps on her feet. Her dark hair was pulled back from her face, and she wore square glasses.

None of them spared us a glance as they passed, like we were beneath their notice, and Rathmore's secretary quickly took them back to his office. When she returned, she sat down without a word, leaving us to wonder what was going on.

After a few minutes, Shelby turned to me. "So... how's the trial going?"

In hushed tones, both Creed and I explained what had happened.

"Sonny lost it all?" She shook her head. "I can't say I'm sorry. I just wish he was going to jail too. Rathmore must have pulled a lot of strings for that to work."

"Yeah." I didn't want to say too much, but she needed to know what she was getting into.

The secretary picked up her phone and glanced our way. I got ready to stand, but Shelby put a hand on my arm. "I have a feeling that it's going to be another few minutes." She shrugged. "It's possible that everyone hasn't arrived yet."

"Oh... I guess that means your premonitions are working." I raised my brows. "Good thing, since that's why Rathmore wanted you. Too bad he found out, right?"

Shelby's gaze focused on me, and she nodded. "Yeah... that's for sure." She glanced between me and Creed, and her eyes widened. "Oh my gosh! I forgot. Congratulations on your marriage."

"Thanks," I said. "We're living in L.A. right now and figuring things out."

"How's it going?"

"I'm working at a hospital, and Creed just got a starring role in a new TV series. We're so excited."

"Oh yeah? That's wonderful. What's it about?"

"He's a detective on a cop show, only with a fun twist." I smiled at Creed. "Tell her."

Before he could utter a word, Shelby's eyes widened and she gasped.

"Is something wrong?" Creed asked, glancing behind him.

"No… not at all. I love twists." She cleared her throat. "What is it?"

Creed grinned. "My character is a detective who can read minds. I know it sounds kind of nuts, but I'm hoping it will go over. In the first few episodes, no one knows… but I keep answering their unspoken thoughts, and the main character, who is my new partner, can't figure it out. I mean… it's this big secret that I have, and no one is supposed to know."

Ramos burst out laughing. My eyes widened with shock to see such a cold, dangerous man laughing his head off. Shelby shook her head and pursed her lips together to hold back, but she couldn't do it, and laughter bubbled out of her, too.

Creed smiled with delight. "Wow. I hope everyone likes the idea as much as you guys." At their continued peals of laughter, he glanced my way, and his brows dipped. "Are they okay?"

I shrugged. "I guess. It must have hit them at just the right moment or something."

He nodded, and we both waited for them to get under control.

"Sorry," Shelby sputtered, waving her hand in front of her face. "I don't know why that hit me so funny." Little bursts of laughter kept escaping from her, but she took deep breaths in between to tamp them down.

Actual tears wet her cheeks, and alarm buzzed over me. I thought the show's concept was brilliant, but I didn't think it was that funny. Maybe she had a lot of stress in her life, and meeting with Rathmore had just made it worse.

The double-doors opened, and the downstairs receptionist showed another man inside. Tall and thin, with dark hair and glasses, he moved a little stiffly, more like an older man. He wore a suit and tie, like the others, and apologized for being detained. The secretary immediately took him to Rathmore's office.

Seconds later, she hurried over to us, and we all came to our feet. "Mr. Rathmore is ready for Shelby. The rest of you will have to wait."

Everyone froze, then Ramos stepped into her space, towering over her. "Where Shelby goes, I go. It's not up for debate."

She swallowed, and a glint of fear shone in her eyes before she managed to replace it with her usual haughty expression. "I'll have to check. Give me a moment." She hurried back to her desk and picked up her phone. A few seconds later, she set it down and came back.

"You may accompany her, but the rest of you must stay here."

Ramos nodded, and Shelby turned back to us with a tight smile. "I'll be fine."

We watched them disappear down the hall before we sat down. Creed sat beside me on the couch and let out a sigh. "I wonder how long it's going to take."

"Yeah... me too. But just think..." I took Creed's hand and squeezed. "Once they're done, we can get Avery back."

"That's right. And this whole thing will be over." He didn't sound like he believed it any more than me, and I hoped we'd both be proved wrong.

The uncomfortable couch made it hard to wait. Each minute seemed to take longer than the last. After only five minutes of waiting, Creed's phone rang. His gaze caught mine. "It's Nash." He answered the phone and listened while Nash spoke. "Yeah... thanks for letting us know." He paused.

"I don't know, but we're working on it. I'll call you back when I know more."

Creed disconnected and pocketed his phone. "It looks like Sonny got his wish. He was found not guilty and acquitted of all charges. Nash said that Avery's testimony alone wasn't enough for the jury to convict him beyond a reasonable doubt. So all the damage Rathmore did worked. He did say that Sonny didn't look as relieved as he should have, so I guess that counts for something."

"That makes sense. I guess he kept his freedom, but lost everything else. It still doesn't seem like enough though."

"No, it doesn't, especially when I think about what he did to Avery."

My phone began to ring, and I pulled it out of my purse. "Hello?"

"Ella... it's Dom. I just wanted to tell you that Sonny beat the charges."

"Yeah... we heard."

"How are things going on your end? Have you got Avery back yet?"

"Not yet." I didn't want to tell him anything, especially if Sonny had put him up to calling us to find out. "What's Sonny doing?"

"I don't know... I guess he's headed home."

"I'd think he'd be out celebrating... he did just beat a murder rap."

Dom huffed. "Yeah... but I'm afraid he's not in the mood. Listen... will you let me know when you have Avery?"

"Why? So you can tell Sonny?"

"No. I just want to make sure she's all right. That's all."

"I'll think about it. Goodbye Dom." I ended the call and let out a sigh.

"Let me guess," Creed said. "He wants to know when we have Avery."

"Yup. Both him and Nash." I shook my head. "Next time she starts dating someone, make sure she clears it with you or me first, okay?"

Creed let out a mirthless chuckle. "No kidding."

We waited for another half hour before the sound of a door opening brought our heads up. All of the people who had gone in ahead of Shelby and Ramos passed through the office, and the secretary took them down the hallway to the elevators. Hopefully, Shelby and Ramos would be coming next.

It took another fifteen long minutes before the door opened again. Shelby and Ramos stepped into sight, and I sighed with relief. Ramos's countenance hadn't changed, but Shelby's face looked paler than normal, and a weight seemed to fall over her shoulders.

As Shelby passed me, she stopped, placing her hand on my arm and leaning in to whisper. "Be careful. There's something... off... about him."

Alarm ran down my spine. "We will."

She nodded. "Good. Please let me know this worked."

"I will. I'll call you."

"Thanks." Dropping her hand, she quickly left, Ramos hovering protectively at her side.

As they disappeared inside the elevator, the secretary stood from her desk. "Mr. Rathmore will see you now."

I took a deep breath, and we followed her down the hall to the double doors at the end. After a quick knock, she pulled the doors open and motioned us inside. Rathmore sat behind his desk, a satisfied gleam in his eyes.

He stood, motioning us into the chairs in front of his desk. We sat down, and he took his seat behind the desk. "Thank you for arranging that meeting with Shelby. She's everything I hoped for." He met my gaze. "You mentioned that you met in New York. Could you tell me what she was doing there?"

"I only know that she was helping the police with a murder case."

"Are we good?" Creed asked, done with the small talk. "We've done what you wanted. Where's Avery?"

Rathmore frowned, showing his displeasure. He sat back in his chair and opened a drawer in his desk before answering. "As you know, she's at the ranch. I'll take you there, and you can collect her."

"That's not necessary. We know where it is."

"I insist. I'm done for the day, so it's not a problem. I just have one request."

Creed frowned, his eyes filling with wariness. "What's that?"

"A demonstration." Rathmore pulled a small handgun from his desk drawer and fired, hitting Creed in the chest.

CHAPTER THIRTEEN

C reed's body jerked from the bullet's impact, and blood blossomed on his shirt. With a terrified cry, I jumped to my feet and pulled his shirt apart. The bullet had entered his chest below his left shoulder. I quickly placed my hand over the wound to stanch the bleeding, and felt along his back for an exit wound. There wasn't one, and fear tightened my throat. That meant the bullet could have gone anywhere, including his heart.

"Creed! Hang on. You need to lie down."

Creed's breathing became labored, and his face turned white. He was going into shock. I put my arms around him, and he leaned forward, his heated gaze focused behind me on Rathmore. "You... bastard."

I pulled Creed's weight into my arms, and he slid off the chair to the floor, his face contorted with pain and his breathing labored. "Creed. Stay with me."

With my hand over his wound, I concentrated on finding the path the bullet had taken. Closing my eyes, I felt the torn flesh beneath my fingers and followed the damage. The bullet's course had missed his heart and entered his lung, filling it with blood.

I sent my healing energy into the wound, concentrating on the trajectory of the bullet. First, I began to repair the damage around the bullet, hoping to force the bullet out of his lung. Healing the damaged air sacs and bronchiole tubes in his lung was an intricate process, and it was slow going.

With raw determination, I managed to speed up the process and stopped the internal bleeding. The healing tissue forced the bullet to come out in the direction it had entered. Unfortunately, I couldn't remove the blood that had already flooded his lung.

Healing him seemed to take forever, even though only a few minutes had passed. Still, by the time I got the bullet closer to the surface, my vision had started to blur. I broke my concentration, needing a moment to catch my breath. My own stress and terror didn't help the situation, but at least Creed was out of the woods. Without my intervention, I had no doubt that he would have died.

Anger burned in my chest, but now was not the time for that. I needed to be calm so I could concentrate on healing him. At least the blood coming out of the wound had slowed, and Creed's pain and distress had leveled out to something more manageable.

Knowing that helped calm me, and I studied his face to see if he'd passed out. His eyes fluttered open, and my terror subsided. I loved him so much, and it hurt to see him in such pain. "I've almost got it," I whispered. "You're going to be fine."

He gave me a slight nod and held completely still, taking small, shallow breaths. Not being able to draw a proper breath sent most people into a panic, but he was doing his best to remain steady.

Once again, I immersed my focus into his wound and knit the torn flesh back together. Soon, the bullet became visible beneath my fingers. I pulled it out and palmed it, not wanting Rathmore to see what I'd done.

Using another blast of power, I knit Creed's skin back together, determined that Rathmore wouldn't leave a scar to brand him. Finished, I took deep, gulping breaths and sat back on my heels, pulling my bloody hands away.

Creed began to cough, and I helped him sit up and lean over as he coughed up blood. I glanced over my shoulder to find Rathmore standing beside his desk, studying us. With a satisfied gleam in his eyes, he tilted his head. "There's a bathroom in the back where you can get cleaned up."

Suppressing a scream of anger, I helped Creed to his feet. His coughing had worsened, and more blood coated his hands. With my arm around him, we shuffled to the back of the office where a short hall led to a bathroom.

I pushed the door open and led Creed to the sink. I turned on the water, and he leaned over the basin where he continued to cough up blood. His coughing soon turned into deep gasps until I was afraid he would pass out.

Finally, his coughing subsided, and I relaxed my hold on him. While he caught his breath, I rinsed the blood from my hands and quickly dried them on a towel. Wrapping an arm around his waist, I held my hand against his forehead.

My touch soothed his labored breathing, and I sent another wave of healing power into his body. Immediately, his breathing deepened into a steady rhythm, and the blood cleared from his lungs. Taking several deep breaths, he closed his eyes and relaxed his shoulders.

"Does your chest feel better now?"

"Yes. I can finally breathe again."

He cupped his shaking hands under the running water and washed the blood from his face and rinsed out his mouth. I handed him a towel and he dried off, leaning against the counter. Our gazes met in the mirror, and he pulled me into his arms. I closed my eyes and let my head rest against his shoulder. We held each other for a long while, each of us shaken and drained.

I lifted my head to look up at him. "I almost lost you."

His haunted eyes turned brittle with anger. "How did he know?"

I shook my head. "I don't know." Exhausted, I turned toward the sink to scrub the remaining blood from my hands. We both took our time to wash up, getting as much blood off our skin as we could.

Creed's gaze dropped to the mirror and the blood that still marked the skin on his chest and stomach. With a paper towel, he scrubbed the blood away, revealing the perfect skin underneath. "Rathmore's going to love this."

There was no way around it. If this was a test, I'd just passed with flying colors.

"Maybe you shouldn't have done such a good job."

His worried gaze met mine, and I shook my head. "Maybe. But I wasn't about to let him mark you, consequences be damned. Whatever happens next, he's not going to get away with this."

"Ella... I know you're mad, but don't show all your cards. You might need them later. Okay?"

I shook my head. Anger and shock weakened my knees, and I took a deep breath to fortify my strength. "Fine. But there's nothing he can say that will make up for what he did to you. Nothing."

Creed closed his eyes. "I know, but he still has Avery, so we've got to see this through. Until we have her back, we have to play his game."

I swallowed. "You're right." The fight went out of me, and I dropped my head. "Okay, I'm good... let's get this over with."

The blood on Creed's shirt was still damp, but he pulled the shirt back together, and we stepped into Rathmore's office.

Rathmore had taken his seat behind his desk, but, as we entered, he got to his feet. He motioned toward the chairs we'd been sitting in earlier, and we started that way.

Although Creed's wound had healed, he still suffered from shock and loss of blood, so I wrapped my arm around his waist and walked beside him to the chairs. As we passed Rathmore, he held out a hand to stop us and flicked Creed's shirt aside to look at the wound.

His brows lifted, and he met my gaze with a satisfied gleam. Dropping his hand, he sat back down in his chair and waited for us to take our seats.

A large circle of blood had soaked into the rug, a big reminder that Creed had almost died. At least this expensive rug was ruined, but that was hardly satisfying enough to make up for him shooting Creed. Skirting the blood, we pulled our chairs around it and sat down.

"It's truly miraculous," Rathmore said. "Without that bloody shirt, no one would ever know that you'd been shot."

His gaze found mine and his eyes narrowed. "Now that we have that out of the way, I think we're ready to come to an agreement. I know you want Avery, and you fulfilled your end of the bargain by bringing me Shelby Nichols."

His assessing gaze locked on mine. "But now you must understand that your value has changed dramatically."

I sucked in a breath, ready to battle it out, but he held up a hand.

"Don't worry. I'm not going back on my word. I'll return Avery to you as promised. There's just one condition."

Anger burned in my chest. I'd had it with all of his threats. When would it ever end? It was always one more thing with him, and I was tired of playing this game. "No. You promised that if I got Shelby Nichols here like you wanted, we'd get Avery. We're done bargaining."

His brows rose. "Of course you'll get Avery. I just need to know that I can count on you for any special needs I may have."

"After what you did to Creed, why would I ever agree to that?"

He took a deep breath and pursed his lips like it pained him to have to explain. "Are you certain that Creed can survive a bullet to the head? Or an accident that mangles his body beyond recognition? Or any number of other ways there are to die? Especially if you're not there to save him?"

I clamped my teeth together to hold in my scream of rage. I'd never been so angry in all my life. I wanted him dead. If it wasn't for Avery, I would have grabbed his hand and pulled the life out of him right then and there.

Sensing my rage, he leaned forward to press his point, his hard gaze capturing mine. "Can you bring someone back to life?"

I inhaled sharply. "No. Of course not." His words penetrated my anger, and I felt the blood drain from my head. These weren't empty threats. He'd do it, and he'd make sure I knew it was him.

The moment I realized it, he sat back in his chair, a satisfied gleam in his dark eyes. "Then it's simple. All I need is your agreement to help me out when I ask. As a show of good faith, I'll give you Avery. I'll have my man drop her off at your place in time for dinner tonight."

I turned to Creed and met his gaze. His clenched jaw and thin lips told me how much he hated this, but he couldn't stop it any more than I could. There was nothing to do but agree.

I met Rathmore's gaze with all the disdain I could muster. "Fine. But we're leaving right after that."

"And you'll agree to my terms?"

I had to force the words out of my mouth. "Yes. I agree."

"Wonderful." He checked the time. "Then I'll make sure Avery will be at your place at six o'clock sharp."

I slowly rose to my feet, counting on my anger to keep me from falling over. Creed rose as well, but staggered against me, and I caught him around his waist to steady him.

Rathmore stood and motioned toward Creed with narrowed eyes. "You can't leave looking like that. We're about the same size. I've got a spare shirt in my closet." He stepped toward the corner of his office, next to the bathroom, and opened a closet door, revealing several changes of clothes.

Pulling out a white shirt, he took it off the hanger. He held it out to me, and it took all my will power not to throw it back in his face. Rathmore's eyes narrowed with a challenging stare. Before I could refuse, Creed tugged the shirt from my hand, averting the confrontation.

He'd already discarded his bloody shirt, and he slipped the new one on. It pleased me to find that the shirt was a little snug over Creed's broad shoulders, so they weren't as alike as Rathmore hoped, and I calmed down.

As Creed buttoned the shirt, I couldn't resist asking Rathmore the one question that kept buzzing in the back of my mind. "How did you know I could heal him?"

If my question surprised him, he didn't show it. "I didn't exactly. But I was willing to risk it. You see, I couldn't figure out how Avery's condition had changed so drastically. I read the accident report and her hospital files. She shouldn't be walking right now, let alone talking in coherent sentences.

"So I made a large donation to the care center where she stayed, and my private investigator found several people who were willing to share the story of her miraculous recovery. They were eager to tell my agent about her brother's girlfriend who visited her the day before she recovered her ability to walk. That's when I discovered you were a nurse, and it piqued my curiosity.

"Naturally, I had my investigator start digging into your background. After that, she began watching you, and it seemed that, everywhere you went, people suffering from all sorts of problems got better. I think it was that boy who was paralyzed at the hospital that convinced me of your abilities."

He shook his head. "I heard that you call your power 'healing hands,' but you and I both know it's much more than that. You really should be more careful, or more people will figure it out. We certainly don't want that."

Creed finished tucking in his shirt and was ready to go. I pinned Rathmore with a hard stare, putting as much outrage into my tone as I could. "You could have killed him."

His brows rose. "Yes... that was a distinct possibility, but I don't have a problem thinking outside the box, so it all worked out." He sat back down in his chair and gave us a dismissive wave. "I'll be in touch."

With clenched teeth, I took Creed's arm, and we stepped into the hall. As soon as the office doors closed behind us, I could finally breathe again. Between my rage and fear, I was shaking like a leaf. It also didn't help that healing Creed had drained most of my energy.

Rathmore's secretary glanced up as we left, telling us to have a nice day. I wanted to flip her off, but managed to ignore her instead. We finally stepped onto the elevator and I sighed, relieved we'd gotten out in one piece. I wasn't sure I'd ever get over the shock of watching Rathmore pull a gun out of his desk and shoot Creed. It would probably haunt my dreams for the rest of my life.

But now he knew my secret. It was just about the worst thing that could happen. How was I ever going to get out of this? The thought of killing him with the other side of my power held a certain appeal, but I pushed it away. It went against everything St. John had told me, but... how was working for Rathmore any better?

Of course, with the enemies Rathmore was sure to have, maybe someone would do it for me. Maybe that was the answer, and I'd just have to be patient. At least we were done for now, and, once we had Avery, we could finally go home.

It seemed like weeks had passed, rather than days, and I was eager to get back to my life. Still, as much as I wanted to believe we were finally done... I knew it wasn't going to be that simple.

It scared me to know that the one friend I'd had at the hospital was working for Rathmore. And I was such an idiot that I'd invited her to my wedding. Reyna knew my secret, and she'd met the people I cared about most in the world.

With her connection to Rathmore, it was like a tight vise had just closed around my heart. He pulled all the strings, and there was nothing I could do about it.

We made it back to the rental house with half an hour to spare before Avery was supposed to show up. After a quick change of clothes, exhaustion overwhelmed me. Creed may have been healed, but he was still light-headed from the loss of blood, and I wasn't much better. We were both too tired to think about driving back to L.A. right away like we'd planned.

Since there were still a few days left on the rental, staying another night would work, as long as Rathmore actually came through and sent Avery back like he'd promised. Unfortunately, I had doubts that he would, and the stress was eating me alive.

At quarter to six, Creed and I stood in front of the window, watching the street. I didn't know if Avery remembered the security code for the gate, but I doubted that would stop

Rathmore's people. The minutes ticked slowly by before a black SUV turned the corner and headed our way.

As it pulled into the driveway, my heart began to race. Creed pulled the door open and stepped outside. Avery jumped from the car and ran into his arms. He held her tight, then reached over and pulled me into the hug with them.

"It's so good to be done with this!" Avery exclaimed, pulling away. "What a few crazy days."

"That's for sure," I agreed, surprised she seemed so cheerful. "Come on, let's go inside, and you can tell us what happened."

Avery carried a small bag of belongings, and I followed her and Creed inside. I paused at the door to make sure the SUV left with Rathmore's men. Only after they'd turned the corner could I relax and head inside the house.

Wasting no time, Avery sat down on the couch next to Creed and began her story. She told us how frightened she was when she woke up in a strange place. "But then they told me that Martinez had arranged it to keep me safe, and that both of you knew all about it.

"He explained that there was a leak in the police department, and that's why Nash couldn't know what was going on. I was sorry they wouldn't let me talk to you at the courthouse. And the worst of it is that I don't even know the outcome of the trial. Did they convict Sonny?"

Creed's brows dipped. "So you thought you were in protective custody this whole time?"

"What do you mean? I was in protective custody. They took me to this great house in the desert with armed guards and everything. Martinez even came to see me the night before the trial." She glanced between both of us, her lips turning down. "What's going on?"

I didn't want to burst her bubble, so I let Creed explain what had actually happened. She didn't take it very well, but it made sense that they'd led her to believe the lie, since it guaranteed her cooperation. Trying to escape had never even entered her mind.

"Seriously? So Rathmore was behind it, and Martinez went along?" Shaking her head, she slumped back against the couch. "What happened to Sonny?"

"After your testimony, he got worried. So he met with Rathmore to make a deal." Creed sighed. "He signed the hotel and casino over to Rathmore in exchange for staying out of jail. Rathmore used his powers of persuasion, and considerable resources, to compel the rest of the witnesses to forget everything. In the end, your testimony alone wasn't enough to convict Sonny, and he was found not guilty."

"What? You mean he got away with it?" She glanced between Creed and me, her eyes full of misgiving. "So what else is going on?"

Anger tightened Creed's jaw, so I told her the rest of the story, ending with Rathmore's test of my abilities. Her wide-eyed gaze jumped to Creed, and I patted her arm. "He's okay. I healed him."

"But Rathmore saw the whole thing?"

"Yes. And now he expects me to jump when he calls, or he'll hurt someone I love...maybe permanently."

"What the effing hell!" Avery jumped to her feet, her chest heaving with anger. "Coming here didn't help anything." Her stricken gaze met mine. "It just made it worse." She wrapped her arms around her chest and closed her eyes. "I never should have gone through with this. Mom was right. I'm so sorry."

"It's not your fault," Creed said. "Come back and sit down." He patted the cushion beside him. "I'd drag you down here myself, but getting shot in the chest kind of wore me out."

Immediately contrite, Avery sat beside him. "What can I do? Do you need anything?"

"What we need is some food," I said. "We'd planned on leaving tonight, but both of us are too worn out. Do you mind staying here until morning?"

"No. Of course not."

"Good. Then let's order some take-out and have it delivered. What should we get?" After talking it over, we decided on pizza and a salad and called in our order.

"While we're waiting, I need to call Shelby," I said. "She deserves to know what happened."

"Yes," Creed said. "Without her, none of this would have been possible."

I wandered out to the backyard and put the call through. She picked right up. "Ella? Did it work?"

"Yes. We got Avery. How about you? Are you okay?"

"Yes... we made it home."

"I hope your Uncle wasn't too mad at you, but I have no doubt that Avery would be dead if you hadn't come. I'll never be able to repay you for that, but if you ever need me for anything, I'll come. That includes my healing touch. Promise me that you'll call if you need me. Okay?"

"I will. So what's going on? Are you still in Vegas?"

"Yeah, but we're leaving in the morning."

"Good. Get as far away from Rathmore as you can."

"That's the plan." I couldn't tell her everything right now, even though I wanted to.

I heard Shelby sigh. "I have a feeling it's not the end... for either of us. When this is all over, and you're back home, let's talk."

"I'd like that."

"Good. Thanks for letting me know it worked out."

"Of course. And Shelby... if Rathmore ever contacts you again, will you let me know? Maybe we can help each other where he's concerned."

"Sounds good. Thanks Ella. Don't forget to call me when things settle down."

"I won't. Take care."

"You too."

I put my phone down and closed my eyes. Even though I was totally exhausted, it helped me feel better to know that I had a friend in Shelby. Because Rathmore wanted something from both of us, we were in this together. It made me wonder if I should confide in her. She already knew I had healing hands, but could I tell her the rest? It was definitely something worth thinking about.

I headed back inside to find Avery gone and Creed resting his head against the back of the couch. "What's going on?"

Creed opened his eyes. "I called Nash to let him know that Avery was back, safe and sound. Before I'd even finished, he said he was coming over. When I told Avery, she ran upstairs to... I don't know... freshen up?"

I sat beside Creed and smiled. "She likes him, but she's not sure he feels the same. What do you think?"

Creed shook his head. "I say we relax and enjoy the evening. After everything we've been through, I don't want to think about it."

"Sounds like a good idea."

"How's Shelby?" Creed asked.

"She made it home, so that's good. I'm going to call her once we get home and things go back to normal. I'm not sure what I'm going to tell her, but I think she'd be a good ally to have."

Creed nodded. "That's true. I just worry about what her Uncle will want from us. We already owe him, and now we're even more in his debt."

"I wouldn't worry about him so much. He's nothing like Rathmore." I sighed. "But at least we're leaving tomorrow, and we can put this behind us."

"Yeah... until Rathmore wants something."

I shook my head. Just thinking about it was almost more than I could handle. "We'll figure it out. For now, let's try and forget about him."

"I like the sound of that." The doorbell rang. "That must be the pizza." Creed opened the door to find Nash there instead. "Hey... come on in."

"Is she okay?"

"You can ask her yourself." Creed closed the door as Avery rushed down the stairs from her room. Nash swallowed her up in a tight hug that seemed more than friendly to me.

They finally pulled apart, and Nash stepped back. "So tell me what happened."

"Martinez told me that I was in protective custody, and I had no idea what was really going on. And now Sonny is off the hook. It makes me so mad."

"I'm sorry Avery. This is my fault. It never should have happened. You did the right thing, don't ever doubt that. In fact, you impressed the hell out of me, and I can't tell you how relieved I am that you're safe."

"I'm safe because of Creed and Ella."

Nash met Creed's gaze and frowned. "What did you have to do?"

Creed met my gaze and gave a slight warning shake of his head. He turned to Nash. "It's complicated, and I'm not sure how much we want to share. Just be happy that we did it, or Avery might not be here."

Nash snapped his mouth shut and tightened his lips. "Well... whatever you did, I'm grateful, and I'm sorry it went that far." He ran his fingers through his hair. "We've got some problems in our department, and I apologize. I'll do what I can to clean it up, you have my word."

I shook my head. "Just don't get killed while you're at it. In fact... have you ever thought about moving?" I glanced at

Creed. "Hey... maybe Nash could give you some pointers for your new show."

"What show?"

The doorbell rang, announcing that our pizza had arrived, and we took it into the kitchen. While we ate, Creed told Nash all about being cast as a detective who could read minds.

Nash got a kick out of that. "You know... that could be a great thing to have in my line of work."

"Exactly. I can't wait to get started."

"What's the name of the show again?" Nash asked.

"Crossfire."

"Nice. Yeah... I'd be happy to keep in touch if you need some pointers." He glanced toward Avery before looking down at his food. "Maybe I'll look into relocating... it wouldn't hurt to check out all my options."

My phone rang, and the caller ID said it was Dom. "Excuse me, I need to take this." I quickly left the room and answered. "Hey Dom."

"Is there any news about Avery?"

"Yeah. She's here. With us."

"Thank God. Can I talk to her?"

I let out a big sigh. "I don't know. It depends on if she wants to talk to you."

"Please... just ask her. Tell her there's something I need to say."

"Okay, give me a minute." I leaned around the door to the kitchen. "Avery... Dom's on the phone. He wants to tell you something, but you don't have to talk to him if you don't want to. I'd be more than happy to tell him to get lost."

She froze before pushing back her chair and reaching for my phone. As she answered, she walked into the other room, and we couldn't hear her clearly.

Frowning, Creed shook his head. "I don't know why he cares now. He never did before. I wish she wouldn't talk to him."

"Yeah. I know," I agreed. "But maybe she'll tell him off, and it will be just the thing she needs in order to move on."

Nash clenched his jaw, clearly upset that she'd have anything to do with Dom. "She wasn't there when he gave his testimony, otherwise, I don't think she would have spoken to him."

"That's right." I nodded. "And we haven't had time to fill her in. Oh well... it doesn't matter. It's not going to change anything." I rubbed my eyes and sat down at the table.

"You guys both look tired." He leaned forward, catching my gaze. "I can go if you want."

"No... this is the first time I've felt normal in days. Please... stay as long as you like."

"Thanks... but I won't stay long. When are you leaving?"

"In the morning," Creed said. "We're hoping to get a good night's sleep and leave around nine."

Avery came back to the table, her eyes stormy with anger. She handed my phone back and let out a breath. "I told him I didn't ever want to see him again, so I hope he won't be calling me anymore."

"Good." Creed glanced between Avery and Nash. "Before more time passes, I think you need to call Mom. I basically told her the same story you believed, so stick to that and she'll be fine."

"So you don't want me to tell her the truth?"

"Not really. Do you think you should?"

Avery sighed. "No... she'd freak out."

"I should go," Nash said, pushing away from the table. "Thanks for the pizza."

"You don't have to go yet."

"Yes I do. Thanks for letting me come over. I'm glad you're okay... I've been worried."

Avery nodded. "I'll walk you out."

They left the kitchen, and Avery walked outside with him to his car. I glanced at Creed. "Do you think he'll kiss her?"

He shook his head. "I don't even want to think about that."

"Better him than Dom, though, right?"

"Totally."

I woke the next morning, surprisingly refreshed. It helped to know that today was the day we'd finally leave this desert city and go home. It surprised me how quickly I'd begun to think of L.A. as home, especially since I'd only been there a little over a month. But that was because of Creed. It probably wouldn't matter where we lived; as long as I was with him, I'd be happy.

We carried our belongings down to the kitchen, and Creed opened the garage to load everything into the car.

As he opened the hatch-back, a police car pulled into the driveway. The officers got out of the car and approached us. "Sir, could you please step away from the car?"

Dread tightened my stomach, and I froze.

Creed's brows dipped. "Uh... sure. What's this about?"

The cop noticed Avery and me standing behind Creed. "All of you need to step away from the car." He motioned toward the front of the house. "Stand over there."

We did as he asked, while the other officer ducked inside the car and opened the glove box. He pulled out the car registration and safety inspection papers. After looking them over, he nodded at the officer standing near us.

"Sir, this car has been reported stolen. I'm going to have to take you in." He pulled out a pair of handcuffs and slipped them around Creed's wrists.

"But it's not," Creed said. "Sonny Dixon gave me the car."

The officer shook his head and took the car keys from Creed. "I'm sorry, but you'll have to come down to the station."

Creed glanced at me, his eyes full of shock, and I turned to the police officer. "Wait, it's all a misunderstanding, Sonny gave us the car. I know it looks bad, but..."

"Sorry ma'am. Please step away. Don't make this any harder."

"But..."

The officer grabbed Creed's arm and pulled him toward his patrol car. I trailed after them, unwilling to let it go. "Creed... it's okay. I'll call Nash. We'll figure this out."

Before Creed could do more than nod, the officer pushed him into the back seat of the car. The other officer called it in and asked for a tow truck to come and get the car.

"Do you have anything inside the car you want to get out before we go?"

Asking me was probably a courtesy, so I scrambled to take a look inside. Luckily, we hadn't loaded any of our luggage, so the only thing I needed was the remote for the garage. I quickly grabbed it and stepped away.

The cop sent me a nod and locked the car with the key fob before getting inside his patrol car. As they drove away, I shook my head in disbelief. "What the hell? We should have left yesterday." I glanced at Avery. "I should have known Sonny would pull something like this, but I wasn't thinking."

Avery shook her head and stepped into the garage. "Let's take everything back inside and call Nash. He'll know what to do."

With my blood boiling, I grabbed our few bags and hurried after Avery. Once everything was inside, Avery insisted on calling Nash herself. She explained the situation, and he said he'd look into it and call us right back.

Ten minutes later, my phone rang, and I answered. "What's going on?"

"Creed hasn't been arrested, but they put him in a holding cell. It looks like Sonny reported the car stolen yesterday. How did you end up with Sonny's car anyway?"

I huffed out a breath. "He gave it to us after the poker tournament. We didn't have a car, and it was part of the deal he made with us so we could leave."

"So he never signed over the title?"

"No. It was just a verbal agreement."

"Okay. Well... until we get this straightened out, there's not much I can do. When Sonny reported it stolen, he provided them with the address of the rental house. He must have it in for you. The only thing that will get you out of this mess is if Sonny drops the charges. I can keep Creed from being arrested for now, but he'll have to stay in a holding cell until we clear this up."

"Okay. Thanks Nash. I'll see what I can do."

I wasn't about to call Sonny, but Dom might have some answers. He picked right up. "Dom, it's Ella. The cops just showed up and took Creed down to the station. Apparently Sonny told them the car he gave us was stolen. We were just about to leave and go home. What the hell's going on?"

"Shit. Sonny must be pissed."

"No kidding."

"Look... I'll call him and get back to you." He disconnected before I could say another word.

"What should we do?" Avery asked.

"I guess we'd better head down to the station and find out how we can get Creed released." A tow truck came around the corner and pulled into the driveway. "Man, they didn't waste any time."

A few minutes later, the car was hitched up, and the tow truck pulled it away, leaving us stranded. "I don't know what Sonny's trying to prove by doing this, but I'm certainly not going to make a deal with him."

"So what do we do now? Nash can't help us, and, unless Sonny drops the charges, Creed's stuck in jail."

"I don't know." Frustration sent a pounding ache through my head. I knew one person who would be happy to help, but Rathmore was the last person I wanted to call. There had to be another way.

Avery tugged at my arm. "I think grand theft auto is a felony. Creed could spend a year in jail for that." Her eyes widened. "Ella... we can't let that happen. You have to call Rathmore."

"I know... I just... let's wait and see if Dom can do anything first." I knew the chances he could help were slim to none, but I had to be certain.

Ten long minutes later, Dom called me back. "I'm sorry, but Sonny's not budging. You know how he gets. When something doesn't go his way, he lashes out, and Creed was an easy target. He's furious about this whole thing."

"How far is he going to take this?"

"As far as he can. Sonny blames Creed for losing the tournament. He said he'd still have his hotel and casino if Creed had come through. I know he's being unreasonable, but Sonny's out for revenge. He'd probably kill Creed if he could, so he's not about to back off."

My shoulders slumped. "Then it looks like I don't have a choice. I have to call Rathmore unless..." I swallowed. "Do you have a better idea?"

Dom snorted. "No. I'm afraid Rathmore is the only person who could get Sonny to drop the charges."

"All right. Thanks Dom."

Just thinking about calling Rathmore sent a spike of rage through me. But what else could I do? Nash was no help, and neither was Dom. It was Rathmore, or possible jail time for Creed. There was no other choice.

Clenching my teeth, I put the call through. Rathmore's secretary put me on hold, but it only took a few seconds before he picked up. "Ella. I didn't expect to hear from you so soon."

"Yeah... well, I didn't expect to call either." I quickly explained what Sonny had done. "So now Creed is at the police station, and the car's been towed away."

"I see. Don't worry Ella. I'll get this straightened out. Why don't you head to the station? By the time you get there, I should have this taken care of."

"Sure. I'll head over there now." I couldn't thank him since I knew he wouldn't let it go without repercussions. I called an Uber, and the car arrived ten minutes later. We locked up the house, and told the driver to take us to the police station. We arrived several minutes later, and Nash met us in the lobby.

"Any news?" I asked him.

"No. Why?"

"I think Sonny's going to drop the charges."

Nash's brows rose. "Really? How did you manage that?"

I took my time before admitting it. "Rathmore."

Nash frowned. "That's too bad."

"Tell me about it."

It took a couple of hours before we got everything straightened out. Finally released, Creed stepped into the room, looking more angry than relieved. After giving me a quick hug, he pulled away. "They told me the charges were dropped. How did you do it?"

I knew he wouldn't like it, and I hesitated before answering. "I called Rathmore."

His jaw clenched. "Damn. I was afraid of that."

"I know, but at least we can get out of here. Avery and I have been looking at flights to L.A. We found a couple this afternoon. I think there's still time to book the later one."

His expression cleared. "Good. Let's do it."

We asked the police officer at the intake desk to let Nash know we were leaving, and he quickly joined us. "Let me drive you back to the rental house. It's the least I can do."

None of us argued with that. After we climbed into his car, my phone rang. Dread pooled in my stomach to see Rathmore Industries on the caller ID. I answered, and Rathmore's secretary put me on hold. A few seconds later, he came on the line.

"Ella, did you get Creed released okay?"

"Yes. But I don't imagine Sonny was very happy about it."

He chuckled. "No. He wasn't. But I'm glad I could help." He paused and I froze, waiting for the other shoe to drop. "He insisted on keeping the car, but I'm happy to assist you in getting home."

"Oh... that's okay. We're just going to book a flight. There's one leaving later today that we can make."

"I'm afraid I might need you for something before you go."

My breath caught. "Uh... I really need to get back—"

"How about this," he continued, talking over my objection. "You help me out in the morning, and I'll send you home in my jet tomorrow afternoon. That way, we'll both be helping each other."

"But—"

"I insist." His hard tone left no doubt that I didn't have a choice.

I sighed. He'd just cornered me, and there was nothing I could do about it. "Okay... as long as we leave tomorrow, I guess we can stay one more night."

"Good. I'll have my driver pick you up at nine in the morning." He disconnected, and I leaned my head against the seat.

"Damn," Creed said. "That didn't sound good. What did he want?"

"I'm not sure. He needs my help in the morning. After that, he's agreed to fly us home in his private jet."

Creed swore under his breath. "We don't need his help."

"I know, but he got you out of jail. I have to help him."

Nash glanced at me through his rear-view mirror. "What does he want from you?"

Not about to involve Nash, I played it down. "It's nothing to worry about, and it's better for us if you don't get involved. It just means we're stuck here for one more night."

No one spoke until Nash pulled into the driveway. "Look... I feel terrible about all this. I feel like it's my fault. Let me take you all out to dinner. We'll go somewhere special... off the beaten path. I know just the place."

"Okay," Avery said, then turned to look back at us. "I mean... why not? What else are we going to do?"

Creed met my gaze and raised a brow, silently asking what I wanted to do. "Sure. That's a good idea."

Nash picked us up later for dinner, and it was a lot more fun than I'd imagined. It was a nice reprieve from all the drama of the last few days, and, as long as I didn't think too hard about what Rathmore wanted, I could pretend there was nothing to worry about. We stayed longer than necessary, and when Nash drove us back to the house, Avery stayed in the car to talk.

I opted to take a bath in the master suite and enjoyed every minute of it. It relaxed me enough that I should have been able to fall asleep quickly, but knowing I was meeting with Rathmore in the morning drained all the calmness right out of me.

I didn't know what Rathmore wanted from me, but somewhere in the back of my mind, I couldn't shake the feeling that Creed shouldn't come. Maybe it was because Rathmore had nearly killed him, and I didn't want to worry about it happening again.

If Creed wasn't there, I'd have more leeway in my responses to Rathmore's demands. I didn't want to worry about him the whole time I was there. But how was I going to make him stay away? He wouldn't like it, but I hoped he'd understand.

CHAPTER FOURTEEN

The next morning arrived with a bank of dark clouds rolling in over the horizon. I was so used to sunny days that it caught me by surprise. Of course, given that I had to help Rathmore, it totally suited my mood, especially since I'd just told Creed I didn't want him to come.

As I waited for Rathmore's car to arrive, my stomach churned with anxiety. Creed stood beside me, his disapproval coming off him in waves. "Ella... I don't like this. You need me. I'm supposed to be with you."

I turned to face him, hating that we were arguing. I needed his support, not his anger. "Creed..." I reached up to run my fingers along his cheek, feeling the rough stubble of his beard against my skin. "I love you. That's why you have to stay here. You know Rathmore would use you against me. It has to be this way... at least for this meeting."

"But what if you get in trouble?"

"I won't. Rathmore needs me. He's not going to let anything happen to me."

His eyes intense, he turned to take hold of my upper arms like he wanted to shake me. "I know this is hard, but don't let your fear for me cloud your judgement. We're supposed to be partners in this. Don't take that away from me."

"I know... and I'm sorry, but just this once, I need you to stay here." What he said made sense, but I couldn't get my heart to agree. "I don't know why, but I feel like it's what I need to do."

He sighed and dropped his hands. "Fine. I don't agree, but I'll go along with it. Just promise me one thing."

"What?"

"I'm just worried. I know you were angry enough to use your gift to kill him the other day, and I don't want that to happen. I'm worried about the consequences, and that it might change you. If anyone's going to kill him, it should be me."

"Creed, I'm not going to do anything like that... and I'd only consider it if it was the last resort. I'll follow St. John's advice. All I know is that this isn't the last time he'll want me for something. Maybe, the next time, we'll know if that's the course we need to take, but until then, let's see how it goes."

He let out a breath. "Okay. That helps, but I'm still not happy about it."

I swallowed. "I know, and I'm sorry."

A black SUV turned onto the street and then pulled into the driveway. My heart began to race, and I rubbed my sweaty palms on my pants.

Avery came running down the stairs. "They're here." She rushed over to hug me. "Be careful. We'll be waiting with our bags packed."

"Sounds good."

I turned to Creed and patted my purse. "I've got my phone right here, so I can call if I need to, but don't worry, I'll be back before you know it." I leaned in for a quick kiss, and Creed caught my hands.

"I'm trusting you to be okay."

"I know. I won't let you down." I kissed him again and walked out the door.

Creed and Avery both followed me onto the porch. The driver's door opened, and a man jumped out to open the back door. He wore a suit and tie, reminding me of the security detail Avery had with her.

"Ward?" Avery asked. The man's head jerked in her direction. She sent him a beautiful smile, and he flushed. "Take care of Ella, okay?"

"Of course."

"Thanks."

My lips quirked up, and I sent Creed and Avery a quick wave before jumping into the back seat. Somehow, Avery had lightened the moment for me, and it gave me hope.

It didn't last long. As Ward closed the car door behind me, I noticed the gun he carried beneath his suit coat, and a chill ran down my spine. Now I was even more grateful that Creed wasn't going with me.

As Ward began the drive, he glanced at me in the rearview mirror, and I smiled. "Hi Ward... I'm Ella. Nice to meet you."

His lips tightened, then he gave me a slight nod. I counted that as a small victory. He may work for Rathmore, but it didn't hurt to have some kind of connection of my own with him. Who knew when it might come in handy?

I slipped on my seatbelt, hoping I didn't look too casual for the occasion. My black pant suit had blood stains on it, so I had to wear my jeans and a nice t-shirt. This one was white, with blue ocean waves on it. Even if Rathmore didn't approve, at least it matched his office decor.

As we turned onto the Las Vegas Strip, the flashing lights up and down the street drew my attention. How many of these buildings did Rathmore own by now? He was buying them up like they were candy. Why? Was he just after the money?

I doubted it. It made more sense that he craved the power just as much, if not more.

It seemed like every deal he'd made, and every person he'd employed, was calculated to expand his resources. He'd dipped his fingers into the police department, and I had to imagine the state government as well. He was building an empire, and Las Vegas was the center of his control.

Of course, that was all speculation, but it might not hurt to find out as much about him as I could. Once we got home, I could enlist Avery's freaky computer skills to help me dig into his past and his financial holdings.

He had to have some weaknesses, and, if I wanted to get out from under him, I needed to know what they were. Besides that, it wasn't just me. He'd used Shelby as well, and I doubted he'd forget about her anytime soon.

He'd discovered that she had a special psychic ability, and now he knew that I could heal. Was there a pattern here? Were there more people like us out there? I'd never thought about that, but it had to be a possibility.

It hit me that Avery could be one of the special ones. Somehow, my healing power had changed her. She was like a human calculator with a photographic memory. Was that part of my purpose? Part of the reason I had this gift?

Who else had I healed that could be different? I didn't know for sure, but I'd have to keep track of them, just to see if they developed anything out of the ordinary. I shook my head. What was I thinking? I was getting carried away. Still, I couldn't stop that small curiosity that I might be onto something.

Ward made a sharp turn into the parking garage of Rathmore's corporate offices, ending my musings. We continued past the first level and into the lower executive parking structure. He stopped in front of the elevator and jumped out to open my door.

I stepped out, and he shut the door behind me. At the elevator, he pushed the button and the doors swished open. Inside, he used his keycard to unlock the stop for the thirteenth floor.

We went straight up, and the doors opened. Stepping out, Ward ushered me to the outer doors of Rathmore's office suite. Inside, the secretary glanced up. Her assessing gaze examined me from top to bottom and frowned, finding me lacking. With a glare of disapproval, she motioned to the chairs. "Have a seat. I'll let him know you're here."

I sat down in the wingback chair, knowing the couch wasn't as comfortable. Ward sat in the other chair, surprising me. Was he my personal guard to keep me in line? Of course, without a keycard of my own, I needed someone to let me in and out of the building.

The secretary hung up her phone and glanced my way. "He'll see you now."

I stood, half expecting Ward to follow me in. He sent me an easy smile and said he'd wait there for me. Down the hall, Rathmore's door stood open, so I stepped inside to find him speaking on his phone. He glanced up and smiled, like I was an old friend and he was happy to see me. He spoke into the phone. "Thanks Derek, you won't be sorry."

He hung up and caught my gaze. "Ella. Thank you for coming. I hope it wasn't too much of an inconvenience."

How could he act like nothing was wrong? "It was, but I didn't have much of a choice."

His smile didn't even falter. If anything it got bigger. "I'm sure you're anxious to get home, so I'll try to keep it short. That was my associate on the phone. He just called to say he wasn't feeling up to our meeting. Since you're on a time frame, I convinced him to let us come to him. It shouldn't take too long, and, once we're done, I can have my driver take all of you to the airport. My jet and pilots are on standby, so you won't have to wait. Sound good?"

It flustered me that he had everything all figured out. "Okay, sure, but I'd like to know what it is you want first."

"Of course. Let me explain. We're meeting with the owner of the tech giant, Urban AI. His name is Derek Vaughn. He's in the process of developing a smart city just west of Las Vegas. At the moment, he's run into some financial snags, and I've offered a substantial investment to back this dream of his."

"What's a smart city?"

Rathmore's eyes lit up with enthusiasm. "Nothing like you've ever seen. It's the wave of the future, a city built from the ground up with a complete integration of major technology research and development.

"It includes all kinds of things, from autonomous technology to robotics, artificial intelligence, wireless integration, biometrics, and even renewable resource technology. It's the most exciting thing I've ever seen, and it's being built just southwest of Las Vegas on about seventy thousand acres of undeveloped and uninhabited land.

He shook his head in awe. "It's a city that will bring in new businesses at the forefront of technology, and the state government has just offered a special zone permit to allow the company developing the city to be able to form its own government. That means carrying the same authority as counties, including the ability to impose taxes, form school districts and courts, and provide government services."

"So it's a city separated from the rest of the world and run by a corporation?"

His smile turned indulgent. "Not quite, but in a way... I suppose you could say that. I want to be part of it, and I'm hoping to convince Derek Vaughn to agree, and you're just the person I need to persuade him."

"How am I supposed to do that?"

He grinned, but it didn't quite reach his eyes. "You'll see when we get there."

Before I could protest, he left the office, and I had no choice but to follow. Rathmore told his secretary we were leaving. Ward jumped up, and Rathmore motioned for him to follow us, explaining that he needed Ward to drive us to the meeting with Derek Vaughn at his house.

Soon we were in the SUV and on our way. On the drive, I concluded that Derek Vaughn, or a member of his family, had to be sick. It was the only way Rathmore could use me to bargain his way into the project. It didn't bother me to heal someone who needed it, but I hated the idea of healing someone to further Rathmore's agenda.

This was exactly what I had been afraid of, and now I had a choice to make. If I refused, Rathmore would threaten to kill someone I loved. After shooting Creed, I knew he wouldn't hesitate. So what would happen if that awful burning sensation told me not to heal them? Worry tightened my stomach, and I hoped that didn't happen.

We drove out of Las Vegas into the southwestern part of the desert. Thirty minutes later, we arrived at the development. There were several warehouse buildings with machinery at the beginning of the property. Further down the road, Vaughn's company had already begun breaking ground on the city, with his team's headquarters on site.

A large banner between two posts showed an artist's rendering of what the city would look like, and I had to admit that I was impressed. The silver buildings looked sleek, with both round and angular designs, and roofs made of solar panels. The housing communities surrounded them and were interspersed with greenery.

From what I could see, they were nearly halfway done, and things were progressing at a rapid pace. We pulled past the initial staging area into a small community, where sidewalks and driveways lined the empty streets, waiting for houses to be built.

At the end of the development, a street continued to curve up the side of the hill that overlooked the valley. Sitting at the top of a cliff, a fully finished home perched above us, with an incredible view of the development.

It was the only finished house there, and it sat in a perfect spot to overlook the valley. The driveway curved around the house toward the edge of the cliff, giving us a view of the whole area below.

This birds-eye view of the building going on was breathtaking, reminding me of a futuristic city rising from the dust. The downtown area held larger buildings in the center and was surrounded by interconnected buildings that spanned outward towards the neighborhoods where people would live.

Glancing back at the house, I saw that the same ultra-modern architecture made it a showpiece of technology. The lines and angles, along with the sleek solar panels, made it look like a house from some futuristic sci-fi movie.

Rathmore got out of the car and waited for me to join him before heading to the front door of the house. Ward followed us toward the front door, but stood as a sentry while we continued to the porch. From this side, the house didn't look so big, but glancing toward the back, I could see that it was built right into the cliff.

A few seconds after Rathmore rang the bell, the door opened, and the man I'd seen in Rathmore's office stood in front of us. He'd been the last to arrive, and he didn't look especially happy to see us. His hair poked up in the back, like he'd been lying down, and there was a slight tremble in his hands.

"Hello Derek," Rathmore said. "Thanks for meeting with us. This is Ella St. John, one of my newest employees."

Derek's glaze flicked over me dismissively before turning back to Rathmore. "Come in." He left the door open and stepped toward the back of the house. We followed him through the large living room area, with vaulted ceilings and beautiful lines, to the back of the house that showcased floor-to-ceiling windows overlooking the valley below.

Entranced by the view, I still couldn't help noticing Vaughn's stiff gait, even though he tried to hide it. We followed him to the French doors that opened onto a beautiful stone balcony. A low stone wall, following the circumference of the balcony, perched on the edge of the cliff.

The balcony held several lounge chairs near the house, comfortably situated for the best views. Yucca plants bordered the wall, with several mesquite trees standing proudly on the hillside next to the house.

Other desert plants, including cactus and desert willow trees, sat in big pots, strategically placed around the balcony. The late fall sun hung to the south, barely penetrating through the dark threatening clouds, and a soft breeze ruffled my hair, bringing the scent of sagebrush and a promise of rain.

It was the perfect place to witness the coming storm, and mirrored the scowl on Vaughn's face. He sat down in a lounge chair and motioned toward the other chairs beside him. "You can sit anywhere you want. Or you can pull up one of those chairs from the dining table over there."

Rathmore didn't seem to mind Vaughn's lack of hospitality and grabbed a couple of the smaller outdoor chairs for us. He placed them in front of Vaughn, effectively blocking a portion of his view.

Vaughn picked up an iced drink that sat on the small table beside him and took several swallows. He didn't bother to offer us anything, but Rathmore waited patiently for Vaughn to make the first move.

Vaughn finally glanced at Rathmore and shook his head. "I already gave you my answer. Nothing you can say will change my mind. This is my legacy, and I've worked too damn hard to let you get your hands on it."

"I know why you don't look well," Rathmore said, changing the subject. "You have stage four lung cancer, and it's killing you. I don't think you'll still be here when this city is finished, let alone live to enjoy your legacy."

Vaughn huffed out a breath and struggled to sit up. "How did you find out? Who told you?" His face turned red, and his chest heaved. Losing the battle, he sighed and slowly lowered his back against the lounge chair. "I've been trying to keep this under wraps, but it doesn't matter. This is my legacy whether I'm here or not, and I won't have you taking it from me."

Rathmore shook his head. "I don't want to take anything away from you. I just want to be part of it."

"That's not what you said before."

"Maybe that was the case at first, but I've changed my mind. This plan of yours is brilliant, I wouldn't dream of changing it. In fact... I think we could work together. You know you'll never finish it without my help."

"That's not true," Vaughn said. "I've found others who are interested in investing. Now that my link technology has caught up with real-world application, it's only a matter of time."

"They won't invest if they find out about your illness. You're the brains behind this project. Without you, it's dead in the water." Rathmore watched Vaughn with a calculating gleam in his eyes. "How long have you got left? Six months? A year? What happens to your legacy then?"

Vaughn shook his head. "They're giving me a year or two, if I'm lucky. But even if I agreed to your terms, you can't expect me to believe that you won't change everything once I'm gone. I gave you my answer, and I haven't changed my mind. Now please go."

Rathmore pursed his lips and nodded. "I understand how difficult this must be for you. But..." He sat forward in his chair. "What if I could change all that? What if you didn't have to die? What if there was a way to make you perfectly healthy again?"

Vaughn's eyes narrowed before he shook his head. "Are you crazy? There's nothing that can be done. Everyone knows that."

"But there is." Rathmore glanced my way, and my hands began to sweat. "What if I told you I have the solution and I can fix it. Right here. Right now. Would you take that chance to be healed? To live?"

"What you're saying is impossible. There's no cure now. The cancer has spread too far. The treatments should give me more time, but that's the best I can hope for."

"You haven't done everything," Rathmore said. "There is one more thing you could do. The only question is if you're willing to take that chance. You're dying, and I'm offering you the opportunity to live until you're an old man. What have you got to lose?"

Vaughn's brows dipped, and he shook his head, clearly intrigued, but wary. "What could you possibly do?"

Rathmore looked at me, and I shook my head. He would give my secret away. Then what would happen? How many people would this man tell? Where would it stop?

He must have seen the panic in my eyes. "Don't worry, Ella. I know what I'm doing."

Vaughn finally looked at me. "What's she got to do with this?"

"Before we can continue this conversation, I need to know if you want to be cured. Tell me no, and I'll leave right now, no questions asked. You can go back to whatever time you have left and wonder if you made the biggest mistake of your life. Then you will die. Or, you can take a chance that I have the cure, and you'll be free of this terrible disease. You'll live. But the choice is up to you."

Vaughn licked his lips, finally taking Rathmore seriously. "And if your cure works, which I highly doubt, what do you get out of it?"

"What is your life worth?"

Vaughn took a deep breath. "To be cured of cancer? I'd be willing to sign over this whole project to you. But that's not going to happen. You're just messing with me."

Rathmore smiled. "I'm perfectly serious, and I'd take that deal, but we both know that this is your project. Without you... it will fail. So I propose you stay in control until this project is up and running. Once that is accomplished, I'll take over and furnish you with a retainer that will set you up for life. You can live here, or anywhere else you want to go."

Rathmore rubbed his chin. "You see... I have a vision of expanding cities like this all over the world, and I can guarantee that you'll have a place in each one if you like. If you agree to that, the only other condition I have is that you tell absolutely no one about your cure. No one can ever know what happens here."

This time Vaughn sat up. He studied Rathmore for a long time, then glanced my way. "Is this for real?"

"What do you say?" Rathmore asked, pulling Vaughn's attention away from me.

Vaughn took a few deep breaths. He held his shaking hands out in front of him before meeting Rathmore's gaze. "Yes. If you can cure me, I'll agree to your terms."

Rathmore nodded. "Good. Then we will proceed. But just so you understand... if you go back on your word, there are other ways you can die."

Vaughn's eyes widened. "I won't go back on my word."

With a nod, Rathmore turned to me. "Ella. It's up to you now." I hesitated just long enough for him to raise a brow.

Shaking my head, I pulled my chair beside Vaughn's. He stared at me, his eyes holding both fear and skepticism. "I have to touch you. Can I take your hand?"

He huffed out a breath and looked between me and Rathmore. Coming to a decision, he shrugged. "Sure."

I took his hand in mine and placed my other hand on his forearm. "Close your eyes. Try and stay calm. This might hurt a little." He sent one last glance at Rathmore before letting out a breath and closing his eyes.

A sudden fear that I'd be unable to heal him washed over me, but I pushed it away. I didn't have a choice. I also knew that, if I tried to heal him all at once, I ran the risk of passing out, so I had to take it slow.

Cancer cells were mutated cells that could grow and spread, and stage four cancer meant that the cancer had metastasized to other parts of his body. In order to find the mutated cells, I had to look for the places inside his body that felt wrong and use my healing power to burn them out.

Since I wasn't sure where to start, I'd just have to go by touch and follow where my senses led. Gripping his hand, I let my awareness meld through his skin and into his body. My healing power slipped into him without burning, and relief washed over me. Right away, I found a cluster of mutated cells in his lungs.

I concentrated my healing power there for several long minutes until they'd been destroyed. Next, I searched for more clusters and found a mass that had spread into his liver. Purging them took more time, as they were deeply embedded into the tissue.

A wave of dizziness washed over me, and I tried to pace myself, taking a moment to rest before I pressed on. I found a few smaller clusters in the lymph nodes of his neck and burned them out. With my energy draining, I followed the last trail of cancer cells to his brain. A mass of mutated clusters had formed deep inside his brain tissue, which in turn had caused a lot of his pain.

Before tackling them, I took another moment to regroup. It felt like hours had passed since I'd started, and my neck and back had begun to ache. Steeling myself for one more surge, I pulled the last of my healing power from deep inside and trickled it into the mass of cancerous cells.

Little by little, I could feel them burning away. Vaughn's grip on my hand tightened, and a moan escaped his lips. I pushed on, focusing all my energy on them until every last one was gone. Panting, I pulled my focus from his brain and turned one last time to scan his body.

Unable to feel any more cancer cells, I finally pulled back into myself and released my hold on him, letting go of his hand. With my energy depleted, I began to slump forward into darkness. Rathmore's strong arms came around me, pulling me toward him, and my head fell back against his chest.

Soon, my breathing evened out, and the darkness began to clear. I was still too weak to move, otherwise, I would have jumped as far away from Rathmore as I could get. Several more minutes in a semi-conscious state passed before Rathmore held a glass of water to my lips.

I took it greedily, holding it to my mouth and drinking it down like I was dying of thirst. The effects were immediate, and I sat up, pulling away from my perch on Rathmore's lap. He helped me stand, steadying me around my waist until I could regain my balance.

"You okay?" he asked.

"Yeah." I glanced at the lounge chair where I'd last seen Vaughn, but it was empty. "Where's Vaughn?"

"He's bringing you something to eat. Let's go inside."

Still unsteady on my feet, I allowed him to hold my arm as we stepped inside. Vaughn stood at the kitchen counter, buttering a piece of toast. Seeing me, he rushed to my side and handed me a glass of orange juice, which I promptly gulped down.

That helped me even more, and Vaughn took the glass from me, his eyes full of wonder. "You were right. It hurt. A lot. It felt like something was burning inside of me. But... I can't believe I'm saying this, but I feel amazing. What did you do?"

As I opened my mouth to answer, I caught a flicker of movement coming from the side of the house where the bedrooms were located. I turned for a better view, and Sonny stepped out, his face full of indignant rage, and holding a gun in his hand.

He glanced at Vaughn. "I thought you'd never come inside. What took you so long?"

"Sonny... wait," Vaughn said, his hands raised. "This was a mistake. You can't kill them."

Sonny chuffed. "What? You're turning against me too? You can't be serious after what he's done."

Vaughn stepped in front of me. "You can't do this. I don't care about that now. You have to stop. I won't let you hurt them."

"Screw you." Sonny fired his gun, hitting Vaughn in the stomach. He doubled over and slumped to the floor, groaning in agony.

Frozen in shock, I couldn't move. Sonny pointed his gun my way, but Rathmore pushed me down, sending me tumbling onto my hands and knees.

Sonny fired the gun five more times, striking Rathmore in the chest. Rathmore jerked with each impact, then he slowly crumpled to the ground. He lay unmoving, his eyes open and sightless.

"No!" I tried to stand, hoping I could do something, but Sonny pointed his gun my way and pulled the trigger. I dropped to the floor, hearing another loud bang.

The door crashed open, and Ward rushed inside with his gun out. Sonny turned toward the guard, but before he could shoot, Ward fired several times, hitting Sonny square in the chest. As Sonny toppled to the floor, his gun dropped from his hand.

Ward rushed to Sonny's side, kicking the gun further out of his reach. Touching his fingers to Sonny's neck, he shook his head. "He's dead."

Ward stepped to Rathmore's side and felt for a pulse.

Huddled on the ground, I couldn't seem to move. "Is he... dead?" Ward's gaze narrowed, but he didn't answer.

A soft moan came from Vaughn. He was lying on his side, curled into a ball, and clutching his stomach. I knew my legs wouldn't hold me, so I crawled to his side, worried that I wouldn't have enough strength to save him.

His pleading gaze caught mine, and I placed my hand over his wound. "I'll do what I can, but I'm still pretty weak."

"Please... whatever you can do..."

I nodded and closed my eyes, finding a small glimmer of power, I pushed the healing light into his wound. Luckily, the bullet had gone straight through and exited out the side of his back. With sheer force of will, I managed to mend the worst of the damage and heal the major blood vessels before my power fizzled out.

It would be enough to save him, and I hoped, once he got to a hospital, they could repair the rest. I glanced at Ward. "Please... there's no time to call an ambulance. You need to take him to the hospital. Now."

He glanced between me and Rathmore. "I'm not supposed to leave him."

"But he's... he's gone. Look... I'll stay here. You can save Vaughn. It's what Rathmore would have wanted. Just take Vaughn to the hospital, and you can come right back. I'm not going anywhere."

Ward's lips twisted with indecision.

"Hurry... you need to go."

Letting out a breath, he stepped to Vaughn's side.

Grateful he'd listened to me, I spotted a towel on the kitchen counter. "Hand me that towel." He did as I asked, and I placed it over Vaughn's wound before looking into his eyes. "Hold it as tight as you can against the wound."

With a jerky nod, Vaughn held it tight. He winced, and I patted his hand. "You're going to be fine. I stopped the worst of it, and the doctors will finish patching you up."

Vaughn nodded. "Thank you."

Glancing between us, Ward took note of my trembling hands and labored breathing. "Are you okay?"

I sat back and nodded. "Yes... I'm fine... just shaken. Please go."

"I'll be back as soon as I can. Watch over Rathmore."

What did he mean by that? "Uh... sure."

With a nod, Ward helped Vaughn to his feet, and they shuffled out the door, leaving me with two dead men. I closed my eyes and laid my head back against the kitchen island. A few seconds later, I felt steady enough to examine my own wound. It hurt like hell, but I knew it wasn't bad enough to require a trip to the hospital, especially since I could probably heal it once my strength came back.

Glancing down, I found a large, red stain near my waist where a stray bullet had nicked me. Lifting my shirt revealed a nasty two-inch gash. I needed to clean it up before I bandaged it, but I had no strength left to get up off the floor.

Worse, I couldn't seem to catch my breath. Sudden tears gathered in my eyes and trailed down my cheeks unchecked. I couldn't understand why I was crying. Both Rathmore and Sonny were dead. I should be relieved. Instead, all I felt was shock. How had this happened? Sonny must have been here the whole time, just waiting for his chance to kill Rathmore... and probably me as well.

I glanced at Rathmore's still form. He was lying on his back, his arms spread out and his eyes wide open. His chest was covered in blood, and I counted at least three bullet wounds.

If he hadn't shoved me out of the way, he might still be alive. He'd done it to save me. I couldn't understand it. Rathmore was a horrible person. Why save me instead of himself? It made no sense.

One of Rathmore's eyes twitched and I gasped. It was so subtle that I wondered if I'd imagined it. I stared at him without blinking. Nothing more happened. Still, my heart began to pound, and I crawled toward him. His eye twitched again and I froze. Could he still be alive?

His eyes blinked. Once, then twice. Suddenly, he sucked in a breath and his chest filled with air. As he continued to pull air into his lungs, his eyes closed and he moaned. Shocked, I scrambled to his side and raised my hand to feel his pulse. Before I could touch him, a bullet emerged from his chest, followed by two more. I jerked back, my jaw dropping open.

With a groan, Rathmore opened his eyes and pushed up onto his elbows. Taking several sustaining breaths, his gaze found mine, and his eyes narrowed. As his lips twisted into a grimace of pain, he sat up, rubbing his chest.

CHAPTER FIFTEEN

"That hurt."

I stared at Rathmore, hardly daring to breathe. How had this happened? Was he like me? What did it mean?

He sighed and closed his eyes. "I was hoping you wouldn't find out about this yet."

"Who are you? What are you?"

He huffed out a breath and shook his head, his lips twisting into a sardonic grimace. "I need a drink." Rolling to his hands and knees, he pushed slowly to his feet. Standing, he took a moment to find his balance and twisted his head from side to side. Rolling his shoulders, another bullet popped out from his body and bounced across the floor.

"That's better." He glanced my way, and concern tightened his eyes. Dropping into a crouch, he studied me more closely. "Ella?"

A wave of dizziness washed over me, and I lowered my head. Taking deep breaths, I fought against the panic that threatened to overwhelm me. Unable to hold it together, I slumped to the floor on my back and closed my eyes.

Rathmore knelt beside me. "It's okay Ella. Take a deep breath and let it out... slowly...that's right... in... and out... in... and out."

For some reason, his words calmed me, and I concentrated on my breathing. Soon, my heart slowed into a regular rhythm, and I felt more in control. Several seconds later, the dizziness passed, and I could finally open my eyes.

Rathmore knelt on the floor by my side, watching me with concern. His gaze went to the blood on my side, and he frowned. "You got hit?"

"It's just grazed, but I couldn't heal it... not after helping Vaughn. I'm still weak."

"You always get weak like this?"

"Not quite this bad, but healing Vaughn took a lot out of me."

His lips twisted. "Where is he anyway?"

"He got shot in the stomach. I sent the last of my energy into healing the worst of his wound. Then I made Ward take him to the hospital. He should be fine once they're done with him."

Rathmore nodded. "Can you get up now? You should probably drink some water and eat something."

"I think so." He took my arm and helped me up. I stood still for a moment, making sure I wouldn't faint. "Thanks. I'm good."

Rathmore let go of me and stepped to the kitchen. He turned on the faucet and filled up two glasses of water. I moved to the kitchen island and sat on the cushioned barstool, taking the glass he offered me. He found a box of crackers in the cupboard and opened one of the sleeves.

Emptying it out on the counter, we both took a couple of crackers and chewed, washing them down with water. In the silence, it hit me that we were eating and drinking while Sonny lay dead on the floor.

I glanced his way and found it hard to swallow my next bite, so I quickly finished off the water to help it go down. "What's going on? What do we do about Sonny?"

Rathmore finished his water and raised a brow. "I need to call someone. Why don't you get cleaned up? There's a bathroom down the hall."

"But what about you? What happened? How did you heal like that?"

"I'll explain everything, but right now I need to make a call. Go on. It won't take me long, and then we'll talk."

Frowning, I shuffled to the bathroom. After scrubbing the blood off my hands, I leaned against the counter and glanced in the mirror. My blue eyes seemed to glow purple in my pale face, making me look like a stranger. Combined with the dark circles beneath them, my unhealthy pallor shocked me.

Turning away, I examined my wound. Blood oozed from the gash, and the skin around it was tender and painful. I had to keep stopping to catch my breath before I'd cleaned it enough to put on a bandage. Part of me had hoped it would miraculously heal itself. But that would make me like Rathmore, and I cringed just thinking about it.

Opening the bathroom cupboards, I found a first aid kit and pulled out the supplies I needed. Using plenty of gauze and tape, I finally got my side patched up. I'd hoped to send my healing power into the wound, but I just didn't have enough strength.

After taking a moment to regain my composure, I straightened and pulled the door open. Stepping down the hall, I heard voices, and disappointment washed over me. I'd wanted some time alone with Rathmore for answers, but now I'd have to wait.

Entering the living room area, I found Rathmore speaking with Ward. They both glanced my way, and Rathmore came to my side. He wore a fresh shirt and jacket, and there was no sign of blood on him anywhere.

Catching Ward's gaze, I asked, "How's Vaughn?"

He shrugged. "I didn't stay to find out." Taking in my frown, he continued. "You said he'd be fine."

I sighed. He was right, but what the heck? I turned back to Rathmore and lowered my voice. "Does he know about you?"

Rathmore raised a brow. "Yes. He's been with me for a while now." Before I could question him further, he spoke. "How's your wound?"

"It's okay. I'm not like you. I have to concentrate on healing it myself before it will get better." I shook my head. "Right now I'm too exhausted to take care of it." He nodded and I plunged ahead, meeting his gaze so he couldn't avoid answering. "Are you like me? Can you heal me?"

He studied me, his eyes turning hard. "No. I'm afraid not."

"Then what just happened. You were dead... and now... you're fine. What's going on?"

A car pulled up outside, and Rathmore nodded toward the door. "That will be the police. I'm afraid this conversation will have to wait."

"But—"

Ignoring me, he moved toward the door and greeted a detective and two police officers. While they spoke, I eased into a cushioned chair, knowing any answers I wanted would have to wait. Exhaustion crept over me, and I found it hard to keep my eyes open.

This was all too much, and I didn't understand any of it. Rathmore had come back from the dead. Who does that? My eyes popped open. I had. But if Rathmore couldn't heal people, then he was nothing like me, so what was he?

If he was used to this sort of thing, it suddenly made sense that he'd accept my ability to heal Avery, and why he'd shot

Creed to test his theory, but it still didn't explain what had just happened to him.

Shock and exhaustion crept over me, and my eyes fluttered closed. The men's low voices lulled me to sleep, and I let down my guard. I just needed a few minutes to rest, and then I could deal with this madness.

The sound of my cell phone jarred me back to consciousness, and I automatically searched for it. The police were still here, so I'd only been out for a minute or two. Before I could spot my purse, the ringing stopped, and I remembered leaving it out on the patio.

Heaving a sigh, I got to my feet, swaying slightly before catching my balance. Feeling better, I stepped through the double French doors and sank down into one of the cushioned lounge chairs beside the small table where I'd left my purse, grateful it hadn't begun to rain.

It started ringing again, and I managed to pull it free. Creed's name came up on the caller ID, and I quickly swiped to answer it.

"Creed?"

"Ella. Where are you? I thought you'd be back by now. Is everything okay?"

I wanted to reassure him, but how could I, when nothing made sense? "Yes... I'm okay, but I'm going to be here a little longer."

"He didn't go back on his word, did he?"

"No. It's nothing like that, I just need some answers, and I'm not leaving until I get them."

"Why? What happened?"

Someone stepped onto the deck, and I glanced up to see the detective. "I can't explain it right now. Someone's waiting to talk to me. But I'm okay, and I'll tell you everything as soon as I can."

He sighed. "Fine. But this is killing me. You should have let me come."

"I know... I'm sorry. Look... I have to go, but I'll call you back." I disconnected and glanced up at the man.

"It's Ella St. John, right?" At my nod, he continued. "Mind if I have a seat?"

"Sure... go ahead."

He sat on the edge of the lounge chair beside mine and faced me. "I'm Detective Garcia. Would you tell me what happened here?"

I told him everything, only leaving out the part where Rathmore got shot. He asked me a few more questions, which I answered as succinctly as possible. Through the glass doors, I caught sight of two men entering the house with a gurney.

I watched as they stuffed Sonny's body into a body bag and zipped it up. The finality of his death sent a shiver down my spine. I didn't realize I'd gone silent until the detective said my name a few times. I started and glanced his way, finally hearing his question.

"Is there anything else you can tell me?"

"No, I think that just about covers it."

His lips thinned, and he held my gaze a little longer than necessary. "So you think Rathmore was the target? Or did Sonny want you dead, too?"

His question surprised me. "Uh... I think he was after Rathmore, but he would have killed me too if he'd had the chance. It was a good thing Ward was here. He saved me... us."

The detective waited, but since I had nothing more to say, he got to his feet. "Thanks for your time. Feel free to call me if you remember anything more." He handed me his card and joined the police officers inside, leaving the door ajar.

I heard him say that we were free to leave, but they might have more questions later.

After they left, Rathmore glanced my way. He motioned Ward to his side and spoke to him quietly before heading toward me. Ward left the house, and Rathmore came out on the deck, taking the chair beside mine.

"This really is a great view. That storm coming in is magnificent, and the sunset here would be worth the price of the house." I didn't answer, and we sat in silence for a few minutes. "I was hoping to avoid this, but now I don't seem to have a choice. Before I tell you my secret, I just need to know one thing. How did you get your healing power? Was it from John?"

At my gasp, he narrowed his eyes. "I guess you'd call him *Saint* John now, although I think that's a bit of a stretch."

"So you know St. John? Did he give you the power to heal yourself?"

"Oh no. John doesn't have that kind of power because I didn't heal myself. You see... I'm immortal... just like John."

At that moment, a rumble of thunder sounded in the distance, and my hand flew to my mouth. What was he saying? "That's preposterous. How can you be like him? You're nothing like him."

His lips flattened, and his eyes turned cold. "He wasn't the only one given the choice to tarry on the earth; or did he leave that part out?"

My eyes widened, and I blinked. "No. He mentioned there were others, but— " I studied Rathmore's face, hoping to see something there besides the cold, unfeeling hardness he usually wore. Not finding it, I faltered. "What are you saying?"

He sat back in his chair and huffed out a breath. "My original name is Nicodemus. You may have heard of me."

My mouth dropped open. "The same one in the Bible?"

He nodded. "John and I were friends back then, and we were given the same incredible gift. I was like him at first. Or maybe I was more like you." His piercing gaze caught mine before he glanced away. "I began with noble intentions, wanting to do my part and make a difference in the world. I did the work and helped as many people as I could, always taking the path that had been chosen for me.

"I found people to heal, but there were also many I couldn't help. Through the years, they began to add up." His eyes took on a faraway gleam.

"Mothers dying in childbirth, soldiers fighting for a worthy cause, fathers who wanted nothing more than to provide for their families... and then there were the children. So many of them died, and I could only save a few."

His lips twisted. "I think it was the children that broke something inside of me. Children are innocent... and yet, through no fault of their own, they suffered so much pain. I even took apprentices, like you, but it was never enough. I was supposed to make a difference in the world, but I barely made a dent.

"Other times, I'd get there just minutes too late, and the person had already died." He shook his head. "Even that might not have mattered quite so much, but I hated it when I had the power to heal someone, and I was forbidden to do it." He met my gaze. "Has that happened to you yet?"

I swallowed, remembering the phony reporter's husband who was dying of cancer. The burning had stopped me, and I could only help manage his pain. And what about my own mother? I'd grown up without one because St. John had been forbidden to heal her.

He nodded. "I see in your eyes that it has. But here's a question you probably haven't considered. What makes those you save more special than those you can't? Aren't we all his children?" He shook his head. "I'll never understand it. He's given you this power, and then he won't allow you to use it. Why? When you're right here? It's not right."

He tilted his head back to watch the darkening clouds, and I followed his gaze, feeling the same swirling turmoil in my chest. Yes, it bothered me. It wasn't fair, and it hurt that I had this gift and couldn't always use it.

"So much suffering in this world," Rathmore continued. "Even with the gift to help a few, it doesn't really change anything. People still kill each other, the serial killer gets away with torture and murder. Good people die in accidents, or they get cancer, or any number of other diseases, and nothing ever changes. I soon came to realize that what little I could do meant nothing in the larger scheme of things."

"You're wrong," I said. "It meant something to them."

He huffed in derision. "Yes... I knew you would say that with your clear-eyed idealism. And maybe it did for the moment, but are they really better off? Sure, there are some things worth living for, but in the end, everyone dies anyway. Why try to save them when they could just as easily die later in an accident, or suffer from a different illness?

"I mean... look at Vaughn. He's a great example. You just healed him, giving him everything you had, and Sonny shot him only moments later. Sure... he's alive because you pulled him through. But if you weren't here... he'd be dead."

He shook his head. "In my many years on this earth, I've saved a lot of people, only to have them die a day... a week... even a few years later. What's the point in saving them in the first place?"

I opened my mouth to argue, but he raised his hand. "I know what you're going to say... one more day of life on this earthly plane is worth it. And if it were just that... it might have been different, but there's so much more."

His expression turned harder than I'd ever seen it. He glanced at me with fire in his eyes. "I hated the fact that my choices were taken from me. My path was chosen. My fate was sealed. And it didn't matter what I wanted." His vitriol shook me. He was so full of rage that he couldn't see anything else.

"But surely you agreed to that. Wasn't it part of the deal?"

He huffed out a breath. "Yes... you're right. I agreed to it, but I didn't know then what I do now. Sure... at first it didn't bother me, but, after a while, it began to chafe. It felt like I had a collar around my neck, and my short leash was being pulled to and fro by the winds of fate.

"None of it was of my choosing. I was just supposed to go wherever fate led me. Like a guessing game with none of the answers spelled out. The oppression pulled me down until, one day, I stopped using my gift to heal.

"It was so liberating to be out from under that heavy weight. I could finally be my own man and make my own way for a change." Another roll of thunder sounded and the clouds shifted to completely block the sun's light.

He met my gaze, his eyes darkening, just like the clouds above us. "Don't tell me you haven't questioned your path. Questioned who you should heal and who you shouldn't? Questioned where you should go and what job you should take? John told you it was all based on feelings, didn't he? Trust your feelings and go with the flow. How is that working for you?"

I didn't like the sneer on his face. "It's not easy, but I'm managing." I shook my head. "So is that why you can't heal anymore? Was it taken from you?" He didn't answer, so I continued. "It must have been, otherwise, you wouldn't need me. So what happened?"

Derision replaced his sneer, and he looked down his nose at me. "I may not be able to heal, but that hasn't stopped me from accomplishing my goals. I could have gotten Vaughn's cooperation by other means, but, since you were here, it was much quicker, and he will be in my debt for the rest of his life." He shrugged. "However long that lasts. I have to admit that I was surprised you had enough energy left in you to save him after he got shot."

He hadn't answered my question. "Did your ability to heal stop because you quit using it? Or was it something else?"

Rathmore's eyes tightened into narrow slits. "Maybe I'll tell you at some point. But you're not ready to hear it now. Still, I am curious." He turned to study me, and a prickle of unease ran down my spine. "Healing Vaughn took a lot out of you. Why is that? Didn't John teach you anything?"

His disrespectful use of St. John's name bothered me, but I still took the bait. "What do you mean?"

His answering smile sent indignation through me. "He didn't." Rathmore clicked his tongue and shook his head. "He's slacking in his job. He should have taught you how to harness the healing power without depleting your own strength. Draining your own energy will have a lasting effect. It could shorten your life by years."

I couldn't believe that. St. John would have told me. Even so... my energy always came back. That's what mattered. But what if there was something to it? In the mirror just now, I had looked sick and unhealthy. Was it draining me? If I used too much of it, would it kill me? "What are you saying?"

He sighed, as if I was too stupid to figure it out. "You'll have to ask *Saint* John the next time you see him. Did he tell you when that would be?"

I didn't answer, and his eyes grew round. "He didn't give you a time and place to meet again? He just left you with this amazing power and taught you nothing?"

"He was busy." I knew right after I said it that I shouldn't have.

Rathmore laughed. "Oh this is rich. Of course he's busy... much too busy saving the world to help you." He shook his head and let out a heavy breath. "I can help you with that... if you want. Although I doubt that you think I'm worthy."

What game was he playing now? He had to know I hated feeling so weak and helpless after using my power, but how could I trust anything he said? "I think St. John would have told me if such a thing were possible."

A tiny smile tilted his lips, causing the back of my neck to prickle. "Fine. Suit yourself. Just make sure you don't completely drain your strength, or you could burn yourself out. Do that enough times, and it's not something you'll survive... at least... not as you are now."

Was he saying I'd lose years of my life? Or have permanent physical damage? Or lose my healing power all together? "I think it's time for me to go."

His brows rose. "So soon? No more questions?"

I didn't answer him. I wasn't sure I could without opening myself to more of his lies and criticisms of St. John.

"I can see that you're not ready for the truth." He stared at me, and didn't continue until I met his gaze. "Maybe if you have someone to talk to, who's been there, you won't lose what you've been given." When I didn't jump at his offer, he shrugged. "But that's entirely up to you."

He glanced over the valley below. "So much potential lies down there. This is just the beginning of a new era. With my backing, I'll cut the years it would take to get this project off the ground in half. Imagine a world of self-governing communities like this? The peace it could bring to a world of chaos. It may take a few years to reach its pinnacle, but time doesn't matter to me."

He turned to me with a smile, and a flash of lightning lit up the sky. The accompanying thunder pounded through my heart, and the wind whipped through my hair. The rain began to fall, slowly at first, but coming harder with each passing second.

With a shake of his head, he rose to his feet and offered his hand to help me up. I ignored him, and managed to stand on my own. Sure, I was a little wobbly, but I could feel my strength returning. All I needed was some food and rest, and I'd be fine.

He shook his head at my folly, but didn't seem to take it personally. Inside the house, Rathmore shut the patio doors, blocking the rain. "That's quite a storm, but I doubt it will last long." Already, the clouds had begun to roll to the south, taking the rain with them.

We walked through the house to the front door. "I sent Ward for my car, so I won't be going back to the city with you. He'll take you back to your rental house, for your husband and his sister, and then take you to the private airport where my jet is waiting to take you home."

At my raised brows, his lips flattened. "Don't worry. You helped me a great deal today, and I always keep my word."

"But—"

He held up his hand. "Using my jet won't change anything. You're part of my team now, whether you like it or not. Beyond that, I want you to know that I'm not the enemy... or at least, I don't need to be. I have more to offer you regarding your unique abilities than you know, and I'm happy to share my knowledge when you're ready. You may not know this now, but there's a whole side to your power that you haven't even begun to explore. You really have no idea what you're capable of."

He pulled a business card from inside his jacket pocket. "This is my personal number, where you can reach me any time, day or night. I rarely give this number to anyone, but you and I share something special, and I'd like to help you however I can. Nothing is too small. Even if it's just to answer a question, I'll always take your call. In the days ahead, I think you'll find that I'm a very good friend to have."

Swallowing, I hesitated. He offered more than just answers to my questions; he offered me guidance that I sorely lacked. Still, confiding in him was the last thing I wanted to do. But I couldn't let the opportunity pass. It didn't mean I'd ever call him, but at least I'd have the option. Chewing on my bottom lip, I grabbed the card, even though everything inside warned me not to. "I'm taking it, but that doesn't mean I'll use it."

He held back a smile. "Fair enough."

Rathmore opened the front door and we found Ward waiting in the relative safety of the porch. The rain had already begun to subside, leaving the air smelling of earth and sage. We stepped toward the driveway where a bright red Lamborghini waited for Rathmore. He smiled with pleasure and strode to the car. Before climbing inside, he glanced my way. "I'll be in touch."

A moment later, he backed out of the driveway and sped away.

Ward pulled into the subdivision at just past one in the afternoon. The dark clouds and rain had moved on, and sunshine filled the blue sky. I'd sent Creed a text to tell him I was on my way, so he wouldn't worry. Jumping out of the car, I hurried inside and into Creed's embrace, grateful to feel his strong arms around me.

I held him for a long time before pulling away. "I'm sorry I left you here. It won't happen again."

His lips tilted in that sexy smile I adored. "Can I get that in writing?"

I grinned back, thankful he'd forgiven me, although, with the way things had turned out, I was glad he hadn't come. Sonny could have shot him too, and, with my healing powers so depleted, I wouldn't have been able to save both him and Vaughn.

"So what happened?"

"First, you need to know that Ward is waiting outside to take us to the private airfield where Rathmore's jet is waiting."

He opened his mouth to protest, but I held up my hand. "I know you don't want to use it, but we're going to take it anyway. It's the fastest way to get out of this city, and I want to go home before anything else happens."

"Fine. I get it, but I still want to know what happened."

"Oh, you will. Let's just get our stuff together first."

"Already done." Creed motioned to the bags by the door.

"Where's Avery?"

"I'm coming!" She rushed down the stairs with a smile that turned into a frown. "Ella, is that blood? What happened to you?"

"Oh... I forgot. I'd better put a different shirt on." I rummaged through my bag and pulled out a clean shirt.

"Is that your blood?" she asked.

"No. Let me change, and I'll be right back." I hurried up the stairs with Creed at my heels. In the bedroom, he closed the door behind us. I pulled off the shirt, revealing the white bandage I'd applied.

"I thought you said it wasn't yours."

"I lied. But it's okay now. I healed it in the car on the way back. Can you help me take the bandage off?"

Creed gently tugged at the tape, and I explained that we'd gone to Derek Vaughn's house. "He's the one who came in late for the meeting with Rathmore when Shelby was there."

"The thin one?"

"Yes. Anyway... there's so much more to tell you, but, to sum it up, Sonny was there at Vaughn's house waiting inside to kill Rathmore. Of course, that didn't work, and now

Sonny's dead, but everyone else is okay. I was too exhausted to heal myself until a few minutes ago."

The bandage came away, showing a slight pink color where I'd been wounded. "See? All better."

Creed heaved a big sigh and shook his head. "You left a lot out."

"I know. I can't wait to tell you everything, but let's get on the plane first. We can talk there."

"Why the rush? I'd like to know now."

"It's going to take a while, and, to be honest, I want to go home before something else stops us." I slipped my clean shirt on and frowned over the ruined one.

Creed took it from me and examined it before chucking it in the garbage. "All right. But don't forget that Avery will be there. Is it something she can hear?"

That gave me pause. "Not all of it, but I've been thinking about that. She knows I healed her, and now she's smarter than anyone I know. Maybe she's more a part of this than we realize. What do you think about telling her the whole story?"

"You mean about St. John and everything?"

"Yeah."

He took a moment to think about it before answering. "She's grown up a lot these last few months, so... yeah. I think she could handle it."

"Okay... let's see how it goes."

CHAPTER SIXTEEN

We arrived at the private air field, and Ward drove right up to a sleek-looking jet. As we got out, he opened the back of the car and retrieved our luggage. The pilots and steward welcomed us aboard, and we climbed inside to a luxurious interior, just like those I'd seen in the movies. The leather seats along the sides faced each other across a working table, and, further back, a long couch faced a large-screen TV, with a few more seats in the back.

We took three of the four seats in the back for privacy and buckled in. After the jet took off, the pilot announced our flight time of forty-one minutes and told us we were free to unbuckle our seat belts.

The steward came in and offered us drinks. After we each got a soda and some treats, the steward left us in peace. "Okay, Ella," Avery said. "Spill. What happened?"

I glanced at Creed, grateful we'd decided to tell her everything. He sent me a nod, and I began. "In order to understand some of this... you need to know how I got my healing touch."

Her eyes widened, and she nodded eagerly, so I explained my background, along with the visit from St. John and his message to me. She took it all in with wide-eyed wonder, and it felt good to confide in her.

She turned her gaze to Creed. "You saw him? St. John?" At Creed's nod, she shook her head. "Wow. I can't believe it. He's real."

"That brings us to what happened today. Rathmore found out about me, and he wanted me to heal someone." I continued the story, explaining Vaughn's cancer and the bargain Rathmore had proposed to him.

"After I healed Vaughn, we came back inside the house. That's when Sonny confronted us. He'd been waiting inside all that time. I guess he and Vaughn knew each other, and Vaughn must have told Sonny about the meeting.

"Because he'd just been miraculously healed, Vaughn told Sonny to leave us alone. Sonny wouldn't listen, and Vaughn stepped in his way to protect me. That's when Sonny shot Vaughn. Luckily, Ward heard the commotion and came inside in time to shoot Sonny before he shot me or Rathmore. I had to heal Vaughn again, but Sonny died instantly."

"What? He's dead?" Avery shook her head. "Wow... who would have thought. So... it's over. He'll never bother me again. As much as it shocks me, I have to admit that I'm relieved. Mom will be, too. What happened after that?"

"Rathmore called the police. That's why it took so long. We had to explain everything to them before we could leave."

"No wonder you're exhausted," Creed said, studying my face.

Just then, the pilot announced that we would be landing in fifteen minutes. Avery got up to use the bathroom, giving us a moment alone.

"There's still more to the story, but it's not something I felt right about sharing with Avery."

He nodded. "We'll talk when we get home. I'm just glad you're okay."

It took over an hour and a half to get home. We shared an Uber and had to drop Avery off first. Climbing the stairs to our apartment seemed almost more than I could manage. Creed unlocked the door, and we stepped inside to find the bed unmade and dishes in the sink. I didn't care. We were home, and the worst was behind us.

I dropped my purse on the counter and sat down on the stool, placing my head in my hands. "It's so good to be home, but I just want to sleep."

Creed came to my side and pulled me into his arms. "Come on. Let's get you to bed."

"But we need to talk."

"It can wait."

I leaned against him, letting him lead me to our bed without further protest. If he could wait, then I wasn't going to argue. After slipping off my shoes, I took off my pants and climbed under the covers. As soon as my head hit the pillow, sleep overtook me.

I woke to find the last rays of the sunset slanting through the windows. I stretched before pulling the covers away. Stepping from behind the closet, I glanced around the apartment, but there was no sign of Creed.

As I got a glass of water, I found a note on the countertop from Creed, telling me that he'd gone to the store for some food, so I took a quick shower and got dressed, feeling more like my old self.

Creed came in while I dried my hair, carrying a bag of food that smelled amazing. With my stomach growling, I hurried to his side and wrapped my arms around his back. "That smells amazing. What did you get?"

He set the bags on the counter and turned around to take me in his arms. "Chicken Parmesan for you, and spaghetti and meatballs for me, with garlic bread and a salad."

"I can't wait." We quickly set the table and distributed the food. As we ate, Creed told me what he'd been doing for the last few hours. After finishing up, he took my hand, entwining our fingers.

"Feel better now?"

"Yes. So much better."

"Good. Let's have that talk. I'm dying to know what else happened this morning." He pulled me up, and we settled on the couch.

Snuggling against him, I tucked a soft blanket over me. "This is going to sound strange, but I swear it's the truth." I pulled back to meet his gaze. "After Sonny shot Vaughn, Rathmore pushed me out of the way, and Sonny shot him in the chest." I paused to shake my head. "He died."

Creed froze. "What?"

I nodded. "It's true. Ward was outside the house, but he came running when he heard the shots and killed Sonny. My energy was so depleted, that I could only heal Vaughn enough that he would survive if he got to a hospital.

"Ward took him, leaving me with two dead men. That's when I noticed Rathmore twitch. A few seconds later, he began to breathe, and the bullets..." I shook my head again. "...they just popped out of his body." I met Creed's gaze. "He came back to life."

Creed's eyes widened, and he swore under his breath. "What does that mean? Who is he?"

"I know it's hard to believe. I can hardly fathom it myself, but he told me his real name is Nicodemus... from the Bible."

Creed shook his head. "I don't know who that is."

"Remember how St. John said there were others who were chosen to tarry on the earth? Well... I guess Nicodemus was one of them, and he and John were good friends."

"But... that doesn't make sense. He's nothing like St. John."

"I know."

"So what happened to him?"

I swallowed and took Creed's hand in both of mine, running my thumbs over his skin for something to do. "He told me that he quit helping people because what little he did wasn't enough... and that everyone dies anyway." I glanced out the window at the darkening sky. "He told me things... he said he had some of the same struggles I do."

"What do you mean?"

I sighed. "Like not being allowed to heal someone, like that man with cancer I told you about, and not getting there in time to save someone who deserved to live, like that mother in the car accident. He said he felt like he could never do enough and that they all died anyway, so what was the point?"

"Ella... that's not all there is to it."

I closed my eyes. "I know but... it's still part of it." I licked my lips. "He asked me why I got so tired after I healed someone, and why didn't John teach me anything. He acted like John had left me to fend for myself, and he should have done more to prepare me."

Creed squeezed my hands, stopping my nervous rubbing. "St. John told you to follow your instincts and to believe in yourself."

"Exactly. What does that even mean?" I pulled my hands from his grasp, and the words came tumbling out. "I've been trying to do the right things. Be in the right places. But how do I even know? What if I choose the wrong path? Do I just keep going until something happens? What if I'm not there for the person I'm supposed to save because I messed up?

"When my father was here, he said there were other ways to serve besides working at a hospital. But how does that help me? It feels like I'm playing a guessing game, and I don't know which way to go. Shouldn't I have a better feel for what I'm supposed to do than that?" Creed rubbed my back, and I leaned forward, letting his touch comfort me.

His tone took on a hard edge. "So you're questioning your purpose now? What else did Rathmore say?"

"That there was a way to heal without losing my own energy. He implied that if I overdid it, I could burn myself out. I'm not sure what he meant by that, but it sounded like I could shrivel up and die or something."

"And he knew how to keep that from happening?"

I huffed out a breath. "I guess, but I refused his help. He'd just insulted St. John, and half of the stuff he said might not be true." I shook my head. "He did admit that he lost his ability to heal, but he never told me why, or what happened to cause it. Only that he quit using it to help people."

I threw my hands up. "He said something about being tired of not having a choice... and just answering to the whims of fate. I guess he wanted to do things his way."

Creed shook his head. "He sounds like a selfish bastard to me."

"Yeah... I guess he does."

"Angel..." Creed coaxed me to look at him. "I believe in you. You were given this gift for a reason. You were chosen for this. I don't have any doubts about that. I know this path is hard, but you're strong. You can figure it out. Rathmore... or whatever his name is... can go to hell."

I let out a strangled sob and burrowed into Creed's chest. He stroked my back, calming my pounding heart. Creed believed in me. Hopefully it was enough, because, right now, I couldn't believe in myself.

The next morning, Creed left for the studio. Things were ramping up to begin production, and he was excited about his part. He'd shared the first episode with me, and I loved it. Part of me wanted to be on the set and watch the whole process.

I picked up my phone to call the hospital and tell them I was back, but I just couldn't do it. Every time I thought about going back to work, I cringed a little inside. I wasn't ready, and that worried me. Maybe I just needed a longer break.

I slipped on my exercise clothes and walked down to the beach. The cool breeze on my face, and the sound of the crashing waves, helped soothe my shattered nerves. I walked for a couple of hours, just being in the moment and letting the sun warm me.

By the time I got back to the apartment, I felt more balanced than I had in ages. I'd left my phone on the counter and hadn't even missed it. After picking it up, I found a message from Avery, inviting us to dinner with her and Lauren.

I sent a text to Creed and he responded that dinner at six would work, so I texted Avery that we'd be there. Feeling tired, I put my feet up on the couch and promptly fell asleep. I woke as Creed came in and hurried to get ready for dinner.

After we arrived, we had a great time. Avery was so happy to be home, and, without Sonny to worry about, she truly began to live again. She told us of her plans to apply to MIT and Stanford, who had the best computer science programs in the country, and we were excited for her.

Since we no longer had a car, we'd ridden over on Creed's motorcycle. I mentioned that I needed to go car shopping, and Avery begged me to take her. I missed my Jeep, so I wanted to find something similar that was more suited to city driving.

We checked out a few cars online, and Avery complained about the prices, expressing her worry that we could afford it. I realized we hadn't told her or her mom about my inheritance, but I wasn't quite ready to do that yet.

Once we got home, Creed thought it was a good idea to get the car I wanted with my money, since I'd need it to go to work. I had to agree, and we set up a time to go car shopping.

The next few days were more of the same, and I began to look forward to my walks along the beach. It wasn't until later that Creed voiced his concern. He came home from another day on the set and found me asleep on the couch.

"Ella." Creed knelt by the side of the couch and shook my arm.

"Oh... hey." I pushed into a sitting position and blinked the sleep from my eyes. Patting the couch, I caught his gaze. "Here... sit down. How was your day?"

"It was good. We're going to start filming tomorrow."

"Really? Already?"

"Ella... it's been almost a week and a half since we got back from Las Vegas."

"Oh... I didn't realize."

His brows dipped. "I'm getting a little worried about you. I haven't said anything because I thought you needed some time to recuperate, but it's been days. What's going on?"

I shook my head. "I don't know. I guess I'm just worn out with everything."

"Did you call the hospital?"

"No. I tried but I just couldn't do it." Guilt rolled over me. "They called me, but I didn't answer. I've probably lost my job by now." My eyes filled with tears, and a wave of remorse shocked me. "That job was all I cared about... and now I can't even bring myself to go. What's wrong with me?"

Creed pulled me into his arms. "Rathmore. He got into your head when you were vulnerable. You've been pushing yourself so hard to fulfill your role, that it's no wonder you're worn out." He shook his head. "I feel like it's partly my fault."

I inhaled sharply. "What? No way." He stroked my back, and I rested my cheek against his chest. "Why would you say that?"

"Because I saw it happening. Everything we went through with Sonny the first time was draining enough, but meeting St. John in New York changed everything. Finding out about your life, and his part in it, was huge. Then came the revelation of your gift and what that all meant, combined with marrying me. That's a lot of changes to make at once."

"Yeah... I guess it was, but... it was also pretty cool."

"Yes... that's true. But the minute we came back to L.A., you took that job at the hospital and began healing everyone you could. I think it took a lot out of you, even though you didn't realize it."

I closed my eyes and nodded. "I was just trying to do my job."

"I know. I see that. But now I think we should have taken a little extra time to adjust. It all happened so fast." His lips turned into an overly exaggerated frown. "Plus, I should have tried harder to talk you into going on a honeymoon. But that's mostly your fault. I mean... who wouldn't want to go on a honeymoon with me? Am I right?"

My lips twitched. I knew he was mostly teasing, but he was also right. "I know. I'm a terrible wife." I tightened my arms around him and shook my head. "I don't know what I was thinking. It would have been great."

"Hell yeah. But... it's probably okay... I mean... Avery needed us and it would have been ruined anyway." He sighed. "Still, after everything that's happened, it's no wonder that you're struggling. I'm surprised you're doing so well."

I pulled back. "I'm not so sure about that, but I can't argue. I think I've needed this time to regroup. And you're right. Rathmore really did a number on me. I shouldn't have listened to him. He was probably lying the whole time."

"I agree. Are you sure he's who he said he was?"

"You mean that he's Nicodemus? I don't know why he'd lie about that. He is immortal. I saw him come back to life, so that part must be true. I just wish I could talk to St. John. I feel so lost right now."

"We'll figure this out. I'm here, and I'm not leaving. We've got this."

I pulled away to gaze into his clear, blue eyes and admire the determined set of his jaw. Sure he was handsome, but he was so much more to me. "I love you so much." His lips met mine, and I poured all the love I could into that kiss. I wasn't sure I deserved him, but I wouldn't question it. He was mine, and I'd do anything to keep him by my side.

An hour later, we came up for air, both of us starving, and decided to go out for dinner. We ended up on the beach at our favorite restaurant. We sat outside on the deck, and the soft ocean breeze filled my soul with peace.

After a fantastic dinner, we took a walk along the sandy beach and watched the setting sun. "So tomorrow's the day, huh? Have you got all your parts memorized?"

"I think so."

I held his gaze. "Do you think I could come and watch?"

His brows rose. "I guess. You sure you want to do that? It'll probably be pretty boring."

"Oh... I don't know about that. I'd just like to see what it's like, you know?"

"Yeah... okay. I'm sure you can come. Some of the actors bring their kids to the set, so it's a common occurrence to have family around."

"Sweet. In the meantime, let's talk about where we want to go on our honeymoon."

His answering grin sent a rush of excitement through me. "Now that's something worth talking about."

The next day, we took our new hybrid Jeep Wrangler to the set. I wasn't sure what to expect, so I dressed a little nicer than normal, even adding a touch of makeup. The director didn't seem to mind that I was there, and Creed introduced me to the cast, who greeted me warmly.

I found out that today was all about the action scenes, and I couldn't wait to see how they pulled it together. Creed had a stunt double for the dangerous stuff, which definitely calmed my nerves. They began to film a fight scene, where Creed's character jumps from a narrow fire escape and smashes through the window of an adjacent building.

Creed began the run toward the camera, and his stunt double finished by jumping across the space, diving through the window, and landing in a roll, before continuing the chase. He'd been practicing while they set up the shot, and I was excited to see it all come together.

Right before the shot, the stunt double did one more practice roll and came onto his feet a little wobbly. I knew immediately that something was wrong. He shook it off, but I could tell he'd hurt his shoulder.

When the director called for them to start filming, the stunt double just nodded and took his mark. The scene went off without a hitch, but the director made them do it a couple more times to get the lighting right.

By the end of the shot, the stunt double's face was sweating and pale. He left without a word, and I watched him disappear off the set. Concerned, I followed him outside and found him leaning against the wall, cradling his arm.

Our eyes met, and he straightened, like he'd been caught.

I smiled to put him at ease. "Hey... it's okay, I'm a nurse. I think you'd better let me take a look at your arm."

"It's fine," he said. "Just bruised."

"Uh... sorry, but I don't believe you."

He shook his head. "Look, I know you mean well, but I need this job. I can't be injured right now."

"I understand. I won't tell anyone. Just let me see if I can help. Maybe your shoulder is just dislocated, and I can put it back."

He closed his eyes. "I think it's worse than that. Sorry I snapped at you. But this is just the worst timing ever."

"Let me see if I can help. Maybe it's not as bad as you think."

He let out a resigned breath. "Okay. Go ahead."

I took his arm and probed his shoulder with my fingers. He flinched, and I knew he had a bad sprain, and maybe even a tear in his ligaments. But it wasn't so bad that I couldn't fix it pretty quick.

"I'm going to try something, if that's all right. Just hold still. It might burn a little, but I think it will feel better after I'm done."

"Sure. I'm ready."

I placed my hand over the injury and concentrated on the muscles. The ligaments had stretched almost to the breaking point, so I focused on them, sending my healing power into the tissue.

A moment later, the swelling was gone and the muscle restored. I pulled my hands away and stepped back. "That should help, but be sure to take it easy for a day or two."

He moved his shoulder and his eyes widened. "It doesn't hurt anymore. What did you do?"

"It's a special kind of... massage therapy using pressure points."

"Really? It's amazing. It did burn a little, but it almost felt like it was burning the pain out."

"Good. I'm glad it helped."

"I'm Chad." He held out his hand.

"Oh... Ella St. John. I'm Aiden Creed's wife. It's nice to meet you, Chad." I shook his hand and smiled. "You're doing a great job."

"Thanks. Creed's a lucky man. Thanks for your help."

"Of course. We'd better get back."

Using my healing gift on Chad had hardly made a dent in my energy levels, and I realized it might be because of all the rest I'd gotten lately. Maybe that was the key I'd been missing? But how would that help when I worked at the hospital? I couldn't take all that time off to recharge. Still... it gave me something to think about.

The rest of the day passed uneventfully. Chad managed to do a couple more stunts without incident. After he was done, he sent me a grateful nod, and I smiled back.

At the end of the day, I was ready to go home. Creed was right. It was fun, but also boring; nothing how I imagined working on a set would be. At least Peyton Lind, Creed's co-star, didn't seem too interested in Creed.

I had to admit that I didn't like how close they got on camera, and they did seem to have a certain chemistry going on between them, but, once the filming was over, she was all business. Maybe she was afraid Creed would develop a thing for her?

I knew it was a dangerous profession for things like that, but I trusted Creed, and he didn't seem affected by her at all, so that helped.

"So, what did you think?" he asked on the way home.

"It was fun. I only got a little bored, but I can see why you'd enjoy acting like someone else. I thought you were fabulous, by the way."

He chuckled. "Glad to hear it." He paused. "Chad spoke to me before he left. He said you helped him out and I was a lucky man. What did he mean by that?"

I explained his shoulder injury and that I'd healed him. "I told him what I did was a form of massage therapy. He wasn't about to get help because he needed the work, so I'm glad I was there. He could have made it so much worse."

"When did he get hurt?"

"While he was practicing. After the cameras began to roll, he did the jump two more times." I shook my head. "He should have stopped after the first time, but he just powered through it."

Creed nodded. "Then he was lucky you were there."

I smiled. "You know what? So was I, but not just because I helped him." I took a deep breath. "It felt good to ease his pain, and I realized that I'd missed it. I think I'm ready to go back to work."

His shoulders sagged and he grinned at me. "Good, because you were starting to get on my nerves. All that moping around..."

I narrowed my eyes. "Yeah... right. You just don't like my cooking."

"That's not entirely true. You can make a mean grilled cheese sandwich."

I smacked his arm. "Fine. I guess that means you're cooking tonight."

Two days later, I arrived at the hospital to start my shift. My supervisor didn't bat an eye that I'd been out so long, and she was more than happy to get me back in the rotation. I met most of the staff and greeted the others I already knew.

As I got started, Cody from the night shift, popped up beside me. "Hey, Ella. It's great to have you back. You were gone so long I wasn't sure I'd see you again."

"Yeah... well, I had some personal things I needed to take care of."

"I get that, but it's been a little crazy around here without you. Do you have a minute to look at a patient who just came in?"

I cocked a brow. "You mean like the last time, with that teen-aged girl? You trying to keep me busy?"

"No, I just... I didn't think you'd mind is all."

I sucked in a breath. "No, of course I don't. What's going on?"

"This woman came in with a severe headache, along with neck pain and a high fever. They diagnosed spinal meningitis, but it's a bad case. If she doesn't die, they're afraid she'll lose her hearing."

"Oh... that's not good. Where is she?"

"Over there. They're getting ready to take her up to the ICU. I'll take you to her."

I followed him to the woman's exam room, where the attending nurse was readying her for the move. While I sanitized my hands and slipped on a face mask, Cody spoke in hushed tones to a family member before hurrying back to my side. "Can you do anything to help her?"

"I can try." As the others finished preparations to move her, I touched her arm and forehead. The sickness hit me immediately, and I pushed my healing power into her body. I felt the tension drain, as the bacteria succumbed to my healing power, and I pulled away, knowing the power would continue to work until all the bacteria was gone.

The attending nurse asked me to move out of the way so she could get the woman up to the ICU, and I quickly complied. A moment later, they were gone, and I glanced up to see Cody studying me. He came to my side. "You didn't get much time. Were you able to help her?"

I nodded. "I think so."

"Thanks." He rushed out to catch up with the family member, and I lost sight of them.

I took a moment to catch my breath and shook my head. That hadn't tired me out too much, but what was going on with Cody? Was he turning into a true believer? I headed back to my station and began my day.

After a slow morning, I took my lunch break in the cafeteria. Just as I finished up, Reyna slipped into the seat across from me. It surprised me to see her, especially now that I knew she worked for Rathmore. Was this his way of spying on me?

She took one look at me, and her smile lost its luster. "Hey Ella. It's been a while. How are you?"

"I'm all right."

"You must have gone on your honeymoon. Did you have a nice time?"

"You don't have to pretend with me. I know you work for Rathmore. But why are you still here? He's already got me under his thumb, unless he needs you to spy on me."

Her mouth dropped open, but she tried to hide it under a confused stare. "I don't know what you mean."

I shook my head. "You mean I'm wrong?"

This time she met my gaze. "There's something I need to tell you. Then you can decide what you want to do about it. But not here. Can you meet me after your shift?"

I thought about telling her off, but changed my mind. "I guess so."

"Good. I'll wait for you in the parking lot." She left before I could say another word, and I spent the rest of the day wondering what excuses she'd give me. If she thought we could still be friends after this, she was in for a rude awakening.

At the end of my shift, I started out to the parking lot. I couldn't see Reyna anywhere, so I decided not to wait around and continued to my car. The sound of footsteps came from behind, and I turned to find her hurrying to catch up. Not wanting to make it easy for her, I took a few more steps toward my car.

"Ella, wait. Can we go someplace and talk?"

"It depends. Is this about Rathmore?"

"Yes... but it's not what you think. Just give me a chance to explain."

I sighed. "Fine. There's a coffee shop around the corner. Let's head over there."

Neither of us spoke until after we had our orders and were sitting down at a small table in the back. I kept quiet and waited for her to begin.

She took a deep breath. "You're right. I'm a private investigator, and I've been working for Rathmore, but I wanted you to know that I've had a change of heart, and I want to help you."

I said nothing, and she swallowed. "I've worked for him off and on for a while, doing odd jobs here and there, but it wasn't until lately that I've realized he's not someone I want to do business with. Unfortunately, I'm not sure I have a choice in the matter anymore. That's why I want to join forces with you."

She met my gaze, and her dark eyes hardened. "I believe in you, Ella. In what you are. I've seen it, and I hate that he wants to exploit your gift. So I want to work together, behind his back. I'll keep you informed about what he wants, and, if there's any way you can escape his plans, I want you to take it."

I narrowed my eyes. "But what if he finds out that you're helping me? He's not going to stand for that."

Her lips turned down. "I'll have to make sure he doesn't." At my raised brows, she continued. "But it doesn't matter in the end. You're more important than any of this. You're like... an angel. This world needs you. If I can do anything to help you, I will."

Her determination surprised me. "You're serious."

She nodded and sent me a small smile. "I want to be on the right side of whatever comes next. And that's with you."

"So what about your ten-year-old son? Or was that a lie?"

She glanced away. "It was. I don't have kids."

I clamped my lips together. At least she was being honest. "Okay. I'm listening. What's your plan?"

Hope brightened her eyes. "For now, my job is to keep tabs on you and report to Rathmore weekly. He knows we've become friends, so he won't suspect anything, which will help us in the long run. I'm not sure what he has planned next, but when I find out, I'll let you know."

I studied her for a moment. "You must know a lot about Rathmore."

She nodded. "I guess that's one way to put it. And, just so you know, I took the jobs I did for him because they paid well. I didn't question what he did with the information I gave him."

She shrugged. "It was just a job to me. But then something happened, and I was forced to see how he used my work to hurt people. By then, I knew too much, and I didn't think I could ever escape. That's when you came into the picture. I don't know if it's fate, or something else, but you changed everything for me. I want to help you. So that's what I plan to do."

My breath caught. Could I believe her? "Thanks Reyna. You seem sincere, so I won't pass it up, but I'm not going to lie. I might have a hard time trusting you."

"I get it," she said. "But you can. You don't have to take my word for it. I'll prove it to you. You'll see. Just give me a chance."

A small ray of hope washed over me. "Okay."

She smiled. "In fact, there's something you need to know about Cody."

My eyes widened. "What about him?"

"He's using you."

"What?"

"He's asked for your help twice now, right? Or did I miss one?"

"No. That's right."

Her lips twisted. "He's setting it all up before he asks for your help by telling the family about you. He convinces them that you can only help so many people, but he'll get your attention for their loved one first. All they have to do is pay him a small fee."

I gasped. "Are you serious?"

She nodded. "Yeah... they're so desperate that they're more than willing to pay him whatever he wants."

"That's disgusting. How much have they paid? Do you know?"

She shook her head. "I'm not exactly sure, but probably in the thousands."

"That slimeball."

"I agree. That's why I'll help you straighten him out."

My brows rose. "How will you do that?"

"We'll confront him together and tell him that we're onto him. He'll probably deny it, but it's a start."

"That's not enough. He needs to pay them back."

Her lips twisted. "That might be a little harder, but if we threaten to tell Dr. Kelley what he's done, he might agree."

I shook my head. "I don't know. He could always threaten to tell the wrong people my secret. You know how badly that could go."

"Then I'll do some digging. If he's dishonest about this, he's probably got some skeletons in his closet I can ferret out. Threatening to expose his secrets might do the job."

"Yeah... that could work."

She sighed. "The easiest way to take care of it would be to hire some muscle. You know... someone big and scary who'd threaten to break both his legs if he didn't pay them back."

I chuckled. "Actually, I know a guy who does stuff like that for a mob boss. The mob boss's niece is a friend of mine, and I think she'd be happy to ask him to help us out."

Her brows rose. "Really? Wow... you're full of surprises."

I grinned back. "I'm beginning to find that out."

We left the shop as friends instead of enemies, and it amazed me that Reyna had been willing to risk so much for me. Was it real? Could I trust her? Only time would tell, but I was willing to give it a shot. We parted ways in the parking lot, and I thanked her for confiding in me. "So... you'll let me know what Rathmore tells you?"

"Yes." She paused, frowning over my uncertainty. "Ella... I know you may have your doubts about me, but I was raised with a simple faith, and I've seen what you can do. I promise, I won't let you down."

"Thanks Reyna. That means a lot."

"You working tomorrow?"

I nodded. "Yes."

"Okay... see you then." Her brows tightened. "Maybe while we're on a break we can figure out what to do about Cody?"

"Sounds good." I drove home, grateful that she believed in me. It helped to have someone else on my side, especially after everything Rathmore had said. He'd done more damage than I realized, and I knew that if I needed the right answers, I had to do the work to get them.

Creed got home just before me, and I could hardly wait to fill him in on the day's events. After telling him about Reyna, he was shocked that she'd been around for so long, feeding information to Rathmore. I finished filling him in, even telling him about Cody and his devious ways.

Creed's eyes darkened. "I can lean on him if you want."

"Let's wait and see what he says."

"Sure, but I have a mind to go visit him right now. Preying on people who are at their most vulnerable shows a definite lack of character. He doesn't deserve your lenience."

"I agree. But let's wait and see what happens first. Reyna's got some ideas up her sleeve, and I'd like to see what she comes up with."

Creed let out a husky laugh. "Sure... but if you need me, just say the word."

"Okay." I didn't have the heart to tell him that I'd already considered asking Ramos to do the honors. Even so, I had a sneaking suspicion that between me and Reyna, we could lean on Cody ourselves. Two determined women could be pretty scary, and that might be all the motivation he'd need.

I closed my eyes and leaned my head against Creed's chest. I was tired, not just physically, but emotionally, and it was only my first day back on the job. How was I going to keep this up without getting burned out?

"I wish I knew how to heal people without getting totally drained. Rathmore said there was a way. Maybe I should have asked him." I shook my head. "No... that's not right. He was trying to entice me to his side. I think he wanted me to trust him because he had all the answers, and St. John left me high and dry."

I tilted my head back to meet Creed's gaze. "But if there is a way, why didn't St. John tell me? It seems kind of important, you know?"

Creed nodded. "Yes, I see your point. But maybe he didn't tell you because he wanted you to figure it out."

My shoulders sagged. "It always comes back to that, doesn't it? Would it be so hard to just tell me something... anything?"

Creed's lips quirked. "I get that, but I don't think it works that way. I mean... after all this time, when it comes to your gift, has anything ever come easily? Maybe you're supposed to figure it out for a reason." At my frown, he continued. "So you can get better. Maybe you'll grow into something more."

It reminded me of Rathmore's words, that I had no idea what I was capable of, but he was probably lying his head off. I shook my head. "Yeah... right. I don't think so."

He shrugged. "Hey... I'm just throwing things out there. I'm as clueless as you are. I'm just saying that maybe you should try figuring it out for yourself. Who knows? Maybe it's not that hard."

I pursed my lips. He had a point. I hadn't thought there was a way to heal someone without draining my own energy, but, since Rathmore seemed to think there was, it only made sense that I could figure it out.

Too bad I had no idea where to start.

My first week back to work came to an end, leaving me exhausted and ready for a break. Luckily, Creed had the next two days off as well, and we decided to take the motorcycle for a ride along the Pacific Coast Highway.

He'd been eager to get away from the stress of his frantic work schedule, and we began the drive, heading toward Malibu and taking our time to pull off the main road and stop at all the different beaches along the way.

We grabbed some lunch before continuing on to Point Dume, a tranquil coastal area featuring some great viewpoints and trails. We explored the rocky coves and totally enjoyed the day just hanging out.

Too soon, it was time to head back. A gas station came up on the left, and I signaled to Creed to stop. He pulled around to the back entrance and parked. After dismounting, I explained. "I need some lip balm since I forgot mine."

Inside, I found the brand I loved, and Creed went to the restroom. I stepped to the register to pay, and a man came in from the front entrance and stood behind me. Something about him made me uneasy, so I quickly finished my transaction. Since Creed hadn't come out yet, I glanced around the store and stepped toward the sunglass display case to wait for him.

The clerk asked the man what he wanted, and he suddenly pulled a gun out of his waistband, yelling at the clerk to give him all the money in the cash box. The clerk raised his hands and backed away, causing the man to scream even louder.

The clerk rushed back to the register to pull out the cash, and I inched backward, hoping to get out of range of his waving gun. I glanced behind me, wanting to find a way to warn Creed before he joined me, but it dead-ended at the drinks machine.

As the clerk placed the money on the counter, the gunman began to stuff it into his pockets, while still holding the gun pointed at the clerk. Just then, the jingle of the bell sounded, and a young man stepped inside, totally oblivious to what was going on.

Startled, the gunman pointed at the newcomer and pulled the trigger. The young man fell to the ground, clutching his chest. Creed came running, and the gunman pivoted toward him and fired. Creed ducked behind a shelf, and the shot went wide.

The gunman twisted my way, and I sucked in a breath. As I ducked lower behind the sunglass display case, Creed threw a can of food at him, hitting him in the chest. He kept up the barrage, hitting the man a couple of times, but not doing any real damage.

The young man who'd been shot began to inch his way toward me, and I took a chance to step beside him. I grabbed his arms and pulled him behind the display case where I'd been hiding. As I knelt beside him, I placed my hand over his wound to access the damage.

Shots rang out, and I ducked over the wounded man. Glancing up, I realized the gunman had taken a couple of shots in Creed's direction, and my heart raced. What if Creed got shot? I didn't think I'd have enough strength to save both him and this man. My mouth went dry and I concentrated on the young man in front of me, knowing instantly he would die if I didn't do something quick.

"Oh God... help me." Taking a deep breath, I sent a blast of healing energy into his wound. His back arched and he gasped. As he exhaled, all the pain and tension went out of him, and his wide-eyed gaze found mine.

Abruptly, the shooting stopped, and the gunman fell to his knees, dropping the gun harmlessly to the floor. As his eyes rolled back in his head, he toppled over. Creed rushed toward him and kicked the gun away, then stared down at him in confusion.

Shaking it off, Creed reached down to feel his neck for a pulse. "He's alive."

Until then, I didn't know I'd been holding my breath. Finding Creed unscathed was such a relief that I almost didn't hear what he'd said.

"I'll call the police," the clerk said. "Should we tie him up?"

"I think he's out cold, but yeah... sure." Creed turned his attention to me and the young man. "Is he going to be okay?"

"Yes. He'll be fine."

The young man began to sit up, so I took his arm to help prop him against the side of the drinks machine. With a flurry of movement, he tugged at his bloody shirt, pulling it away to expose his chest. Finding no wound of any kind, his breath caught, and he looked at me. "What just happened?"

I wasn't sure how to respond, so I just shook my head. "You look okay to me."

"But... I felt it. The pain was excruciating. Now it's like it never happened. What's going on?"

"Uh... it must be a miracle."

The kid's eyes rounded, and he swallowed.

Knowing he was okay, I grabbed a few napkins to wipe my hands and stepped around him to Creed's side. He'd just finished tying the unconscious man's hands together. "I'm going to go to the restroom. Can you show me the way?"

Picking up on what I didn't say, Creed nodded. "Sure." After making sure things were under control, he stepped down the aisle, and I followed. The restrooms were around the corner, close to where we'd come in.

"Wait here." I rushed inside and quickly washed my hands. Hurrying out, I grabbed Creed's arm and pulled him to the exit.

"What's going on?"

"We need to leave."

"But we can't. The police will be here any minute."

I shook my head. "We have to go. It will be okay. Trust me."

Creed met my gaze and only hesitated a moment before nodding and following me out of the gas station. The bike sat right where we'd left it, and we slipped on our helmets. Creed started the bike up, and we pulled out onto the road.

Sirens and flashing lights headed toward us and quickly passed us by. We continued down the road for another ten or twenty minutes before we came to a scenic turnout.

Since we'd been stopping at these little turnouts all day, it wasn't unusual to pull off the road. Creed cut the engine, and I got off. He did the same, and we pulled off our helmets. Looking toward the ocean, we wandered to the edge of the lookout. A couple of rocks beckoned, and we settled down to watch the cresting waves and the coming sunset.

"That was... a little nuts." Creed rolled his shoulders. "That gunman just fell over, like he had a heart attack or something."

I nodded my head in wonder. "Yeah... I think I know why, but I'm not sure how to explain it." I swallowed and turned to Creed. "I did something different this time. When I healed that guy, I was so worried about you getting shot that I sent a single burst of healing power into him, along with a prayer for God's help. Right after that, the gunman fell over."

Creed's brows drew together. "So you think God had something to do with it?"

I let out a chuckle. "Yes. I do. Because it's not just that. I'm not tired... not even a little." Excitement washed over me. "After healing someone as injured as he was... with one burst of power..." I shook my head. "It would normally take so much out of me that I'd hardly be able to stand. But not this time. I put everything into God's hands, and it..."

I took a deep breath and sighed. "It all worked out. I've never done that before... not once. But that gunman... he collapsed at the exact same moment. Almost like the exhaustion went from me and straight into him."

Creed's eyes widened, and his breath hitched. "You really think that's what happened?"

At my nod, we both turned to look out over the waves. The sun was setting behind a bank of clouds, leaving a stunning show of golden color, shining like spotlights through the clouds into the turquoise sky and across the deep blue water.

The waves crashed below us. With the cry of seagulls overhead, it was the perfect end to a beautiful day. My soul filled with contentment and peace, and I knew I'd cherish this moment for a long time to come.

"Is that why you wanted to leave without talking to the cops?"

"Partly. I mean... how were we going to explain what happened? And the young man... he knew I'd healed him. He was dying. He asked me what I did, so I told him that it looked like a miracle." I sighed. "Do you think there will be surveillance footage of the whole thing?"

"Maybe. That could be a problem, but I don't think we'd be in trouble for leaving... at least I hope not."

"I wouldn't have left but... I just felt like it was the right thing to do."

We sat quietly for several more minutes, watching the sky darken until a chill settled over us. "Let's find the nearest motel and get a room for the night," Creed said. "There's nothing we need to hurry home for."

"Sounds good to me."

We found a motel along the way and settled in for the night. Before going to bed, Creed turned on the news. One of the last stories was a special interest story about the robbery at the gas station. We both sat up straight to hear the newscaster telling the unusual story about the mysterious couple who stopped a gunman intent on killing the clerk and an unwitting bystander.

"They were here..." the clerk said. "And then they just disappeared. I'm a little confused because of everything happening so fast... you know? A guy even got shot, but he's totally fine now. Then the gunman just fell over. I thought he was dead, but he'd just passed out. After we tied him up, the police came and the man and woman who'd helped me were long gone."

The reporter continued. "Video footage of the incident has the police baffled." The video footage came on, and we watched intently. "Right here, you can see the outlines of two people involved in the incident. It's easy to tell that it's a man and a woman, but, for some reason, they're blurred. We can't make out their faces, or really anything more about them."

The camera switched back to the reporter. "With no way to identify these good Samaritans, the police are asking anyone with information to please come forward. So, if you're watching this, and you're the good Samaritans, please contact the police."

The reporter turned to the clerk. "If you could talk to them, do you have anything you'd like to say?"

"Yeah... just... thanks for helping. You probably saved my life, and the other guy who was here. He was certain the woman was an angel or something."

The camera moved back to the reporter who smiled indulgently. "And isn't that something we could all use more of today? This is Chelsea, reporting live for KRTX news. That's it for now. Back to you, Henry."

Creed clicked off the TV and turned to me, shaking his head. "Wow. I guess you were right about leaving."

"Yeah..." I flopped back down on the pillows and studied the ceiling without really seeing it. "What does it all mean?"

He chuckled. "Hell if I know." He took my hand and squeezed. "But at least you know how to keep from losing your strength now, so that's good."

"Yeah... but this was different. Almost like karma for that robber. I mean... that was really cool, but how does it work in a hospital setting? Most of the people I help are there because of accidents. Where would the power go then?"

Creed shook his head. "I don't know. But maybe that's not something you have to worry about. It sounds like you just need to give it to God, and he'll take care of it. I mean... isn't that what happened today?"

"Yes, that's exactly what happened."

"Then I guess that's your answer."

I let out a deep breath. "That makes sense, but, in a way, it just leaves me with more questions. Are we supposed to be looking for trouble so we can help out? Or are we just supposed to do our thing and let trouble come to us? It's all so confusing."

"Angel... everything about this is confusing. But after today, at least we know we're on the right track. I mean... our faces were blurred in the video... how does that even happen?"

"I know." I nodded, just as shocked as he was.

"I guess it's just something we have to figure out as we go."

"Yeah."

We both stared at the ceiling, lost in our thoughts. Minutes later, Creed turned toward me, tugging me against him. "At least we're in this together, and right now, I can't imagine any other place I'd rather be."

He kissed me tenderly, almost worshipfully, showing me that I was the most important thing in his life. I responded in kind, grateful for his love and acceptance of me for what I was, and not once trying to change any of this to suit him.

Loving him filled me with a light so bright that it almost hurt. I accepted it, marveling that the pain could also be amazing and beautiful. There weren't words to describe all my feelings for this man I loved, so I showed him with every kiss and every touch. All my barriers came down. Some

I didn't even know I still carried, until there was nothing left but pure raw feeling. He was mine, and I would be his forever.

Later, as we drifted off to sleep, my mind wandered to what came next. I doubted that Rathmore would have told me that turning to God would rid me of my exhaustion. Of course, that didn't mean there wasn't another way... probably a way that would be much darker.

He'd turned his back on God and all that was good, and he'd nearly convinced me to do the same. But none of that was right. I couldn't let doubt creep in and muddy the waters. Sure, I had questions, more than I could count. But, like Creed said, we were on the right track, and I'd just have to trust in that.

I had Creed on my side, and now Reyna. I knew I could count on Shelby as well. I also had my father, John, to confide in, and now that Avery knew the whole story, she could help me too.

Maybe it was time to gather my friends close, even look to a special few I'd healed for support. If I had to battle Rathmore, I didn't have to do it alone. There was strength in numbers, whether they were closely involved, or involved from a safe distance. I didn't need to be the victim. There had to be a way to stop him.

If Rathmore was coming for me, I couldn't just go along with what he wanted. I couldn't let him dictate my life or my beliefs. I wouldn't be a pawn for his plans, whatever they entailed. No... I had plans of my own, and now, it was my turn.

It was time to take a stand.

FROM THE AUTHOR

Thank you for reading **DESERT DEVIL: Sand and Shadows Book 2**. I am currently hard at work on the next book in the sand and shadows series, **Twisted Fate: Sand and Shadows Book 3**, and promise to do my best for another exciting adventure!

If you enjoyed this book, please consider leaving a review on Amazon. It's a great way to thank an author and keep her writing.

The Sand and Shadow Series is a spin-off from my Shelby Nichols Adventure Series. If you are new to my writing, please check out **CARROTS: A Shelby Nichols Adventure, Book 1** in the series. It is available in kindle, kindle unlimited, paperback, and audible formats. Get your copy today!

For news, updates, and discounts, sign up for my newsletter here. By signing up you will receive a FREE ebook, Behind Blue Eyes: A Shelby Nichols Novella. Sign up today!

About the Author

USA TODAY BESTSELLING AUTHOR

Colleen Helme is the author of the bestselling Shelby Nichols Adventure Series, a wildly entertaining and highly humorous series about Shelby Nichols, a woman with the ability to read minds.

She is also the author of the Sand and Shadow Series, a spin-off from the Shelby Nichols Series featuring Ella St John, a woman this a special 'healing' touch. Between writing about these two friends, Colleen has her hands full, but is enjoying every minute of it, especially when they appear in books together.

When not writing, Colleen spends most of her time thinking about new ways to get her characters in and out of trouble. She loves to connect with readers and admits that fans of her books keep her writing.

Connect with Colleen

Website | Amazon | Facebook | Bookbub | Twitter | Instagram | Shelby Nichols Consulting | Amazon Series Page